FOR A MOMENT HE HUNG SUSPENDED, HURTLING INTO DARKNESS. THEN THE SOUNDS OF LIMBS CRACKING, SHATTERING—AND THE SILENCE OF THE NIGHT . . .

When he looked up he saw them standing squarely in the headlight beams. He was pinned under the truck. "Get help," Peter begged.

"We will help," they said together. "We are helpers."

The strawberry-blonde marched forward and giggled: "I start fires!" She jerked up her hand. A flame exploded near the front tire. The black girl stepped toward him. "I control things. Like that ball that hit the girl who lied about you."

"You killed her?"

"It was necessary."

"I find hidden things," the brown-skinned brunette announced. "Something important is near you now. Exactly under the tree."

"Stop!" Peter shouted. Helpless, he watched as their dark forms floated through the fields, disappearing into the grove of eucalyptus trees . . .

IN THE NAME OF THE FATHER

John Zodrow

A DELL BOOK

Published by
Dell Publishing Co., Inc.
1 Dag Hammarskjold Plaza
New York, New York 10017

Copyright © 1980 by John Zodrow and Gerald S. Paonessa

All rights reserved. No part of this book may be reproduced or
transmitted in any form or by any means, electronic or mechan-
ical, including photocopying, recording or by any information
storage and retrieval system, without the written permission of
the Publisher, except where permitted by law.

Dell ® TM 681510, Dell Publishing Co., Inc.

ISBN 0-440-14198-2

Printed in the United States of America

First printing—July 1980

For Griff, pal, confessor
and second father

ACKNOWLEDGMENTS

To Bill Grose, for his confidence and friendship; to Jerry Paonessa and Tom Klassen, talented men, who nurtured an idea; and to Jeanne Bernkopf, my editor, who walks in giant steps but never condescends.

"All things truly wicked start
from an innocence."
Ernest Hemingway

"Do not ask for what you will wish
you had not got."
Seneca

PART ONE

FROM THE CAVE

ONE

Late September, 1948

The olive-green DC-3, props glinting silver, sliced through pools of sunlight as it dropped from the mass of dark clouds, then bounced down in the plowed field. Dust erupted in whirlwinds behind its engines. The plane skidded sideways, then settled into two plowed furrows.

When the Red Cross insignia on the side was clearly visible, a Chinese man and two women in coolie hats broke from the cover of the elm trees near the hill and dashed toward the plane.

The narrow, curved exit door on the DC-3 jiggled and fell inward. A round-faced, horse-toothed young man jumped out.

"Hope this is it," he said. "It sure don't look like no Valley of the Dead!"

A tall man with an aquiline, aristocratic face appeared in the doorway. He was about fifty. His hair, dark and lustrous, was combed back off his face. He was dressed in khaki. On the third finger of his right hand, he wore the sapphire ring of a cardinal.

The American prelate raised his bejeweled hand and shaded his eyes against the sun as he looked at the lush, green valley.

"This is the last stop," the cardinal said to the pilot.

"Suits me. I'm sick and tired gettin' shot at by Chiang Kai-shek on one side, Commies on the other. You'd think they'd know better than to shoot at a plane with a Red Cross!"

Cardinal Livingston Stamp turned from studying the valley and saw the group of Chinese running toward them. "We've got company."

"Christ, I hope they're friendly!" Then, he added, "Sorry, Reverend."

"That's okay. You should have heard me when you landed."

The pilot grinned.

There were three Chinese altogether. They stopped respectfully at the tip of the left wing.

"Eminence, Cardinal Stamp," the man said and dropped to one knee. "I am Kwan."

"Father Kwan! You speak English?"

"Educated at UCLA," the priest said proudly, kissing Cardinal Stamp's outstretched ring. He turned toward the two women. "Nuns, Ling-Po and Da-Nay-Ram. Neither speaks English."

Each of the women swiped off the wide-brimmed peasant hats and quickly kissed the ring. Their faces looked tired and drawn.

"The last of the Kuomintang fled through this valley last night," the priest said when the nuns had finished. "The Communists will arrive any time now."

"I know," the Cardinal said, glancing at the young

pilot, "we've been dodging both sides for the last five hundred miles."

"We do not have much time," the priest said. "Come quickly, please." He spun on his heel and the two women followed. The distant rumble of Chou Enlai's attacking big guns roared up, sending shock waves, through the Valley of the Dead.

"I'm gonna crank up the engines," the pilot shouted to the Cardinal. "Leave 'em runnin' just in case."

The Cardinal waved that he understood and caught up with the Chinese as they moved quickly into the shelter of the elms. They stepped onto a well-worn path and began to climb the hill. It was a gentle ascent but he soon became winded.

To think I used to pitch nine innings, he said to himself. That's what I get for taking a desk job at the Vatican. Ah, the price of ambition!

When the Cardinal gained the level summit of the hill, he saw a massive, wooden enclosure, not unlike a fort. Inside the high log fence, hundreds of Oriental children were carrying planks up ladders and setting them into place over mud frames. Others were atop completed huts, thatching the straw roofs. As he neared, Stamp noted their eyes were strained, like the nuns.

"How many killed in the earthquake?" he asked the priest.

"One," the priest said. "Six hurt. But we are doing all right, thank you."

They arrived at the entrance, a sturdy gate, and the priest jabbered something to the two women in Chinese. They nodded, smiled to the Cardinal and disappeared inside.

"This way, Eminence," the priest said to Stamp,

and he spurted off across the top of the hill descending the back side.

The Cardinal hesitated a moment, looked at the children working now under the supervision of the nuns, then caught up with the priest.

"Father Kwan," he said, "I came here to help your orphanage. To give you money from Rome."

"No money is needed!" the priest said kindly. Yet there was a ragged undercurrent hidden in his voice, a tension barely concealed. He looked up into the Cardinal's face and smiled. "We will fix it all," he explained. "You see, China will be closed to foreigners for a long, long time. Religions must stay unobtrusive, accept no help. That is why we dress like we do now."

"Yes, I know," the Cardinal agreed. "I've met others recently who feel the same. But they accepted money to rebuild."

"It is different here," the priest said. "We are in the country. We survive by the goodness of the peasants. Most welcome communism. We will have to learn to survive side by side." He smiled again as if to reinforce his message.

"Well," the Cardinal sighed impatiently, "my pilot's going to be happy when he hears we flew here for nothing."

"I radioed you here for a reason, Eminence. We must hurry, please!" And he walked quickly down the hill.

"Hurry to what!" Stamp called after him.

"There is something I must show you," the Chinese priest called over his shoulder. He broke into a run.

The wind changed and the sound of the Communists' guns rumbled louder.

With a last glance at the ragtaggle group of children and nuns repairing the buildings, the Cardinal followed Father Kwan down the hill. The path was not easy to pick out. No one had walked it for a long time. Weeds obscured it, stones protruded. As the Cardinal descended, the trail grew wetter until his boots began to slip on the claylike mud.

As he rounded a bend, he tripped. With a desperate lunge, he kept himself from tumbling headfirst down the trail, but his other foot betrayed him and he sat rudely on his ass. Bringing his hands up, he saw they were coated with slime, his cardinal's ring encrusted with it.

He had started to clamber to his feet when something stopped him. Distinctly, he felt a presence, cold and chilling. He looked around. But only the sloping green grasses of the hill surrounded him. In the distance, he heard the chirping of a bird. Then, his name.

"Stamp, Eminence!"

It came from just below.

He searched about. He *had* felt something. . . .

Wiping his hands on his khaki trousers, he plunged downward, seeking as much to rid himself of the place where he had fallen as to join the priest. As he turned a sharp corner in the overgrown path, he saw Father Kwan standing above him, beside a grouping of boulders. He was holding what appeared to be a torch made of moss.

"Here!" Kwan yelled when he saw him approach. "Inside is a cave. It goes deep into the earth."

"I didn't come to see a cave!" the Cardinal said in frustration.

"Japanese soldiers used the cave as a place of torture and death. Hundreds of Chinese were butchered here during the recent world war. That is how the Valley of the Dead received its name!"

"Kwan," Livingston Stamp said impatiently, "my plane is waiting." He turned to go.

"The peasants say a demon named Baz has taken up residence in this unholy place," the Chinese priest chattered anxiously. He saw that the Cardinal was already on the trail and heading back. "A demon of lust and power!" he cried.

The officer of the Church paid no attention. He continued to climb.

"You cannot go!" the Chinese priest screamed. "There is a child inside!"

"A child?" the Cardinal asked, halting.

"An American like you! Six, seven years old. His parents were missionaries, we think, killed by Chinese soldiers. He seems afraid of all Chinese."

The Cardinal stood on the trail below the priest. Something near the mouth of the cave caught his eye. A metal plate full of food. Green bottle-flies buzzed over it.

"We bring his meals here," the priest said, seeing where the Cardinal stared. "But he does not eat. If we take him out forcibly, he returns." He fumbled in his pocket, brought out a sulphur stick match, lit the torch, and immediately ducked inside.

As he followed Father Kwan into the mouth of the cave, a blast of dank air struck the Cardinal. In two steps, the dim sunlight disappeared totally. For a moment, he stood in darkness. Then, the priest turned and Stamp saw his yellow face in the flickering light of the torch.

"Stay close to me," Kwan said. "There are terrible things here yet."

As they walked, hunched over now because of the

sloping ceiling, Stamp saw hundreds of roaches and sowbugs scurrying across the earthen floor. He heard the crunch of the hard-shelled bodies beneath his boots.

Walls glistened in their wetness. Somewhere ahead, there was the sound of water dripping.

Suddenly, he saw the priest straighten, and he felt colder air.

"The cavern itself," the priest said. "Even you can stand up now."

The Cardinal straightened. Piles of skeletons, rotting corpses. The gleaming red eyes of rats. A stench of rot. The Cardinal put his hand over his mouth as if to strain it out.

The priest swung the torch about in a circling search. At the rear of the cave stood a small creature, standing with hands up, shielding his face against the light.

"Boy!" the priest yelled, his voice echoing in the cavern. "Come here!"

The figure stood huddled, unmoving.

"A holy Cardinal of the Church has come to this stinking place to see you," the priest shouted. "Mind your manners!"

Still the boy did not move. The echoes of the priest's commands died away. When there was silence, the child turned furtively and slipped further into the darkness.

"What's his name?" the Cardinal asked.

"Peter. We have not discovered his last. And to ask him is useless. He remembers little about his parents."

"Maybe he chooses to forget. Some have the ability to seal out things too horrible to remember.

"Wait here," the Cardinal said. He reached out to the torch and raised it to illuminate the cave.

Picking his way carefully across the cavern, the prelate tried to keep his eyes focused on the rear wall. He felt himself grow dizzy. There was no air in this vile place!

As the light of the flame refracted off the slimy wall, he saw the child, standing, his back to him. His clothes were filthy from the mud of the cave.

"Peter?"

"G-g-go away! I-I hate you!" the trembling voice said.

"Peter," the Cardinal said. "Look at me. I am not Chinese."

The boy reluctantly peeked over his shoulder. Stamp saw that his face through dirty was strangely angelic, framed with curly, golden hair. His eyes were dark and piercing.

The Cardinal squatted. "Come here," he said.

The boy ran headlong into his arms. As the Cardinal enfolded his thin body, a soaring feeling of love enveloped him. The child, as if feeling the bond also, wrapped his little arms tighter around the prelate's neck.

"What are you doing here?" the Cardinal managed.

"I-I c-co-come to see S-S-Starbright," the boy stammered, relaxing his grip.

"Oh? What does he look like?"

"He has a l-l-long nose and his eyes are bulgy. B-b-but he smiles all the time."

The Cardinal tried to laugh but the boy stopped him by saying, "He g-gave me this!" And he held up a round, stone talisman about the size of an American half-dollar. Engraved on it was a bulbous-eyed, grinning, dragonlike creature. Then as if to show its preciousness, the child hid it suddenly in his filthy trouser pocket.

"Come on," the Cardinal said. He reached out and hauled the boy up into his arms and strode quickly toward the dim light at the entrance. He passed Father Kwan and, wordless, ducked low as he walked, cradling the boy. When they came near the sunlight at the mouth, he set him down. But the child became frightened and clung to him.

"N-n-no!" he squealed in fright. "Don't leave me!"

"I'm not going to leave you," the Cardinal whispered. "Don't worry. You're safe with me."

"You promise?"

"I promise."

He squeezed the Cardinal's neck tightly and kissed him on the cheek. Then, he wriggled from his arms and sprang toward the entrance, whooping as he ran into the sunlight outside.

"I'm g-g-going away!" he screamed at the top of his lungs.

Father Kwan and Stamp stepped outside. The sun was very bright now. They stood there, allowing their eyes to adjust to the light.

Peter was charging up the muddy path. The Cardinal watched him, feeling strangely relieved and warmed inside from the sunlight.

"Has he always stuttered like that?" the Cardinal asked.

"Ever since we found him in the Se-Chuan forest." Then the priest added pointedly, "You know you cannot leave him here. The Communists will kill him."

"You're very clever, Father. You knew I would take him, didn't you?"

Near the top of the hill now, far above the cave, Peter was still cavorting. He swung around momentarily, hands to mouth in a megaphone.

"C-c-come on!" he called down. "Co-come o-on!"

"I'm coming as fast as I can," Stamp shouted, sliding down to the path with Kwan.

"I'm t-ta-talking to my f-f-t-friend!" the boy corrected him. "C'mon. S-S-Starbright!"

There was a strange low reverberating noise. The Cardinal and Father Kwan spun. The entire overhang of the mountain above the cave collapsed. In a moment the mouth was concealed with boulders. Only dust hung in the air, marking the spot.

"He follows!" Father Kwan murmured, crossing himself.

But when the Cardinal turned to ask him what he meant, the priest was already scurrying fearfully up the hill.

TWO

OUTSIDE MILAN: *November 13, 1954*

The rain had been falling for two days in central Lombardy. The Arno, Po and Ticino rivers were swollen above their banks. The Mercedes Benz picked its way carefully toward Milan. Cardinal Livingston Stamp, dressed in a simple black suit with red buttons and piping on the coat, sat uncomfortably in the back seat, enduring the long ride from Rome. He could have taken one of the commuter flights that Air Italia offered, but he was not fond of flying. It made him feel helpless and out of control. And one of his great pleasures in life was being in control, always in power, whether it was saying Mass, hearing confessions or moving around a hundred million dollars.

He was used to hundreds of millions. His hours were spent managing Vatican investments. A former stock analyst, he had, at the request of Pope Pius XII, taken over the portfolio of the vast Lateran Treaty dowry. In less than twenty years, he had quintupled the amount of the Church's fortune.

The car swung past the coastal naval base of Spezia and turned inland to cross the Apennines that separated the Mediterranean Romans from northern Italians. Here, people were blonder and fair-skinned and therefore considered *stranieros*, foreigners. Rome, he mused, that small narrowminded country unto itself. The Cradle of Western Civilization with all its history and wisdom subtly refused to regard as equal an Italy that was not Roman.

The Cardinal smiled inwardly at the thought of how the Vatican would shudder if there were someday a foreign pope. Yet it was becoming more and more a possibility. Cardinals from faraway nations were getting the idea that the church was not just the Holy *Roman* Church but also the *Universal* Church. Led by Cardinal Josef Kruger, an arch-conservative from Austria, the movement to elect a non-Roman pope had gained ground. Many foreigners were openly seeking to unite behind a popular candidate.

Stamp's own appointment to the position of Prefect of Relations with Non-Christians—in charge of foreign missions—made him the first non-Italian to hold the post in three hundred years. Now his name was beginning to be mentioned as a future "Papabile."

Cardinal Livingston Stamp reached up and

grabbed hold of the support strap as the car shot over La Cisa Pass and began its descent into the valley. A small smile edged his mouth as he remembered his first meeting with the crusty old Josef Kruger. It had been shortly after he had received the massive assignment of reshaping Vatican investments.

"So you're the man who'll do it all correctly, huh?" Kruger had asked the young bishop while dining in the Vatican fresco room.

"Either that or go to Philadelphia," Livingston Stamp had joked.

The churchmen around him had laughed. They understood the meaning of his words. The ex-banker, past member of the New York Stock Exchange, present scholar at the Biblical Institute in Rome, had received the challenge of his life. It was a do or die situation. Failure meant being banished to the hinterlands, away from the power of Vatican society, away from advancement.

Working slowly, investing carefully and quietly, Livingston Stamp had funded two life insurance companies, purchased Yankee Stadium, several blocks of apartments along Park Avenue in New York, seventy-odd office buildings in six major U.S. cities; and a large chunk of General Motors stock. His reasoning was simple. The United States would win the war and become the most powerful country in the world. It was the place to put all of the Vatican's billion-dollar treasury.

Recently, Kruger had sent him a message on his stationery. Written in his own hand on the center of the page was a single word: "ITA!" It meant "GO" or "FORGE AHEAD." More importantly, it implied that Cardinal Livingston Stamp was his chosen future candidate for the papacy.

The Mercedes motored past the glass skyscrapers of downtown Milan (a city, he mused, not unlike America's Detroit), past the rain-soaked Duomo Cathedral and on towards Chiara Valle, the highest hill above the city. When the car wound its way through the sheets of gray rain and entered a driveway at the top, halting in front of an imposing stone building that loomed three stories into the clouded sky, Livingston Stamp's euphoric mood changed. The thorny problem that had brought him here was just inside.

For nearly a year, he had kept Peter himself. He knew it was ultimately impossible to raise him but he felt he owed this time to the boy. Gradually, the child's nightmares of the terrible deaths of his parents and the darkness of the cave went away. As Peter grew more relaxed, more trusting, there was a special brightness, a joyousness to the child. The Cardinal looked forward to coming home after work to the apartment on the Via della Conciliazione and being with Peter. Their relationship seemed so completely natural.

Peter had awakened in the Cardinal a paternal feeling he had never known he had. Livingston Stamp saw Peter as a brilliant priest, then a bishop and finally a cardinal like himself. But it was just a fantasy, he told himself. Yet, one day, when they had gone to the zoo, he had asked Peter the question.

"What are you going to be when you grow up?"

"An airplane pilot," the child had replied without hesitation.

"Have you thought of becoming a priest?" the Cardinal asked, and immediately upbraided himself for his selfishness. But to his delight and consternation, Peter had replied, "Oh, I'd n-never w-want to be that! I'd never g-g-get to do anything!"

When the day came that Stamp, with difficulty, announced he would seek parents for Peter—a father and mother who could give him the loving attention he deserved—the boy had locked himself in his room. The Cardinal asked Signorina Calavera, his housekeeper, to get a locksmith. When the artisan arrived and opened the door, the Cardinal was shocked to see the boy kneeling beside his bed, gripping his stone talisman.

"Make it so!" Peter kept praying to it. "Make it so I w-w-won't have to go!"

When the cardinal snatched away the thing, the boy flew into a tantrum. He flopped on the floor and kicked his legs and banged his forehead. Blood flew from his nose. Signorina Calavera had screamed. His behavior alarmed the Cardinal so much that he had given the stone back to Peter. To this day, the boy could not be separated from it. A strange and dark side of his otherwise sparkling, open character.

Was it this part of him that caused the recurring problem, the Cardinal wondered. Was this the reason no one could be found to raise him?

"Eminencia?" the driver from the Vatican car-pool asked. He was standing in the rain, politely holding open the rear door of the limousine. Stamp had no idea how long he had been there.

"*Scusi*," the Cardinal said apologetically. He dashed past the chauffeur, toward the front door of the building, splattering through deep puddles along the brick walk.

An American nun appeared from within, opening the oak door. "Eminence," she said, "it's so good to see you."

"Sister Gertrude, how are you?"

"Well," she chimed happily. "Isn't the rain awful?"

"It's raining in Rome, too," the Cardinal said, brushing drops from his shoulders. "You'd think it would know better."

The young nun smiled girlishly and said: "Mother Mary Theresa is in her office."

They walked into the warm foyer, the tiles gleaming, wood shining and polished. A statue of the Holy Virgin was on a table near the entrance, votive candles flickered at her feet. As he passed beneath the lintel, the Cardinal raised his eyes and saw the small, unobtrusive bronze sign that announced: ORPHANAGE OF ST. CLOTILDE. ALL ARE WELCOME!

He remembered that first day he had arrived here, Peter reluctantly walking beside him.

Like most orphanages, the object of this institution was to place children in good homes. That was not unusual. There were hundreds of orphanages in Italy that did the same thing. But St. Clotilde specialized in putting orphans into *American* homes. Sometimes, members of the Consular corps, stationed in Italy, took the children. More often, a childless couple in the United States adopted an Italian baby. This institution had the enviable record of placing all its orphans. It was particularly annoying therefore that Peter, a handsome, intelligent child and an American to boot, had, after more than five years, never *stayed* adopted.

Sister Gertrude swung open the door, bowed slightly and admitted the Cardinal. Soundlessly, she latched the heavy mahogany behind him. A wizened nun behind the desk, wearing pince-nez, looked up.

"Eminence!" she exclaimed, embarrassed. "I'm getting so deaf I didn't hear the knock." The ancient nun jumped up, pushing her chair away, and hastened to kiss his ring, half-kneeling as she did.

"How are you, Mother Theresa?" the Cardinal asked, passing up the stuffed chair in front of her desk for a hard-backed cane.

"Ah, the finances and the auditors, well . . ." she said. "The usual." She flung her hands toward the ceiling and smiled.

"I'll see what I can do. The Curia has made its budget already but I'm sure there's some sort of 'miscellaneous.' "

"Thank you, Eminence. You know, even though this is Archbishop Montini's territory, we rely on you for support."

"You are close to my heart. All of you," he said.

"We Americans have to stick together. Is it possible we'll get an American pope this next time?"

The Cardinal spread his long fingers and laid them deliberately and carefully across his black-trousered legs. "Perhaps," he said in his measured, diplomat's tone. "We shall see." He dropped his eyes.

"Well," Sister Theresa said, "we continue to pray for you. May God someday reward our supplications." She lifted a bulging manila folder and opened it. "I'm glad you're here. As I said on the phone, it's happened again."

The Cardinal rose from his chair and walked toward the beveled seventeenth-century windows. The imperfect antique glass normally distorted the view of the outside gardens. But the rain, running in rivulets down its uneven surface, obscured the outside entirely.

"Where was he this time?" he asked, long fingers stroking his chin.

"New York," Theresa said, checking the file. "And before that, as you know, Milwaukee, Miami, Los Angeles, Portland, Galveston and twice here in Italy.

Each time the couples were sure, absolutely sure, Peter was the child they wanted and each time, after a short period with him, they brought him back."

"What did he do this time?"

"He was perfect as usual," the nun said, patting the

_____ hild's head. "Absolutely a

_____ nothing to offend any of

_____ g?"

_____ to love them. Not any of

_____ now."

_____ amp offered. "And Peter?"

_____ han ever to return to the

_____ om the ornate rococo win-

_____ ght, starched sides of her

_____ ily her pinched face.

_____ p a creek."

_____ ticing for the annual bicy-

_____ e made captain of the var-

_____ e know I'm here now?"

_____ want to get him excited.

_____ e hears you're coming."

_____ deep in thought, walked

_____ un asked. "There is one

_____ with the face? Well, after

_____ , I took it from him. Or

_____ She forgot that she left it

_____ ent to bed that night. She

awoke in the middle of the night to the sound of cackling."

"Cackling?"

"Yes, she said it was coming from her pocket."

"Nonsense."

"Of course, Eminence. Sister Francis needed a sabbatical anyway. Overworked. She's soaking up the sun now on the Italian Riviera."

"And the stone?" the Cardinal asked, put off by the odd story.

"Peter's got it again. I don't know how. It just disappeared and turned up."

"Okay," the Cardinal said. "I'll talk to him about that too."

The orphanage was in the shape of a large "T" with the hippodrome immediately adjacent, arrived at through covered, aluminum walkways. Count Vicenzo Amalfi, who had bequeathed his estate to the good sisters of St. Mary's, had enjoyed indoor bicycle racing. He had had the concrete hippodrome built at considerable expense, but legend had it that he had paid the hippodrome off with the many wagers he had won from the guests who had come to watch the cyclists race.

The structure was a modified geodesic. To enter, the Cardinal walked down a sloping concrete ramp, then through iron doors. Inside he mounted the empty bleachers and sat down.

In the air were the not unpleasant smells of sweat and pine boards. Below him, he saw the laminated wooden track. Everytime he had seen this track, he had been impressed by the closeness, the claustrophobically engineered turns. The oval track had been built for professionals, not grade-school boys. Yet, the orphanage was lucky to have it.

In the center of the track, a half dozen boys in leather helmets stood around the heavy-set coach. Professore Eugenio, as a young man, before his sins of pasta, had been one of the champions of the Cinzano circuit.

Looking up, Eugenio saw the Cardinal and waved. Then he said something and the boys parted and Peter appeared from the group. He tossed down his helmet as he approached. The Cardinal marveled at how he had grown in just six months. His shoulders were broadening into manhood already and his legs were strong, no longer a child's.

Peter sprinted across the track, up its steep side, vaulted the wooden railing and bent quickly, kissing the Cardinal's ring.

"E . . . Eminence!" he stuttered gladly.

"Hello, Peter," Stamp said, patting the seat beside him. The boy sat obediently.

"I thought I would surprise you," the Cardinal said, smiling.

"I . . . I'm glad you're here," Peter said, his eyes sparkling. "But I-I knew you were c-coming."

"Who told you? Not Mother Theresa?"

"Oh, n-no!"

"Then, who?"

"Oh . . . I j-just knew," he said, turning his face away.

"Sister Theresa tells me you didn't like New York."

"Oh, I l-l-liked it," Peter said.

"But not Mr. and Mrs. Domenico?"

"Th-they we-were fine," he said. "I-I s-s-saw an opera w-while I-I was there. The s-s-story was about

Doctor F-F-Faust and how he sold his s-s-soul t-to the d-devil."

"They made that into an opera?"

"Y-yes," Peter said, "it w-was v-v-very powerful. I-I-I liked Doctor F-F-Faust b-but I h-h-hated M-M-M-Meph . . ."

"Mephistopheles?"

"Y-y-yes, him!" Peter blurted. He smiled in relief at getting it out.

Three cyclers below whizzed by them, bent low over their sleek machines. A tall kid with the oily black hair of a seal was in the lead.

"That's A-A-Antonio," Peter said. "He's the b-b-best."

"I thought you were the best."

"Only at s-so-soccer," Peter said. "He's the b-b-best here. He c-ca-calls me 'football head' because he s-s-says my head i-is round."

"And is it?" the Cardinal teased.

"I-I-I don't think so," Peter admitted honestly.

"I don't think so either," the Cardinal assessed. "I think you have a fine head."

"Th-th-thank you," Peter said. He turned and watched as the riders circled the track. The seal parried every feint the riders behind him made. He was in control and they could not pass him.

The Cardinal saw that Peter was concentrating to- tally on the action on the track. He seemed removed. His eyes were riveted to the lead racer, his cheeks growing redder as if he were holding his breath. Unconsciously, the boy lifted his hand to his shirt and grasped hold of something inside. In a single breath, he blew out, "S-sometimes I-I wish. . . ."

"Peter?" the Cardinal asked.

The boy swung his face up. Immediately the

darkness that had gripped it fled like shadows before the sun.

"You don't like being second best, do you?"

"No," Peter said, "I-I like to w-win very much."

"Be careful of your pride," the Cardinal said. "You have quite a bit."

"But the b-best d-d-deserve to win, don't they?"

"Yes," the Cardinal replied, seeing his chance to move to the subject, "but *you* haven't been winning with your adoptions."

The boy shifted nervously and drew his legs together so his silk trunks pressed tightly and billowed, making his hips appear smaller.

The riders sped past again, legs pumping, torsos nearly horizontal to the mount bar.

"Tell me," the Cardinal pressed. "There must be a reason. You're twelve now. In a few years many couples will not want an older boy."

"T-t-that's the w-w-way it should b-be," Peter mumbled. "I w-won't ever be adopted."

"Who told you that?"

"My f-friend."

"Peter," the Cardinal objected, "you shouldn't go to someone your age for that kind of advice."

"My, m-my-my *old* friend," Peter said. And reaching inside his green jersey, he drew out the stone. It was hanging around his neck by a leather thong.

The Cardinal wanted to snatch away the grinning face that lay cuddled in Peter's palm. The precious place around a child's neck was reserved for holy medals, not this cursed thing! It took a great deal of effort for him to get control of himself.

"How did you get it back?" he asked lightly.

"Oh, Sister Francis gave it to me. Just before she left." Peter was gazing at the bulging eyes and snout.

"You change when you hold that thing," the Cardinal said. Again, the impulse to grab the talisman swept over him. But he knew that such a violent act would only add to its importance. So he finished softly, "It's a child's thing, you know. As you grow up, childish things should be put aside."

"He's my f-f-friend," Peter said. "I won't ever out-out-outgrow him. He *tells* me things."

"Oh, like what?"

"Well, he knew you were coming today."

"He told you that?"

"Y-yes."

"What else?" the Cardinal probed. It was more than time to shatter Peter's illusion about this rubbish.

"My f-f-friend says even th-though you w-want t-to v-very m-m-much, you will never be p-pope."

The Cardinal's heart jumped. He had never spoken of his ambition to anyone—not even to Kruger. He was convinced it would be politically foolhardy.

Blood racing, the Cardinal managed to lean back into the seat and ask "Did he say anything else?"

"He s-s-said there was o-o-only one f-fa-family I would ever b-be adopted i-i-into."

"What family is that?" Livingston asked, his jaw held firmly, lips white.

"The f-family of the Church," the boy said. "He m-meant you w-would be my fa-father."

"I can't do that! I'm a Cardinal, Peter!"

"You f-found m-me in the c-cave. My r-re-religion p-professor t-told me sometimes such things are pre-preordained."

A tingle like an electric shock ran down the back of the Cardinal's neck. From that first day in China, all during those days together in Rome, he had felt Divine Providence had planned his meeting with this special child, that it was somehow a destiny. Is that what all this lack of adoption meant? Still, how could he commit himself to Peter as a father? If fate had that in mind, then let it show him how to proceed.

"I have things to do," the Cardinal said, "many, many responsibilities. I couldn't adopt you. It wouldn't be fair. I would only be playing at being your father. I am not your father, and you are not my son."

"Y-you c-could get someone to look after m-me like Signorina Calavera did," Peter offered quickly. "I-I could go to s-school here and v-v-visit you in R-Rome w-when you w-w-wanted to see me! I-I-I know who you are," Peter said when the Cardinal didn't reply. "I-I w-wi-will be happy with the time you can s-sp-spare."

The bikers screamed past, making the never ending revolutions on the track. Professor Eugenio raised a large cardboard that said "1" signifying it was the last lap. Then he grabbed up the checkered flag in preparation for the finish.

"I don't see any other way," the Cardinal said almost to himself.

"Th-thank you!" Peter stammered, overcome by his happiness. Tears of gratitude wet his face.

"Wipe your face," the Cardinal said, climbing down the bleacher steps. "Then we'll go find you a house and someone to take care of you."

The sound of skidding tires burst up from the track. A boy screamed in pain. The Cardinal quickly pulled himself up onto the wooden railing.

The two smaller boys were coasting around the track, spokes whirring in easy fluid motion. They were looking back over their shoulders toward Antonio, the best rider of the school. He lay amidst shattered spokes, his knees bleeding, the smashed front wheel of his cycle wobbling near him. He had never crossed the finish line.

The Cardinal turned to see that Peter had pulled himself up also. He was staring at Antonio, his hand unconsciously around the amulet beneath his shirt.

THREE

ROME: *October 28, 1958*

A flock of white pigeons swooped across St. Peter's Square. The throng below watched as the birds dipped, then resettled in Bernini's colonnades with the one hundred and forty travertine marble saints. The crowd of over two hundred thousand stood, drinking and eating, jostling one another in the unseasonal heat. Many men took off their shirts and stood half-naked. But despite the blistering noon sun, despite the close-packed bodies, despite children screaming and the thousands of aching feet, no one left. They had assembled sixteen hours before to see who would be the successor to Pope Pius XII. Already black smoke had appeared twice from the tall, thin metal pipe above the Sistine Chapel. Two ballots cast. No pope.

And still the faithful and curious waited and watched, jamming the huge piazza.

From across the adjoining, smaller piazza of Pope Pius XII, at the rear of the crowd, came a willowy young woman, followed closely by a blond-haired boy. The woman was perspiring, her olive skin glistening as she walked. The boy, in coat and tie, was carrying two light overnight bags. He trailed behind the woman as she carved a path through the people, crying *"Permesso, Permesso!"*

A priest refused to move. The woman raised her hands and shrieked "I work for a cardinal!" then pushed him aside, moving finally between parked, empty Roman buses with the numbers 64 in their windows, denoting the Vatican as final destination.

The woman and the boy-man turned briefly up Via della Conciliazione, the only street in Rome that ran directly to the Vatican, to number 52 near Via Rusticucci. Then she took one of the bags from the boy, and together they climbed the red-tiled steps, pushed open a heavy glass-paneled door and stepped inside.

The interior was cool and darkened. Vases of bright yellow chrysanthemums filled the foyer.

"The flowers are worthy of his Eminence, no?" she asked. She was from Bolzano and spoke with a clipped Italian-Austrian accent.

"They are l-lovely, A-A-Anna," he agreed.

They ascended the stairwell, passing the two stained-glass windows depicting Adam and Eve and St. Michael casting Lucifer into Hell, and trudged up to the top story. Anna found the key the Cardinal had given her and opened the door.

She walked through the ascetically furnished living room to the far bedroom. She had long ago chosen the room with the softest bed for herself. But the boy went to the tall glass doors, opened them and stepped out onto the sunlit balcony. He stood there, dark piercing eyes riveted to the smoke stack on the Sistine roof.

"Peter?" Anna asked. "Where are you?"

"Out h-he-here!" he shouted.

She emerged with a dampened towel, wiping the beads of perspiration from her face and neck.

"Aren't you hot in that wool suit?" she asked.

"N-n-no!" he stuttered, turning and smiling at her.

"It's a hundred and ten degrees and you are not even warm! *Santi!*" She shook her head, leaned over suddenly and kissed him on the cheek.

"Anna!" he complained and his face flushed in embarrassment.

"Soon you'll be a man," she said. "And what a man! You will have women waiting in line for your attentions!"

"Anna!" he begged, his face reddening deeper. *"Prego!"*

"You're nearly sixteen," she said. "Every time I talk about girls you stand there and blush like a beet! That girl, Marcellina, she keeps asking me to get you out."

"I-I-I'm in the care of a C-Ca-Cardinal," he said, suddenly stiffening. "I-It is m-my duty to be well-behaved."

"Ah, the old-tune again," she said, pirouetting about the veranda. "They call you the 'virgin' in your boys' school. They say you are a saint. But I don't think so! I see the way you look at the girls when you think no one sees you!"

"I-I-I don't need g-gi-girls!"

"Is that why you pray on your fingertips and your hands swell up from the pain?"

"It's the o-only way I can p-p-pray p-p-p-perfectly,"
he said frowning. "I have impure t-te-temptations if I
do not kneel on my f-f-fingers!"

"Aha!" she cried, teasing him mercilessly like she
always did. "Visions of naked girls, little man? You
see? You do need us! *Capisce*?!"

He turned and ignored her, gripping the balcony
railing, staring down at the Egyptian obelisk. The tall
stone tower had been hand-carried from Caligula's
circus and placed in the Vatican. A temporal symbol
of an enemy vanquished.

"Ah, Pietro," Anna said, draping an arm around his
shoulders, a touch that made him shiver since it was
unexpected. "You are always so serious. I am only
teasing. Women do that when they see a man is un-
reachable."

Still he did not turn toward her.

"The Cardinal hires me to cook for you, wash your
clothes. I see you get to school every morning in Mi-
lano. We live together but you know I don't really
know you."

"I-I use my t-time for m-my studies. Livy is v-very
p-proud of my knowledge of the C-Church."

"That dry old stuff."

"I-it's important t-to know history," Peter said
solemnly. "Th-that w-way I-I won't make the s-same
s-stupid mistakes as o-others."

"What mistakes, little man?"

But Peter did not answer. He only appeared to
study the crowd below.

"What goes on in that head of yours anyway?" Anna
wondered, placing the coolness of the wet towel
against her cheeks. "I know you don't tell anything to
your friends because you don't have any. And you
certainly never tell me what you think. You are mys-

terious, Pietro. Is it because you are trying to prove worthy of becoming his son?"

Without turning from the crowd below, Peter said: "I-I will be. S-s-so-someday."

"You don't know that!"

"I-I-I know!"

"When the earth turns to cheese."

"You j-just wait. You'll s-see!" He was gazing fixedly at the crowd below.

"You love him too much," Anna said, pulling her arm away. "*Che amore!* I like you, my little Pietro. I hope you won't be disappointed."

He turned and unexpectedly smiled warmly to her. "I-I like you t-t-too," he said shyly. Then he turned again to the sea of people at his feet. "So many . . ." he wondered. "So-so very many! T-the Ca-Ca-Catholic Church is very p-p-powerful."

"They have come to see the new pope. Maybe it will be Cardinal Stamp?"

"I-It won't be h-hi-him."

"His Eminence is a very important man. Very big!"

"Oh, despite S-Starbright, I-I-I hope he d-d-does win!" Peter said between clenched teeth. He spun toward the tiny tin smokestack, as though expecting an immediate answer. "S-S-Stamp for P-Pope!" he cried.

Anna laughed. "*Prego.* It is not polite to cheer for a candidate. It is adult to keep quiet and hope secretly."

"I don't c-c-care!" Peter shouted. "I hoped he d-d-does win!" And with a great burst of enthusiasm, he bent down over the crowd and chanted: Cardinal Stamp for P-Pope! S-S-Stamp for Pope!!"

Several onlookers below glanced up at the dark-suited boy. But they paid him no attention. Very few in the crowd had even heard him, such was their own din and shouting.

"I am going inside to take a cool bath," Anna said. "You should get out of this sun or you will go crazier!"

"I'll just stay and w-w-w-watch," he said, turning his gaze to the pipe again.

"These conclaves can take days and days," she said.

"I don't c-c-c-care," he said. "I w-w-want to see the white smoke when it co-comes out!"

She shrugged and went inside, unbuttoning her short-sleeved, cotton dress. Finding his luggage still sitting in the livingroom, she took it to his bedroom, then went to hers. When she was in her bedroom, she pulled her dress off completely, unclipped her bra and stepped out of her panties. Then, she picked up her suitcase and flopped it on the bed. She took out a blue bathrobe and slipped into it, cinching it around her tightly which accentuated her slim waist. For a moment, she gazed into the bureau mirror and remembered where Roberto, her lover, had touched her.

Then she rummaged in her suitcase until she found her green portable radio.

"They don't know how to enjoy themselves here in this Vatican," she said. Grabbing up her toiletries bag, she flounced into the high-ceilinged marble bathroom and twisted on the taps over the bathtub. Water began to pour into the ancient marble tub with its bronze legs in the shape of griffin's claws. She tested the flow until she found the hot water, then shut it down until it was only a trickle into the cold. She did not want a hot bath on this day.

She set her radio on the shelf above the tub and reaching over the running water, flipped it on. Nothing happened. Dismayed, she pulled it down, shook it, and twisted the knobs.

"Ah, the batteries," she said. "I forgot to buy the new ones."

Opening up its plastic compartment in the rear, she uncoiled a cord and set the radio back on its narrow shelf. Searching quickly, she spotted the plug near the corner of the tub and connected it. Classical music by Beethoven emerged through its tiny speaker. Annoyed, she twisted the dial and found Elvis Presley singing "Blue Suede Shoes." She stepped back and did a little dance, shaking her hips to the music. Then, she dug into her toiletries bag and searched for something.

"*Santi!*" she muttered.

Leaving the water running, she strode to the bathroom door and flung it open.

"Pietro," she called.

"Yes," he said, sticking his head inside. And when he saw she was clad only in her bathrobe, averted his eyes like a gentleman.

"I have left my shampoo," Anna said. "Did you bring yours?"

"In m-m-m-my suitcase," he said modestly. "Do you want m-m-m-me to get it?"

"Never mind," she laughed, tossing her silky, black hair over her shoulder. "I'll get it. Go back to your smokestack!"

He turned quickly, glad to get away. Anna scampered across the cool marble floor of the living room and into the bedroom where she had placed his suitcase. She unsnapped the leather bag and flung it open. The shampoo was there on top. Grabbing the bottle up, she turned to go back to the bathroom. But something she had seen in the bag made her look again.

Reaching in between the layers of Peter's shirts, she pinched a worn leather lanyard between her fingers. She withdrew it, wrinkling her nose in distaste as the round stone talisman with the fat, grinning dragon emerged.

"Pagan!" she whispered. "How often have I told him to throw it away!"

Anna glared at the grotesque leering face a moment longer. Then she slipped the amulet into the pocket of her robe and darted back toward the bathroom.

Closing the door, she set the shampoo on the edge of the bathtub and withdrew the stone. She held it dangling momentarily in the air, then dropped it into the toilet.

"Goodbye," she whispered. *"Ciao!"* And she pulled the chain.

The tub was very full. She shut off the taps and felt the water, shivering deliciously at its coolness. Then she wriggled out of her robe, letting it fall around her brown ankles. Drawing in her breath in orgasmic gasps, she slipped bit by bit into the cold water and finally lay full out, eyes closed, breasts bobbing.

Overhead, on the shelf above the tub, the Kingston Trio was beginning "Jamaica."

An odd noise was in the music. It sounded like fingers snapping to a different beat. Opening her eyes, she peered upward.

To her astonishment, she saw her green radio bouncing up and down, rattling its plastic skin against the wooden shelf. It scooted forward, balancing precariously. Too late, Anna realized what was about to happen.

Outside, Peter stood on the balcony, his eyes

riveted to the roof of the Sistine. Suddenly, from within the apartment, came a shrieking cry.

As he spun, the crowd below erupted. A throaty cheer went up, drowning the cries behind him. He turned and saw a stream of white smoke spurt from the thin metal pipe. A pope had been elected!

But from inside the screams continued.

"A-Anna!" Peter shouted, realizing something was wrong. He ran from the balcony to the bathroom and turned the brass doorhandle. The door would not open.

He pounded on it. Her screaming stopped in midbreath. He listened a moment, then tried the handle again. The door swung open easily.

Smoke hung in lazy curls around the bathtub. A stink, like sulphur and melted plastic, floated in the room.

"A-A-Anna?" he asked, stepping forward and immediately felt his shoes slosh in standing water.

Anna lay face up in the bathtub. The radio, still zapping and crackling, floating like a green plastic fish near her feet. Backing from the room, Peter pulled the door shut behind him.

From the piazza, a roar like rolling thunder exploded. Dazed, Peter crossed the room. Through the open doors, he could see directly across the courtyard. The tall doors on the little balcony of Saint Peter's Basilica were being opened. A rotund little man emerged. Cardinal Livingston Stamp was immediately behind him, dressed in the full regalia of his scarlet robes. He stepped in front of the small man, adjusted the microphone and announced in Latin: "We have a new pope. He is John the Twenty-Third!"

A chant began in the crowd. It rattled the windows near Peter.

"*Viva Il Papa! Viva Il Papa!* viva il papa!'

The new pope raised his hand and gave his first blessing. "*Urbi et Orbi:* To the City and the World." Absently, Peter crossed himself. Then he saw Cardinal Stamp dejectedly slip from the balcony and close the gray doors behind the new pope.

* * *

The Cardinal conducted Anna's funeral himself. There was a small gathering of relatives and friends at the Santo Refugio Cemetery. The weather had turned chilly and each hurriedly threw dirt on the coffin as it was lowered and then departed. Anna's mother shook the Cardinal's hand and kissed his ring. She had accepted his offer of a plot here in Rome, rather than taking Anna's body back to Milan. She thanked him for it again, telling him how poor she was.

Peter watched, feeling strangely detached from the scene. He had loved Anna, but really knew none of her relatives or even her boyfriend, Roberto, who stood alone, sobbing, even when everyone was departing.

A chauffeur who drove for the Vatican was waiting in the long, black Mercedes as the Cardinal and Peter approached. They were walking up the slope of the green lawn.

"Anna was w-w-wonderful," Peter said. "Sh-she w-was the p-p-prettiest w-woman on our street!"

The Cardinal, striding beside him, turned suddenly at the comment, realizing the boy had regarded Anna in some other way than as a mere housekeeper. Was it the first awakening of a young man's sexuality?

"Was there no one prettier?"

"I-I-I saw the way the m-men looked at her," Peter said evasively. "Dirty-mi-minded Italians! Pinching and c-c-curling their f-f-fingers, making sl-sl-slurping sounds with their mouths."

"Perhaps your next housekeeper should be someone older, then. Someone not so pretty, huh?"

Peter, gaining the top of the slope, stopped suddenly.

"I-I-I could just l-live with y-you," he suggested.

"No, my boy," the Cardinal replied as gently as possible. "I think the answer is another housekeeper. But come on now. Annuncio is an impatient driver. He may just leave us here." And Peter followed Livingston Stamp as he ducked into the rear seat of the limousine.

The car picked its way through the cemetery. Peter watched as the Cardinal stared out his window, lost in thought. Somehow, he looked much older than before the Conclave. Gray hairs seemed to have sprouted overnight on his head. Even his skin, normally ruddy, appeared sallow.

"E-E-Eminence," Peter asked quietly. "Why are you s-s-sad? Is i-i-it Anna?"

"Partly," the prelate said after a moment.

"The e-e-election?"

"You're a mind reader," the Cardinal said, checking to see that the plastic partition was closed between them and the driver.

He sighed heavily and continued: "New things have happened. The Italians after Pius XII have unexpectedly resolved their differences and regrouped under Pope John. The Vatican, it is rumored, will become all Roman once again. There is even talk I may be relieved of my Prefecture of Non-Christian Relations."

"W-w-what w-would y-you do if you were p-pope?" Peter asked, cherubic face inquisitive.

Normally, Livingston Stamp would not have answered that question. But in the privacy of the automobile, gazing at such a guileless mien, he felt safe.

"Save the Church," he said simply.

"F-from w-w-what?"

"Itself," the Cardinal said. "From men like John who want change too fast too soon. From those who would abandon tradition."

The car was moving swiftly now on the Via Tuscolana which led back into the city of Rome.

"My f-fr-friend predicted y-you will n-never get what you wa-want!"

"I'm afraid he's right. My time is over. Perhaps they tried me too soon. In the future, the press will put my name in the list of 'Papabili,' but they won't understand that I can never again be a serious candidate. Italians and their allies know me now. They'll be lobbying continuously against me until the next election. I will gain many enemies. We underestimated the Italians' ability to regroup."

"B-but maybe if you did what D-D-Doctor Faust did?"

"Who?"

"You know, the m-m-man who m-made the c-contract with Me-Me-Mephi. . . ."

"Mephistopheles. That was only a story, Peter."

"B-b-but h-he did it! A-a-and there is a d-devil!"

"Yes," the Cardinal said. "Lucifer and his cohorts do exist. But that's not the way they work in real life. A man doesn't make one deal. He makes hundreds, thousands of them. Little acts of greed, ethical corners cut, omissions of good he could have done. The selling of a man's soul takes a lifetime."

The Cardinal, feeling introspective, continued.

"The devil works quietly. He does very little that's dramatic or exciting. He chisels away, wearing a man down. He's the most persistent force in our world and he has a startling nose for our weaknesses. We fight and fight with God's help. But by the end, most of us become pretty ragged. We all wind up making compromises of some sort. *That's* the "deal" you're talking about."

"But w-what i-if i-i-it could all happen at once? W-what i-if you c-could just m-make a c-contract with him? And be pope?"

For a moment, the Cardinal hesitated. Then, he turned to Peter with a smile. "It would indeed be a temptation," he said.

The car turned onto the Via Appia Nuova and immediately entered heavier traffic. Horns were blowing angrily, everyone inching along in short stop-and-go spurts.

On the shoulders of the road stood whores, warming themselves over the open fires burning in fifty-gallon gas drums. The number "9" Sewer Treatment Plant, its white paint peeling badly, floated slowly by.

Behind the primitive plant were the ancient chemical flows and the foul pit into which anything solid was deposited. The squalid smell of the open flows and the pit beyond now seeped inside the car.

The car stopped completely. The chauffeur lowered the plastic screen a slit and swiveled in the front seat.

"*Mala fortuna!*" he said and threw his hands up at the hopeless snarl outside.

A figure suddenly appeared at Peter's window. It was one of the whores from the road. She was grotesquely fat and the bulging folds of flesh on her neck were coated with an oily grime. Two purple eyebrow slashes limned her heavily madeup eyes.

"*Malissima fortuna!*" the chauffeur exclaimed, seeing her. He motioned her to go away.

Instead, she pressed herself close so the glass disfigured her gross flesh. She bent and grinned, revealing broken, yellowed teeth. Then she beckoned seductively with her finger and as she did the front of her low-cut dress fell away from her fat breasts and out swung a round, silt-caked face.

"Impulsively, Peter reached for his electric button and whirred down the window.

The whore, sticking in her face, saw the Cardinal's red finery. She shrank away. "*Scusi!*" she mumbled.

"E-e-eminence!" Peter cried pointing. "M-my s-stone! I've b-b-been looking all over for it!"

"Impossible!" Stamp said incredulously. "How could that be yours?"

The hag, noticing where Peter pointed, caught up the small object in her meaty hand.

"P-p-please!" Peter said. "I-i-it *is* my stone!"

At a loss, Cardinal Stamp turned toward the staring chauffeur but the man diplomatically turned in his seat and put both hands on the wheel, ready to go should traffic permit.

"*Permesso,*" the Cardinal beckoned to the whore. He made a motion to let him see it.

Admiring his courtliness, she smiled her most feminine and shy smile and with great delicacy lifted the leather lanyard from around her neck. Then she reached carefully into the car and handed it past the eager boy to the red-robed priest.

Now it lay in the Cardinal's palm. The face on the stone periapt was coated in filth. Using his thumbnail, he scraped at it and in one swipe revealed the gross-lipped grin. It was unmistakable.

"Where did you get this?" he asked her in amazement.

She backed away suddenly, shaking her head, the slight delicate smile disappearing.

"S-s-she s-stole it!" Peter said. "Th-that's where sh-she got it!"

"*Eminencia,*" the driver said, banging on the plastic partition. And he motioned to the traffic ahead of them which was moving now.

"P-p-please get it b-b-back," Peter begged, sensing he might lose it forever.

The Cardinal dropped his eyes to the beastlike face. "On one condition," he said softly. "That I can bless it."

"*Affretta!*" the whore interjected suddenly, seeing the limousine now inch forward.

"Deal?" Livingston Stamp asked Peter. "Can I bless it?"

Peter, feeling the car gather speed, nodded.

Livingston Stamp fished into his soutane and drew out a five-thousand lira note. He held it before the hag's hand. She glanced at the numbers, was about to dicker for more, when the car began to move faster. Like a hawk swooping on a mouse, she snatched the bill from the Cardinal and fled. Livingston Stamp lunged across and brought up Peter's window. Immediately, the limousine roared away.

"M-m-may I h-hold it?" Peter asked.

The prelate handed it to him and the boy looked very happy. He began to rub the amulet against his suit pants, cleaning it.

"Thank you," he said. "Oh, b-b-boy! Th-thank you!"

The Cardinal looked out his rear window and saw

that several whores had gathered in front of the re-
ceding sewerage plant and were joking with its operator, an emaciated man with a caved-in chest. He was
holding a basket of some sort and out of it he pulled
a rusted iron lamp. One of the whores was shaking
her head at such a trade.

In Peter's hands, Livingston Stamp noticed that the
face on the stone was emerging from its muck.

"Give it to me now," he said.

The boy stopped his polishing. Reluctantly, he
handed the talisman to the Cardinal who made a fist,
eclipsing the lusting face.

"I'll bless it after my vespers."

"And then c-ca-can I have it?"

"Not tonight," Stamp said. And turning his face
once again to the landscape outside, he held the amulet tightly, deep in thought.

PART TWO

PUBLIC LIFE

FOUR

The mountain valley lay baking in the late afternoon sun. It was past five and the air was unmoving and heavy. Hillside lupines, normally lush purple, were a wilting gray; the sparsely snow-capped Sierras in the east; the westerly Santa Marias were scorched brown already, showing clear boundaries where their lower slopes met the valley's green crops. The new spring leaves on the oaks and eucalyptus had dropped, leaving limbs bare and autumn-looking, as if reaching to the sky, begging for rain.

Only one lonely cloud had passed overhead during the last week. As in most other places in California, the drought had been here for two years.

Below the Santa Maria valley, the gigantic bread-basket of the San Joaquin was drying up even faster. The farmers there, large landowners, had pumped millions of gallons of water from their underground tables. Others had sunk wells as deep as two or three thousand feet. The smaller farmers of Santa Maria, most with less than a hundred acres apiece, borrowed money to drill wells. They had always been able to rely on the runoff from the Sierras but that had diminished to trickles.

But even the water brought up by the red, electric pumps from underground was not enough. And each of the eighty-odd farmers in Santa Maria, as he lay alone or with his wife those hot muggy nights, listened to his pump as it whined in the darkness and prayed he would not hear the dreaded rattle of ball bearings—the sound that meant the pump had burned itself out because there was not even enough water to cool it.

Normally, the sun would have cooled by this hour. But even this close to evening, the hot ball hung mercilessly in the sky, as though refusing to set. Down the neat, straight-furrowed fields of Santa Maria, the farmers shuffled forward with their hoes and weeded their lettuce, onions, strawberries, tomatoes and cabbages.

A battered 1940s pickup, its sides rusted from lack of paint, rumbled past a field of onions and stopped at the light green rows of lettuce. The driver, a tall, thin, ascetic-looking man, stepped from the running-board and slammed the door. Several workers looked up from the backbreaking labor.

"*Padre granjero,*" they exclaimed. The farmer priest.

The priest took off his hat and the hot sun played on his dazzling blond hair. He waved to a man and woman.

"Ho!" he yelled and leaped carefully into one of the rows. As he neared, the woman saw he wore his usual faded jeans, blue chambray workshirt rolled to the elbows, and workboots. His face was sunburned, his arms and hands a deep brown. The woman noticed too, as she always did, the eyes of the young priest. They were intense and dark brown, unusual for a blond. "They seemed to peer into one's very soul," some said. There were those who said that this young priest was not aware of physical things such as touch, taste and smells that other men complained about or took comfort in. He seemed on some higher plane. Still others said categorically that the farmer priest was a saint. One woman claimed she had seen him scourging himself outside the rectory on the hill.

"Lerda!" the priest cried happily to her, "I s-s-see you are well."

"I am, thank you," she said. "I took the medicines you gave me." She was a big-boned ugly woman, a foot taller than her husband. Half-Irish, half-Mexican, Lerda was known for her quiet, strong devotion to her husband and her church.

"And how is the h-hu-husband?" the young priest asked, turning to the man at the woman's side.

"Well, also, Padre Peter," the bantam-sized man said. "But our *crop* could be better." He said this last cautiously since he did not want to be negative to this priest who always seemed optimistic.

"I've p-p-prayed every d-d-day for rain," Father Peter Stamp said. He straightened and examined the golden hills surrounding them, dark eyes flashing.

"The drought is God's will," Lerda offered, seeing the anguished look on Father Peter's face. "He will give us rain when he wants to."

"Hope it's not too late," Francisco said.

"*Paco!*" Lerda scolded. "Do you doubt God?"

"I see the brown on the lettuce. I feel the mushiness in their heads. In a week or two, we'll lose everything! Does God know that?"

"H-He-He knows," Father Stamp said, lowering his eyes to Francisco's face.

"Then why doesn't He help us? You would if you were God, wouldn't you, Father Granjero?"

"I-I-I would in-indeed," Peter said. "I-I'd g-give you w-wa-water." He smiled broadly at his mildly blasphemous jest. "A-anyone here w-wish t-to confess t-t-t-today?"

"No," the man said, shaking his head.

"You should," Lerda said to him. "You got drunk two nights ago and threw up all over the house."

Francisco swiped off his cowboy hat. He was obviously embarrassed.

"You shouldn't p-p-pu-push him, Lerda," Peter said. "Will I-I s-see y-you both at the meeting t-t-tonight?"

"We'll be there!" Lerda said.

Peter waved to them and continued on down the rows to the other farmers.

"You should not tell everything between us," Francisco accused his wife.

"Forgive me," Lerda said. "I was stupid. But you'll confess?"

"In my own time."

"Before tomorrow?"

"*Santo Niño!*" the man cried. "Yes, by Sunday!"

"Good," Lerda said. "You should be in a state of grace for Sunday. It's not only the Lord's day but Father Peter's birthday!"

"I had forgotten," Francisco said, turning now from his work of piling weeds and seeing the young priest sitting alone with Ramirez, an old man. The old man was talking, telling him his sins. "How old is Father Peter this Sunday?"

"Thirty-three," Lerda said. "You remember how old he was when he came to us?"

"Everyone knows that," Francisco said. "He was barely twenty-one. The youngest priest ever!"

"He's a saint," she said. "Everyone knows that too. He treats us Chicanos the same as the other farmers. We're lucky to have a saint."

She straightened and saw that the young priest had finished with the confession. He slapped the dust from his jeans and stood up. Then he walked toward the pickup.

"He's not of this world," Lerda said quietly to herself, watching him lope in an easy gait to his ancient Ford. "He does not even remember tomorrow is his birthday. It will be a wonderful surprise, huh, Francisco?"

"Do the weeds, woman," he said.

Father Peter Stamp drove the rattling pickup along the edges of the fields. The tangy smells of the crops floated to him through the open window. As he passed each field with its upright water pump, he noted with a practiced eye that the crops were not deep green as they should be. The drought was strangling them.

He had studied every technique for stretching the available irrigation water, had spent his own money on slow-drip watering sprinklers, had advised on conservation of topsoil, even dew collection. All without any success. The water table beneath the soil had receded until now it was hardly reachable. If something were not done soon, he thought, the "L"-shaped valley of Santa Maria and the town of Bethany which nestled in its angle, would disappear altogether. Already, some of the poorer families were talking of pulling out.

He bumped off the dirt road and turned the pickup onto the paved highway 57. Below him the picturesque town of Bethany lay cool beneath the mountain, shaded against the setting sun. How clearly he remembered coming here that early morning in the winter of '63. It was also, unfortunately, the same year his father had lost the election again. Cardinal Montini had been chosen and he had taken the title of Pope Paul VI. Poor Livy. He had been right about his chances. But Peter had managed to make his father forget somewhat by pleasing him. That same year, he had been ordained.

Peter had completed his B.A. in philosophy and his Doctorate in Theology at an accelerated pace. From start to finish in four years, four months. And with never anything less than an "A."

"To imagine," Livingston Stamp had said proudly after ordaining him that day in San Francisco, "I find him in a cave and he turns out to be a genius!"

Peter smiled at the memory of the party that his godfather Archbishop Neil Wright had thrown in his old house on Nob Hill. His father had sat to one side, face beaming proudly, telling people about the fantastic things his adopted son had accomplished. Peter had left the crystal-chandeliered room and gone outside to kneel in the solitude of the garden and give silent thanks to God for his good fortune.

As he knelt there, he relived that distant day in Rome. It had been November 4, 1950, shortly after the election of John XXIII and less than a week after Anna's death. A day that changed his life forever. The long walk to Livy's office. Each determined step across the Piazza.

* * *

Once past the Vatican train station, he had turned toward the gardens and the Ethiopian College. Several African seminarians in their cassocks waved to him as he passed and trundled up the wide, marble entrance. Cardinal Livingston Stamp had only recently moved his office here into the college—forced to give up his previous important one in the Apostolic Palace. The Vatican wags had put it well: anything fifty feet distant from the Pope's Palace was not Vatican at all.

At the second floor, past the classrooms, Peter turned down a plushly carpeted hallway and knocked on a polished rosewood door with a simple bronze "6" fastened to its surface. In a moment, he felt, rather than heard, footsteps on the carpeted floor. The door swung open.

"Ah," Cardinal Stamp said, wearing a frown. "I wasn't expecting you."

Behind his father, down the long stretch of scarlet rug, Peter spied three men sitting around his desk. The room was filled with smoke.

"Is that Peter, my godson?" a booming voice asked. "Come in! Let him in, Livy!"

A short, powerfully built man with thick dark hair and bushy eyebrows rose from the chair in front of Livingston Stamp's desk. Taking the cigar from his mouth, he threw his stevedorelike arms open and clasped Peter tightly.

"It's been four years!" Neil Wright bellowed. "How old are you now? Almost sixteen? My God, look how you've grown! Practically a man!"

Peter grinned. He had always liked his joking godfather, the man who had stood up for him at his baptism. As busy as he was, the Archbishop had always answered Peter's letters, usually enclosing a few dollars for "crazy things."

"Hear you earned all 'A's' in your school! That true?"

"I-I-I got a "B-B-B" in Italian literature," Peter managed to spit out.

"Figures!" Neil Wright roared.

"I-I'm sorry to have d-disturbed you," Peter stuttered, turning to Cardinal Stamp. "But I-I h-had t-to tell you s-something. Th-there w-will be no n-n-need t-to get me another h-housekeeper."

"Oh?" Stamp asked. "Are you all grown up now?"

"I-it's j-just," Peter stumbled, "I-I have o-other plans." He paused, pursed his lips together tightly as if to regain control. "You s-s-s-s-see," he said, "I w-w-want to be a p-p-priest!"

The Cardinal's eyes uncontrollably moistened. He appeared deeply, profoundly shaken. "To say that I had wished for this," he said, voice quivering from emotion, "would be an understatement."

"Do-d-d-d-do you approve?" Peter stammered.

"Approve?" the Cardinal smiled. "Peter, you have made me the happiest man in the world!"

"Congratulations!" Wright said and he shook Peter's hand. "You can come to San Francisco and study at the same seminary your father and I went to. I'll be your guardian! By the way," he whispered conspiratorially, "becoming a priest is a great way to avoid having another housekeeper!"

Peter spun away. His face darkened. Then he turned solemnly to Cardinal Stamp. "There-there is something else. I-I want you to know that I want only to lead a s-s-simple, quiet life as a priest. No-n-n-nothing like you. I'm j-j-just not made of the same material. No church p-p-politics!"

"Well, let's have a toast!" Cardinal Stamp cried. "I have some good American bourbon." He opened a carved wooden chest with doves on its front and took out three crystal tumblers.

"Should take you two years, maybe three," he calculated, planning already, "to complete Philosophy, another three for your Doctorate in Theology."

"That's pretty fast," Neil Wright cautioned.

"Nonsense," Livingston Stamp said, pouring the third shot. "Peter's very mature already." He passed a glass to Archbishop Wright.

"Now," he said, handing one to Peter, "You've given me a great gift today. Someday you will realize how dear a gift it is. In return, I give you mine."

He raised his tumbler in a toast.

"To Peter Stamp. My Son!"

Throat aching from emotion, Peter silently lifted his glass.

"His future," Neil Wright joined.

"Drink! Drink!" Livingston Stamp shouted merrily. His eyes were bright and hard as diamonds. And he was the last to drink and the only one to down his whiskey in one zestful gulp.

The truck shook Peter back to the present as it dropped down one side of the Santa Marias and coasted into Bethany. Eighteen hundred souls. Six streets. Railroad station at one end. School, rectory and church on the hill at the other. In between on Main Street were a Safeway supermarket, Frostee Freeze Hamburger, two hardware stores, a beer hall named The Flying Saucer, the Baptist church, a laundromat, three gas stations and a bakery. Not big. But cozy. Very much home. His sleepy town in the sun.

Doctor Jimmy Heim, the balding, merry-eyed town physician, was parked in front of the supermarket, loading groceries into his Dodge. He waved, taking the ever-present pipe from his mouth and slammed the truck. Peter braked his pickup and waited for him. He and the doctor had become good friends soon after Heim had moved to Bethany.

Doctor Jimmy had been a physician in San Francisco, owner and operator of one of the biggest abortion clinics. Then, one day, during a saline abortion, out had come a squawling, fully developed fetus.

Now, he worked Bethany. Saving lives, he said, not taking them. Not much money involved. But his conscience was mending. "An *atheist* with a conscience?" Peter liked to tease him.

"How you?" Heim asked in his easy style, propping one foot on the old runningboard of the pickup.

"P-p-praying for r-rain," Peter said.

"You feel you *owe* this town rain?" Heim asked. "More Catholic guilt. Arrogance too. You better confess that."

"P-p-people here deserve i-it." Peter stuttered over the chugging of the truck's engine.

"Bothers you, huh?" Heim teased. "You can't get God to make it rain." He wiped at his forehead with the back of his hand. "Damn heat," he said. "Gets to you. I just bought a carload full of junk food. Maybe that's what I'm trying to do, escape this heat by eating myself to death!"

"Y-you should get a h-hat," Peter suggested.

"Hate hats," Heim said. "Reminds me of a joke I heard. Seems this guy was a traveling salesman who sold hats. Three women bought his hats and he wound up in bed with them and a pig."

"I don't w-w-want to hear a-anymore," Peter stopped him.

"Want to hear how the pig got there?"

"No."

"You never want to hear my dirty jokes," Heim said mock sorrowfully, relighting his dead pipe. "But I bet you *wonder* about such things."

Three girls in drab-green suspender dresses trooped past them on the sidewalk. They waved and called out, "Hello, Father!"

"Who are they?" Heim asked, taking the pipe from his mouth. "Don't remember seeing them before."

"New kids, I-I-I think. They j-just started at our s-s-school."

"Something odd-looking about them," Heim noted as they passed. "All colors too." The girls were black, brown-skinned and white.

Peter watched them as they moved in and out of the shade of the buildings. He too had thought them peculiar-looking the first time he saw them a week ago. Young bodies with faces that were adult. An aged look about them. Like they were children but not children at all.

The girls continued down the street, walking together as though they were fastened by an invisible thread.

"Ugly ducklings," Heim said.

"What?"

"They'll outgrow it."

"Oh, sure," Peter said. He put the pickup into gear.

"You on for backgammon tonight?"

"N-no," Peter said. "Th-think I'll just g-go right to b-bed after the t-town meet."

"Savior complex," Heim kidded. "You figure you're their leader and you've got to save them, huh?"

"W-we're looking for a s-s-solution together," Peter denied. He threw out the clutch. "See y-you." The pickup whined off up the street.

"Hey!" Heim shouted, standing in the middle of the asphalt. "I got the solution for their water problem!"

"What is it?" Peter asked goodnaturedly, sticking his head out of the truck.

"WORK . . . A . . . MIRACLE! HOLY AS YOU ARE, WE'D GET RAIN TOMORROW!"

Peter waved him off. In his outside rearview, he could see Heim enjoying his prank, standing in the middle of the street. Peter grinned. That was Doc Heim. Outrageous, but you couldn't help but like him.

As he drove the last bit of road through town, he heard church bells begin to ring. He glanced at the watch on his wrist and saw it was exactly six. Father Thomas Brinkley, the frail, white-haired old pastor, was right on time. As the bells for Angelus pealed through the town, Peter crossed himself and then as so often happened a wave of goosebumps spread across his neck, down his back, buttocks and legs. It was like a blessing from God, reminding him how very happy he had been for such a long time.

All those difficult days in the seminary. Studying until theology and philosophy oozed out his ears. Sleeping a few hours a night. Uptight, driven.

When the other seminarians went on their weekly outings to relax, he would hide in his room and study. And if his Prefect found him and forced him to go hiking or play baseball or do whatever the others were doing, he would sneak along a volume of Husserl, Nietzsche or Aquinas, reading pages as he walked or waited his turn at bat.

Naturally he was ridiculed for it. Yet his fellow seminarians secretly admired him for his single-mindedness, his zealotry. They saw clearly his whole life was aimed at one goal: ordination.

But after ordination, he had changed. Perhaps because he got the assignment he had asked for. Archbishop Neil Wright, his diocesan superior, had given in to his pleas and placed him in this out-of-the-way parish, seventy miles southeast of San Francisco. Arriving, he had relaxed, lost his grim-mouthed obsession, become part of the town. The change was almost magical. It seemed Peter had intuitively prescribed Bethany for himself, realizing the kind of priest he wanted to be. A priest of the people.

He guided the pickup toward Emma's bakery and sniffed the pungent odors drifting out. A small pang in his stomach called attention to the fact he had not eaten anything since last night. Sometimes, unless he was reminded, he would go for days without eating. Like other worldly matters, it did not seem very important.

He waved to the short, aproned woman who stood in the window, arms covered to her elbows in flour. When the farmers of the valley came to town, they usually gathered at Emma's to drink coffee, eat her doughnuts and trade stories. Several were now sitting at the counter. They waved as he passed.

As the nose of the truck rose and the engine labored into the climb, Peter saw the whitewashed adobe church gleaming above in the setting sun. To the right of the church was the three-classroom grade school. Children of high-school age went to Rusy, nineteen miles north. There were only forty students in the eight grades here.

Two teachers, short, bespectacled Rick Hospeth and the free-thinking Amy Coombs, taught all classes. Peter helped during the week, teaching religion, and on Sundays, after Mass, coached the kids in soccer. Tomorrow would be their weekly game.

A faint scent of foxgloves drifted into the open window of the truck and Peter turned to see the rows of marble angels and arch-shaped tombstones. Tufts of saw grass waved in the wind between the markers. And the image came to him again, the same image that had recently sprung up in his mind every time he passed the cemetery.

He would see himself standing before a mirror, clad only in his undershorts. Suddenly, the shorts disintegrated, melting downward like so much heated wax. Then in the mirror would appear a darkened cemetery. A cemetery that looked exactly like Bethany. Shadowy rows of marble angels and weathered stone markers.

A knocking came from one of the tombstones. Then his name being called.

"PETER! PETER? NOW!"

He focused on the rows of tombstones. Some tall, others squat. They were like marble soldiers marching to eternity. He took a deep breath and realized it was the foxgloves again.

Turning, he saw that his hands were gripping the steering wheel. He had stopped the pickup in the middle of the road. Forcing himself to uncurl his white knuckles, he found his palms clammy, perspiring.

For a brief, puzzling moment, he turned back to the graveyard, seeking the answer. Why did he lately have the feeling that something was about to begin?

He noticed that the white picket fence surrounding the graveyard needed paint. And the gate's top hinge was broken. He made a mental note to repair it.

With a last look at the cemetery, he gunned the engine. The truck wheezed up the low hill and rolled across St. Michael's asphalt parking lot and into the rectory garage.

FIVE

Since the garage was at the rear of the rectory, Peter did not see the black limousine at the kitchen. When he rounded the corner, old Father Thomas Brinkley, in his summer cotton cassock, threw up his arms.

"Look who's here!" he shouted joyfully. Then as he did whenever he became excited, he began to rub his soft, womanlike hands together.

The man next to him was older and heavier than when Peter had seen him a year ago. Tufts of gray studded his sideburns. New lines creased his face. But his huge bushy eyebrows were black as ever.

"Godfather!" Peter exclaimed and he embraced him.

"Notice anything different?" Neil Wright asked, stepping back and twirling around like a bear on a leash.

Peter glanced at Father Brinkley, then ran his eyes

up and down Neil Wright. He was dressed in a simple black suit with Roman collar, gold chain and cross on his belly which protruded through his coat.

"N-n-nope!" Peter said diplomatically. "You haven't changed a b-b-bit."

Wright leaned forward. A scarlet, instead of a purple, beanie sat on his head.

"You're a C-C-Ca-Cardinal! When did it h-h-h-happen?"

"Couple of days ago," Wright said. "Hasn't been announced yet. Paul's really appointing 'em. College has over a hundred and more to come."

"What does it mean?" Father Brinkley wondered.

"Don't know yet," Wright said. "But a lot of the new Cardinals are Third World. Rumor is he's divvying out power to keep us foreigners happy."

"You were in R-R-R-Rome then?" Peter asked, interjecting.

"I was."

"How is my f-f-fa-father?"

"Overworked," Wright said. "I've got a letter and package from him for you."

"Cardinal Wright has also come to tell you something important," Father Brinkley confided.

"W-w-what is it? Peter asked.

"Good news," Wright said. "But not now. You'll hear it before I go." He motioned to the driver of the car. "Hal, bring my bag, will you?"

"I'll c-c-ca-carry it," Peter said. He moved toward the car. "You come up and e-ee-eat with us!" he told the uniformed driver.

"I'll take my meal with the help," Hal said, eyeing his employer.

"Come on," Cardinal Wright beckoned, smiling. "You've seen me eat before."

Peter led the way into the old farmhouse that had been converted into a rectory. The house had been moved from one of the earlier ranches in the valley and trucked up the hill and set on a new foundation. The exterior was plankboard, and inside were dark stained floors and high, white ceilings.

The group tramped through the screened back porch and entered the big kitchen. A round, middle-aged woman was at the stove. Next to her was a young girl holding a platter which the woman was filling with fried chicken.

"Auntie," the girl whispered, seeing the group.

The woman spun. "Archbishop," she cried, her eyes widening in recognition. She put down her utensils, wiped her hands on her apron and knelt to kiss his ring.

"He's a C-Ca-Cardinal now," Peter exclaimed, setting the suitcase on the floor.

"A Cardinal?! Well, Glory Be!" she said, rising.

"How are you, Mrs. Riley?" Wright asked the smiling woman. "Been nearly a year, right?"

"Over a year, your . . . Eminence," she said, picking the right word. "And we are all fine, truly fine. A little more rain would be welcome. But we are all truly fine."

"Father B-B-Brinkley," Peter said, his face alive with an idea. "It's co-cozier here than in the d-d-d-dining room. And w-we-we n-nor-normally eat in here anyway."

"We do normally eat in the kitchen," the old priest agreed, "but we have company, Father."

"Nonsense," Cardinal Wright said. "Peter's got a good thought. Mrs. Riley and everyone will sit with us tonight. No arguments! And do you have some wine, Father Brinkley? I haven't celebrated my red hat yet."

"We do have a bottle," the old priest remembered. "A gift from Christmas."

"Then get it by all means!" Wright bellowed. And Brinkley opened a side door and thumped down into the basement.

"D-d-do you need any help, Mrs. R-R-Riley?" Peter asked the cook.

"Just put around more chairs, Father," she said. And then to the girl who was at the stove, "Susan, bring a fresh tablecloth!" She leaned close to Cardinal Wright and confided, "She's just a little bit retarded. Has trouble with the studies. She's staying with me while her parents are in Ireland. Gone home to visit the old sod, you understand. Excuse me!" And she went toward a cupboard and began lifting down dishes.

As Susan spread the linen cloth, the Cardinal noted her shiny auburn hair and dancing green eyes. She was a beautiful girl indeed.

"Susan," he asked, "how long have you been here with your aunt?"

"Three weeks Monday."

"How old are you?"

"Fifteen," she said, her line-green eyes darkening.

"And where do you live?"

"Stockton."

"Passed it on the way out. It's a nice town."

"I hate it there," Susan blurted suddenly. Then, she turned her eyes toward Peter. She went back to the stove.

Mrs. Riley arrived with a pile of plates and began setting the table. "She's a handful, that girl," she said.

"Is she really retarded?" Wright asked politely. "Seems normal to me."

"*Emotionally* retarded," Mrs. Riley said, shaking her head sadly. "Girl is unstable. Been in and out of reform schools. But she's okay here. Only minor problem is she's got a crush on Father Peter. She's just a silly child."

She stepped back and surveyed her work. "Sit, sit!" she beckoned.

The Cardinal settled into a chair. Lighting up his half-smoked cigar, he relaxed, enjoying the commotion around him. He noticed how Susan, working at the stove, kept stealing glances at Peter and how totally unaware he was of her attentions.

No wonder the girl is attracted to him, he thought. Even in old work clothes, he possesses magnetism. He is, as they say in Rome, "of a piece": ingenuous, yet earthy and powerful. Unique combination.

Old Father Brinkley puffed up from the cellar. "Here it is!" he said, holding the dusty bottle over his head as if he had bagged a game bird. "A vintage red!"

"Well, open it!" Cardinal Wright commanded. "And let's eat!"

Everyone gathered and sat. Peter helped Susan carry the bowls and platters of fresh corn, chicken, gravy and salad to the table. Mrs. Riley brought the white porcelain pot of hot coffee.

"Father Brinkley, will you say grace?" Neil Wright asked.

"Of course," he said. "Bless us O Lord and these Thy gifts from Thy bounty, through Christ Our Lord."

"Amen," concluded everyone but Susan. She had been staring at Peter.

"Mrs. Riley," the Cardinal said, "how did you know chicken was my favorite meal?"

"You're just being polite, Eminence."

"He's not," Hal said shyly. "Do you know why he likes chicken best? It's the cheapest on every menu!"

"Don't tell little secrets," the Cardinal scolded, helping himself to an ear of corn.

"N-Neil," Father Peter stammered, after the laughter had subsided. "You came to t-tell me something. But that's got to w-w-wait until tomorrow. D-d-does the same go for my package and l-l-letter?"

"On that subject," Neil Wright said, "I was given very specific instructions. The letter must be opened tomorrow *after* you've heard my news."

"A-a-and the package?" Peter asked, sensing his godfather holding out for drama.

"Here and now," he said with a flourish. He reached into his coat pocket and withdrew a small parcel, wrapped in plain brown paper. There was a card attached by Scotch tape.

"Read the note first," the Cardinal admonished.

Quickly, Peter opened the envelope. "My dearest son," he read out loud. "I think it is time for this now. Treat it as a memento. Your loving father, Livy."

"Open it!" Susan squealed, unable to stand the suspense.

Peter grinned and pulled apart the paper. Inside was a wooden box, filled with sawdust. When Father Peter snapped it open, something tumbled out onto the table. He did not pick it up.

"It's just an old rock," Susan wailed.

"Livy said something about a memento of where you two met," Neil said, hungrily helping himself to another chicken breast.

"What is it?" Susan wondered. She was watching Father Peter closely now.

Slowly, he reached out and cupped the leering face in his palm.

"What *is* it?" Susan asked impatiently. "What does it mean?!"

"M-mean?" Peter asked, rubbing the stone against the sleeve on his workshirt. "It's f-f-from my boyhood. Something I always c-ca-carried."

"Like a good-luck charm?" Father Brinkley wanted to know.

"Something like th-th-that," Peter answered, pleased to be holding it again.

"What did Livingston mean when he wrote 'I think it is time for this now'?" Father Brinkley asked curiously.

"I can answer that," Neil Wright said, wiping his mouth on a paper napkin. "I remember Peter as a boy. He was overly attached to that stone. A lonely little boy with an odd plaything. Well, Livy took it away until he outgrew it. Right, Peter?"

"I m-m-missed it for a long time. But I m-must admit I f-finally forgot about i-it," Peter said, rubbing the amulet between his thumb and forefinger.

"Well," Father Brinkley said, shrugging, "I had a different impression. I took it Cardinal Livingston Stamp waited for this precise time for Peter to have it again. Funny how we all can hear a simple sentence but get a different notion of what it means."

"Eat, Father Peter," Mrs. Riley scolded him, seeing him yet stare at the gargoylelike face. "Your food is getting cold!"

Quickly, he unwrapped its rawhide thong which

had decayed badly. "Have to g-get a new piece of l-l-leather," he muttered. Then to everyone's surprise, he hung it around his neck.

SIX

Toward the end of the meal, Peter glanced at his watch. "I was en-enjoying this so much, I almost f-f-fo-forgot about the m-meeting."

"Important one?" the Cardinal wondered.

"We're v-vo-voting on the m-m-mo-motion to have the c-cl-clouds seeded."

"Tell them we're suffering even in San Francisco," Wright said. "Each person is allowed only seven gallons a day. Try showering, washing your dishes and flushing the toilet with that!"

Peter slipped from the kitchen. He walked through the living room past the wood-burning stove, past the overstuffed floral chairs and couch, and out onto the front steps, pulling the heavy door shut behind him. The moon was coming up. A full harvest moon that hung huge and orange on the horizon, mocking, it seemed to him, the meager harvest the valley would yield.

The night above was very dark; the stars not out yet. He took a deep breath of the cool air, then hopped down the three wooden steps and started across the darkened yard that separated the rectory from the school and church.

As he approached the school, he could see in the middle classroom burly, adult figures seated in the too-small students' chairs. Some milled around the blackboard.

He leaped up the cement steps of the classroom and stopped momentarily at the top. The desperate reason the farmers were meeting tonight hit him. How puny he felt! Why was it he could not give them what they wanted? Their human suffering was increasingly becoming a reproach to his priesthood.

Mumbling a prayer, he swung open the door.

"Lo, Father Peter, " Willie MacArthur said in greeting. He was thirty-five, looked fifty, and was the largest landowner in the valley.

"*Padre Granjero*," several Chicanos voiced, touching his shoulders as he passed to the teacher's desk.

Seating himself on the desk's edge, he stared out at the farmers who re-wedged themselves into the children's seats. In every pair of eyes, that met his, Peter beheld the desperate need.

"I-I-I know s-some of y-you are n-not Catholic," he said. "B-b-but as usual I will open with our p-p-prayer." He bowed his head, relieved at not having to look at their eyes. "Lord, grant us your g-graces and all g-g-good things!"

"Amen!" said everyone.

"The r-reason for th-this m-meeting tonight is to decide if w-we should hire a r-r-rainmaker! N-now, I-I've d-done some checking and f-found th-that th-there's a g-government grant for this sort of th-thing."

"How much will they pay, Father?" Francisco, the husband of Lerda, asked.

"H-half," Peter said. "If-if we q-qualify."

"And how much will it run total, Father?" queried young-old Willie MacArthur, who had seven kids and six hundred acres and whose pale wife sat beside him.

"B-bout t-ten thousand," Peter said.

There were whistles among the farmers and shifting of feet.

"That's four new wells!" Tippy Gonzalez yelled.

"Or a hundred pigs!" Marjorie Radner added. She and her husband owned the sow farm at the upper end of the Santa Maria. But the drought had hurt them too since they needed their crops for fodder.

"M-making rain i-is n-not ch-cheap," Peter agreed.

"Is it a certain thing, Father?" Lerda asked.

"N-no," he said. "F-forty p-percent chance."

A mumble of talk ran through the assemblage. Peter knew what it meant. Farming was enough of a gamble. New risks did not appeal to them. Yet as so many times before, he had the sudden urge to jump into it and urge them to try. Hire the rainmaker! Take a chance! But instead, he bit his lip and gripped the wooden desk. It was not his right to advise his parishioners in this matter. It was their decision. They were the ones who were suffering.

"We," Francisco said, motioning to Lerda, Ramirez and several other Chicanos in stetsons, "who own three hundred fifty acres near the center of the Santa Maria, vote 'NO'! Whatever money we have will be spent on more seeds. Plant more, maybe harvest more. A more better thing than seeding the clouds."

Others stood and voted. Finally only Willie MacArthur was left. Briefly, he glanced at his wife and pushed himself up. "We don't want it either," he said and sat down heavily.

Peter sighed, nodding. "I-I can't a-argue w-with you," he agreed. "I-I-I j-just don't know what's l-left."

"Prayers!" Lerda shouted.

There was no reaction from anyone. Their silence testified to the way prayers had worked.

"God will give us water yet!" Lerda cried, trying to stir them up.

The farmers and their women bowed their heads or pretended to be occupied with strings on frayed trousers, mud on boots. Anything to avoid the confrontation.

"Sit down, woman," Francisco said. And he reached up and tugged her into the chair beside him. Lerda turned from the crowd and stared up at Father Peter.

He avoided her eyes. The room crackled with the unspoken conclusion. There was nothing left. Despair lay like a smothering substance over all.

"D-don't g-give u-up on God," Peter voiced lamely. Perspiration broke out on his forehead. Suddenly, he wanted to bolt from the room, break into the cool night outside. Flee from this failure!

"L-Let us pray for r-r-rain," he managed, his face red. "He-he-heavenly Father, we are in a p-p-p-perilous situation. You who n-never allow us m-m-more than we can b-bear, h-h-help us now!"

"Amen . . ." scattered voices said.

Peter shoved off the desk and moved frantically for the door.

"Reverend Packett will be back in ten days," a woman who was Baptist said. "I got a card from him in Australia."

"Th-that's nice," Peter said, aiming for the exit.

Several Chicano women appeared from the corridor. Lerda carried in the coffee urn. There were baked cookies on trays.

"No, no-no," Peter said, refusing quickly. "I-I-I c-c-ca-can't stay for co-co-coff-coffee tonight." He smiled the best he could and shook hands all around. Fleeing, he headed toward the door.

But a voice behind him whispered: "Padre?"

It was muttered with such urgency that he held and turned. It was Francisco.

"I need to confess, Father."

"Yo-your s-s-si-sins are f-f-fo-forgiven," Peter whispered into his ear and he blessed the man, then turned again to the door.

"But what is my penance, Father?"

"A r-r-rosary!" Peter yelled over his shoulder.

"A rosary!" Francisco said and he whistled between his teeth. "I didn't do *that* much!"

Peter strode into the night. Though the moon was high and silvery now and the night well-lit, he stumbled as he crossed the yard. Tears began to sting his eyes.

He started for the rectory until, through the living room window, he saw his godfather and father Brinkley huddled, conferring.

He had to be alone. He hesitated a moment then looked toward the empty and darkened church. Quickly, he dashed toward the back entrance to the sacristy. As he passed the side of the rectory, he thought he saw Susan's face at Mrs. Riley's bedroom window.

Pulling out a ring of keys, he unlocked the door and slipped inside the cabinet-lined room.

"God!" he muttered. "W-w-why w-won't you l-listen to-to-to-me? I'm your p-p-priest! Th-they need water!"

He laid his head on the dressing counter below the

stained glass window of St. George and the dragon, and pressed his face down in misery, crushing his lips into the wood as if hoping to smother the thought of this terrible fiasco.

"I-I'm worthless!" he murmured. "What good are You to me?!"

The sacristy door opened. Turning his head, he saw that a girl stood in the doorway. She was loose-breasted, wearing a long, ankle-length white gown. The moon filtered through it from behind. He straightened.

"Father Peter?"

"G-g-go away," he said thickly, trying to regain control of himself.

"Please," she begged. "Can't I just stay with you?"

He did not answer. The moonlight through the gossamer gown revealed silhouettes of her long, slim legs. Her narrow waist. Small pert nipples erect.

"I'll just come in for a little while," she said and stepped through the doorway. The door shut behind her.

In the blue light that flowed strongly through the dragon in the glass window, Peter saw her advance toward him.

"I want to talk," she said as she approached. "I've always wanted to talk to you, but you never let me."

She approached him, stood close in the opaque moonlight. Then, she reached out with her hand and brushed his cheek.

"You've been crying," she said. She smoothed his blond hair off his forehead. Then, she caressed his cheek. Still, he did not move.

"Oh, Peter," Susan said. She put her hand on the back of his neck, massaging it, talking hypnotically.

"We can be friends, can't we? Tell me what's troubling you."

Her chestnut hair was spread sensuously onto her shoulders. She smiled, then guided her arm up and encircled his neck. She brought the other up and leaned close into his face and kissed him delicately on the cheek.

"Tell me," she said. "Please, I'm your friend."

"I'm a f-f-failure," he whispered. "I-I c-can't even t-talk right! What k-kind of p-priest am I?"

She pressed into him.

Tentatively, he lowered his arm to her slim waist. His palm encountered the hardness of her hipbone.

"I can't help myself," she whispered into his ear. "I love you."

"Y-you-you c-ca-can't," he said. He tried to pull away. She clung to his neck and pressed herself tighter against him. She stood on her tiptoes and kissed him full and hard on the mouth.

Then she stepped clear and, in one motion, pulled the long white gown over her head and dropped it to the floor.

For a moment, he stared at her. In the soft blue light, she was a goddess. She opened her arms and he felt the heat from her as she wrapped herself around him. Her warm scent made him dizzy.

"No," he said.

"Don't be afraid. I'm not a virgin or anything."

"N-n-no!" He stepped back. "I'm a p-priest! Not a m-man!"

"Please!" she pleaded. "No one will ever know!"

"L-l-leave me!" he shouted. "Get out!"

She dropped her arms. Her face hardened.

"Get o-ou-out of here!" he said, backing to the far wall. "P-p-please!"

"Peter," she said in a level voice, "you're no saint! Nobody is."

Peter squatted and unlocked the bottom drawer of the dressing counter. He slid it open, reached far into the back and pulled out a short, wide belt.

"I-I-I asked you to go," he said.

She bent to the pile of clothing on the floor, scooped it up and walked toward the door.

"You can't stand being reminded that you're nothing but a man!" she spat. She slipped the gown over her head.

"I hate you!" she whispered and went out.

Peter walked to the door and bolted it.

He opened an inside door of the sanctuary and entered the main part of the church. He knelt on the bottom wooden step, facing the altar. The only light was that from the small red sanctuary candle indicating Christ was present in the tabernacle.

"Jesus, Je-Je-Jesus G-G-G-God!" he blurted.

He wriggled out of his blue cotton shirt and let it hang around his waist, still tucked into his pants. Then he swung the belt across his shoulders.

"F-forgive m-me!" he cried, gritting his teeth as the leather welted his bare flesh. The talisman around his neck bounced to the rhythm of the blows.

"I-I-I will n-n-never l-let my d-darker side gain con-con-control over me-me! Never let m-me doubt you! M-make me a b-better p-p-priest! M-make m-me worthy! Make m-me PERFECT!"

The sound of the belt echoed throughout the empty church.

Everyone had gone to bed. Peter groped his way up the darkened steps of the stairway and climbed toward his room. Turning right on the second-floor landing, he passed the guest room in which Cardinal Wright was sleeping and then Father Brinkley's room on the left. He walked nearly to the end of the dark hallway and turned the knob. His door swung open easily.

He stepped inside. Moonlight streamed in through the raised window. The luminescent hands of the clock on his dresser stated 11:55. Wearily, he mumbled a silent thanks to Almighty God that he had already finished his breviary this morning. He laid his cassock on the nearby chair, ready for tomorrow. Sitting on the edge of the bed, he pulled his brogans off and dropped them on the floor. He undid his jeans, unbuttoned his shirt, wincing as he flexed his shoulders to shrug it off.

Padding toward the bathroom, he saw that his breath was steaming clouds. Dimly, he wondered how it could be so chilly. Was there a frost coming tonight? He *had* missed the weather forecast on the news.

He flicked on the overhead lamp above the mirror and picked up his toothbrush. As he covered the bristles with paste, he felt a stab of pain.

Gasping, he stepped back. A pressure of some sort was centering on his chest! He reached up and rubbed his breastbone, wondering momentarily if he was having a heart attack.

Raising his head for the first time since the pain, he looked into the mirror. A sunken-eyed creature grinned back at him, its eyes wider than a human's, its nose long, squared off at the end.

As Peter watched, his boxer shorts began to melt, flowing into a lump on the floor. A beast stood naked before the mirror, wearing only the stone talisman around its neck.

Then rising slowly, upward from beneath the sink appeared the head of its penis. It rose, tumescent, blood-gorged and monstrous, as long as a man's arm.

In the mirror, a pair of hands appeared behind the beast. Milky white, they reached around and squeezed the swollen shaft. Two more, black ones, wound around the other side of the beast's waist and clutched the penis, caressing it. Brown hands writhed up from beneath the beast's crotch and dug long female fingernails into hardened flesh.

Grinning, the beast looked down, allowing the playful hands to roam about its member. Then slowly, the beast sunk, disappearing down to where the hands were. And now the mirror reflected a darkened cemetery. Shadowy rows of marble angels and weathered stone markers.

A knocking came from one of the markers. Persistent. Annoying.

A name called.

"PETER? PETER? NOW!"

He raised himself in the mirror and saw he wore shorts. Around his neck hung the talisman and in his hand he held his yellow toothbrush, dripping paste.

A rustle came from behind him. A small noise in his bedroom. Not the creak of a house settling. Not wood expanding. But a rustle. Like the flutter of wings.

He turned and listened.

Now a new sound like scratching tickled his ears. What was it? A mouse? Perhaps a furry tarantula on the floor. They were common around this part of the country. At night, driving home, he had often seen them lying on the roads, enjoying the asphalt's warmth. In the dark, they made crunching sounds beneath the tires.

Turning, he approached the scratching. It was coming from his bedroom dresser. Pausing beside the bed, he snatched up one of his heavy boots. Then, ready to strike he pulled the heavy dresser from the wall. But beneath it was no animal. The floor was coated with silvery, untouched dust.

Something behind the dresser caught his eye. He froze and bent down close to the wall. In the pale light of the moon, he saw two crudely formed numbers: "33." And scrawled below, a ragged "S."

"33" and "S," he thought. What does that mean?

Reaching out, he dabbed a finger into the "S." It was still wet! He rubbed it against his thumb. Then bringing his finger closer to his face, he saw that the glistening liquid was dark red.

A sudden pain in his palm make him look down. Blood was seeping like oil from a deep gash in his hand, oozing down his wrist.

He dashed quickly toward the lighted bathroom. Turning on the tap, he held his hand beneath the cool flowing water. When he turned his palm up, there was no longer any blood. And the gash was gone!

Snapping off the overhead mirror light, he went back into the bedroom and flicked on the reading lamp beside his bed. Harsh light flooded the room. He squatted, reached out and felt the painted surface of the wall. Dry and clean. Had he dreamed it all?

"I'm tired, I'm ha-hallucinating," he said. But he did not believe that.

He switched off his reading lamp and the room faded into darkness. In the soft moonlight, the clock showed it was 12:04, Sunday already.

"Lord," he said as he knelt, staring up at the crucifix. "I'm t-terrified. H-help m-me to u-understand what this m-means. S-something is h-happening!"

Still kneeling, he laid his torso on the bed, knees bearing his weight on the hardwood floor. In that position, he slept, startling awake occasionally to pray, until morning.

SEVEN

His travel alarm clock went off at 5:30. Cardinal Neil Wright immediately sat up and said: "Jesus, Mary, Joseph, pray for me!" He reached out, fumbling, and snapped off its ringing bell.

For a moment, he lay still, enjoying the warmth of the covers, allowing his senses to focus. The sunlight was filling the high-ceilinged farm room already, the warmth stealing in through the window.

He wriggled his toes, luxuriating in a last bit of hedonism before throwing back the blankets to meet the morning. So much to be done. Livy had said that. Overworked, overworried, disappointed Livy. Knowing that now of all times it was necessary for the church to become vigorous again! To give guidance as before and not float as Paul was allowing it to do. Fortunately, most American Cardinals, being conservative, were fighting with him.

Neil took a deep breath and sighed. Livy had so few pleasures left. Except when he spoke about his son, Peter. His pride and joy! What great hopes he had for him.

How would Peter take what Neil had to tell him today? Would he think Livy was pushing? Maybe. But put Peter in a lepers' colony and people would recognize his potential for greatness.

Cardinal Wright slid his short, stubby legs from the blankets and hung them over the side of the bed. He eased his feet into brown, leather slippers and stood and stretched. Then he ambled to the window and opened it. Outside, the sun, flat and huge, was pushing up on the horizon. The sky above was totally cloudless and deep blue. No rain today.

As he lowered his eyes, the Cardinal saw that the earth was covered by a low-hanging tule fog. It would vanish momentarily. The sun would see to that. But now the lovely white mist floated over the school and church and the town below. He took a deep breath and exhaled it loudly.

A patter of feet in the parking lot made him look downward. Someone was there. Running. And as if by magic, the fog parted and Peter appeared in shorts and sweat-stained T-shirt, clouds swirling around his long, muscular legs.

"Hey!" the Cardinal shouted.

Peter waved up to him. He did not stop running but kept pumping his feet in place. "Morning!" he hallooed. His face was dripping with perspiration.

"You still run every morning?" Neil Wright asked.

"Five miles," Peter shouted up. "Keeps the spirit in control."

The Cardinal grinned, slightly envious. He had long known about Peter's obsession with self-discipline. Now the thought struck him that for every force there was a counterforce to be balanced. Peter worked very hard at expending energy and if he were not a priest, where would that energy surface? Probably in a high degree of sexuality, he mused. A very high degree.

"Just about finished," the young priest shouted. "Started late this morning." He waved and loped off into the fogbank, vanishing.

Wright watched him go. Then, he closed the window. Something Peter had done bothered him. What was it?

As he shaved at the bathroom mirror, he thought about it. There was nothing unusual or surprising about what he had said. A normal conversation. But as he showered and dried, dressed in red-buttoned black cassock, descended the stairway and walked across the already car-filled parking lot, he still felt there was something . . . something different about him.

He bade good morning to several Sunday-suited farmers as they filed into the front of the church with their families. He opened the door of the sacristy. Peter and Brinkley were vesting already. They would concelebrate the Mass with him this morning.

"Gonna be a cooker," the Cardinal said.

"Hot one, Neil," Father Brinkley agreed. He was dressed already in the white, floor-length alb and was tying the ropelike cincture around his waist. "You sleep well?"

"Dandy," the Cardinal said, kissing the small amice. He took the rectangular white linen from the dressing counter and placed it over his shoulders. Turning, he noticed Peter was totally absorbed in his dressing prayers. He was gazing up at the crucifix that stood above the vesting table, his fingers looping the flat, ribbonlike stole, symbol of priestly preaching, through the cincture at his waist.

Two altar boys in red cassock and white surplice

swept through the door from the sanctuary. One was carrying a burning wick in his hands. "The candles are lit," he announced to Father Brinkley.

"Good. Is there an extra chair on the epistle side for his Eminence?"

"Yes, Father," the older boy said meekly.

"Hope you put out a large chair," the Cardinal said mischievously. "I own a big rear end you know."

Both boys grinned but said nothing. The younger boy saw Father Peter lift the bulky white and gold chasuble and raise it over his head. He ran to assist him.

"*I* didn't get helped," the Cardinal sniffed with a smile to Father Brinkley. He threw his chasuble on and straightened the poncholike garment on his shoulders.

"We're ready," Brinkley said to Peter. "Father Stamp?"

Peter looked down from the crucifix. He nodded in agreement.

Wright glanced at his watch. It was a little before seven. "Is everyone there?" he asked the altar boys.

"The church is packed, Father," the older boy said, now knowing what to call the Cardinal.

"You're delivering the sermon," Brinkley reminded Peter.

Peter nodded but his face was white. The ordeal he hated the most. The thing that made him feel nearly as much a failure as not securing water for the farmers.

They lined up in single file, Wright in last place, the position of honor. As Neil entered the sanctuary and genuflected before the altar that faced the congregation, he still could not pinpoint what was bothering him about Peter. He shrugged it off. Time to pray. He ascended the steps with Peter and Brinkley and kissed the altar stone.

"In the name of the Father and the Son and the Holy Spirit," they intoned. "I will go unto the altar of God."

"To God, the joy of my youth," the congregation replied.

The Mass flowed smoothly. Father Thomas read the epistle which was from Thessalonians. It was an admonition not to let the things of the world invade the soul. Wright turned and gazed at the young priest.

It's fitting, he thought. What I have to tell him today couldn't happen to a better man.

At the gospel, Wright went out to the lectern and read how Jesus prophesied he would rise again from the grave after dying on the cross.

"This is the Gospel of the Lord," the Cardinal finished.

"Thanks be to God," the congregation answered.

The Cardinal genuflected before the golden tabernacle that held the Body of Christ, crossed the short distance to the chairs and sat down between Peter and Father Brinkley. Peter rose. The altar boys who were on the opposite side of the sanctuary fidgeted nervously. Several people in the congregation cleared their throats. Sermons from Father Peter were not easily gotten through.

It was the custom to ask a cardinal's blessing before preaching.

Peter bent and kissed his godfather's ring. "Pray that the words I speak," he whispered in the prescribed manner, "may touch the hearts of all assembled."

"I will pray. . . ." the Cardinal answered but then

he stopped. His lower jaw dropped in amazement and his eyes stared at Peter's lowered head.

Feeling something amiss, Peter looked up.

"You . . ." the Cardinal said and smiled. I know what it is!" His face shone as if he had just witnessed a miracle.

Peter blinked. He glanced across to Father Brinkley who was peering, puzzled, at the Cardinal.

"I will pray that your words touch the hearts of all those assembled," the Cardinal whispered quickly. Then, he added, "Go! Go on!" and gave him a little shove.

Peter hesitantly crossed the sanctuary area. At the base of the pulpit, he stopped. A sudden cold sweat began to pour from his armpits and thighs. He took the first step, the next and finally the third. When he had gained the pulpit, he looked down at the congregation. Mrs. Riley and a sullen-eyed Susan sat in the front pew. Lerda and Francisco; the schoolteachers Amy and Rick sitting together; Willie MacArthur and his brood of seven kids. The church was packed. The entire community of Santa Maria at one Mass. Parishioners stood in the side aisles since all the pews were full.

Eminence . . . Reverend . . . Father," Peter began haltingly, his voice weak. He bowed to the Cardinal and Brinkley. But as he bowed, he noticed he had left his sheaf of notes on his chair. He felt his knees sag. There was no going back now. He did not have the strength to cross the sanctuary again.

Desperately, he turned to the congregation. "Dearest . . . dearest brothers and sisters." He frowned. The words had come easily.

"I wanted to talk to you today about our Lord, Jesus Christ."

A murmur swept through the crowd.

"*Padre granjero* speaks!" Lerda said.

Momentarily, Peter paused. Then, realizing what had happened, he gazed directly at the congregation.

"He promised us miracles." The words poured from his lips like quicksilver. "He also promised us He would be around until the end of time. Not visibly, perhaps, but here with us. Do you feel him, brothers and sisters?"

Several women in the congregation took out handkerchiefs and began wiping their eyes. Sunburnt men sat beside them, shoulders stiff, checking their emotions.

"Jesus will never desert us," Peter intoned, his voice booming now. "He rose and is with us every day of our lives. 'When even two of you are gathered in My name, I am there!'"

It was a miracle! He was whole!

The words tumbled out faster, lips moving in flawless coordination to tongue and brain. Ideas he had only dreamed of speaking stood up clear and pronounced. With newfound zeal, he shared his thoughts, preaching boldly about Jesus, riveting the congregation.

In the rear of the crowded church, three little schoolgirls were standing near the back doors. Prepubescent, about thirteen. Odd-looking. Women's faces on children's bodies. There was a strawberry blonde, a brunette and a black girl. They stood in a row and listened to Father Peter. When he was at his most eloquent, each of them smiled. A fleeting acknowledgment of his new power. Then, they slipped unnoticed out the doors.

EIGHT

Peter knelt alone. The church had long since emptied. The families stood outside chattering about what had happened that morning. Voices drifted through the open windows. Peter was praying, kneeling on the bottom altar step, his concentration on the crucifix above, lips moving rapidly.

The Cardinal was standing in the sacristy with Father Brinkley. Both men were eyeing Peter.

"It's a miracle of sorts," Brinkley said.

"Sometimes people conquer their disabilities," Neil Wright suggested.

"Will you tell him now?"

"As good a time as any."

Thomas Brinkley nodded and left the sacristy through the back door. The Cardinal hesitated a moment and then padded into the sanctuary. He came near the young priest and asked: "Peter?"

His revery broken, Peter glanced up.

"I have something to tell you."

"The reason you came."

"Yes," the Cardinal said, smiling. "You're going to be made a monsignor!"

Peter did not return the Cardinal's smile. He stood up, then looked down at the black, polished shoes that stuck out from beneath his simple black cassock.

Without a word, he turned and stepped out of the sanctuary and eased into a front pew.

"I don't want it," he said finally. "Get somebody else."

"Tried," the Cardinal said. "I offered the job first to Father Brinkley."

"And . . ."

"He turned it down. You know his health is bad. Simply didn't want the responsibility."

"Well, I don't want it either," Peter stated. "Besides, the whole thing smacks of nepotism!"

"Well, I won't lie to you," Wright admitted. "After your father heard about Brinkley, he suggested you. But it was my decision. I've seen your work, noted your ways. You're more than deserving."

"What do you want me for, anyway? I'm not a conservative. You can't count on me to be on your side."

"We'll take our chances. Once you get into the politics of the church, you'll realize we're right."

"Don't be so sure," Peter said. "I have pretty radical ideas."

"Then, become a monsignor and try them out."

"No," Peter shook his head slowly. "I'll stay a simple priest. I'm not cut out to go bigger."

Wright reached into one of the deep pockets of his red-buttoned black cassock and pulled out a white envelope.

"Here's your letter," he said, extending it. "Livy knew you'd make a fuss."

Peter came to the communion rail and took the envelope. Grimly, he ripped it open.

Standing beneath the glass windows showing the patron saint of the church, Saint Michael, leading an army of angels, Peter read:

Dear Son:

Greetings from the Eternal City. This is a most happy occasion. Neil, who has risen in rank recently himself, told me of his decision to raise you to the select office of Monsignor. This brings with it hard work and less time for your spiritual self. It is a sacrifice you must make, my son. We are in perilous times and Mother Church needs holy men like you. Men of persuasion. Men who will continue the tradition of centuries gone before."

"Politics!" Peter said under his breath.

"I have no doubt you will resist this appointment. Do not! I want to warn you, accept this new burden humbly! To refuse it would be a sin of pride."

Peter froze and glanced up at the Cardinal. "A sin of pride?"

"Disobedience too," Wright said.

"But I. . . ."

"Every man has a destiny. You can't fight yours."

Pensively, Peter finished the letter.

"And so, my son, I congratulate you on this marvelous occasion. As you may have heard. Cardinal Josef Kruger died last week. The mantle of our cause has fallen on my shoulders. We need one, strong candidate, capable of uniting all estranged factions within the church. With God's grace, we shall succeed.

Your Loving Father,
Livy.

"P.S.," Peter read. "Happy thirty-third birthday." He folded the letter carefully. The anger he had shown in ripping it open was gone now.

"Peter," the Cardinal said, "I have to leave for San Francisco shortly. Will you become Monsignor? This area needs one."

"I'll accept on one condition," he said softly. "That I be allowed to stay here at this country parish. That way I will never become involved with Church government."

The Cardinal laughed. "You worry too much," he said. Then he stuck his hand out and shook Peter's. "Congratulations!" He draped an arm over Peter's shoulders and, together, they walked down the aisle toward the back doors.

"You know," Neil Wright said. "Jesus was at the height of his powers at thirty-three. It seems a good omen you become a monsignor now."

"At thirty-three," Peter said, with no humor. "Jesus was also crucified."

"Worry, worry," the Cardinal grinned.

They were at the doors and Wright put his hand on the wood to push one open. But Peter grabbed his wrist.

"Godfather," he said urgently, "strange things are happening to me. Last night, I had a . . . a vision and the numbers "33" appeared on my bedroom wall. This morning, I speak normally and you inform me I'm to become a monsignor."

"Who wrote that stuff on your wall?"

Peter shook his head. "I don't know."

"Is it there now?"

"Vanished."

The Cardinal nodded reassuringly. "You've been

working too hard. Time to slow down, huh? As for the last two, trust in God."

The Cardinal pushed open the door. They left the cool recesses of the church and stood blinking in the hot sunlight. The school playground and parking lot were still filled with farmers and their wives. Children scampered around, playing and yelling. Someone had set up a table and everyone was standing around it.

Up on the slightly elevated soccer field, several children were practicing, punting the ball back and forth between them. In a short while, the Sunday soccer game of the schoolchildren would start. Peter felt happy at the prospect.

"Week, ten days, I'll call you up to San Francisco for the ceremony," the Cardinal said.

Peter nodded.

The Cardinal clapped his hands and, on cue, everyone in the parking lot pivoted and faced the church steps. "Just one more thing to attend to." Wright winked.

Father Brinkley appeared from the group, hair white in the sunlight, and sang: "Happy Birthday to you. . . ."

All the parishioners, including Doc Jimmy Heim, joined.

Peter's eyes moistened. These were his people and he was their leader. Was this what a priest felt when he was loved? The admiration . . . respect and . . . and what? The power? Yes, the power, Peter decided. It felt very good indeed. Nothing wrong with being a little appreciated! But deep inside he felt only half-deserving. God had still not sent water.

A cheer went up from the parking lot and the farmers stepped aside so that Peter could see a three-tiered white cake on a table. With thirty-three lighted candles.

"Hurry, Father!" Mrs. Riley commanded. "Blow them out!"

"Wait!" Cardinal Wright bellowed. "I have an announcement!"

"Later," Peter pleaded shyly.

"Now," the Cardinal whispered. "Good time to celebrate." He raised his hands dramatically and yelled to the crowd, "Ladies and gentlemen of Bethany. I have the privilege to announce today that your very own Father Peter Stamp will shortly be elevated to the rank of monsignor!"

The entire group settled into a reverent silence.

A movement on the field above caught Peter's attention. Three girls broke away from the practice. They wore the short, olive, suspender dresses of the school. Their legs were in white knee socks. They stopped their play and faced him. All were smiling.

Taking control, Cardinal Neil Wright nudged Peter down the church steps. "Three cheers!" he cried. "Hip . . . Hip . . ."

"Hooray!" the farmers exploded.

"Hip!"

"Hooray!"

"HIP!"

"HOORAY!" and spontaneous applause echoed between the rectory and church buildings.

"Blow out the candles now, Monsignor!" Mrs. Riley cried. "It's bad luck if the wind does it."

Everybody laughed as Peter walked toward the cake.

"You creep!" a voice cried from somewhere. With violent shoving, the crowd was forced apart. Susan

Riley lunged out, blocking Peter from the cake. The candles sputtered uncertainly in the wind.

"You!" she spat, her face dark. "You can't be a monsignor!"

"Susan," Mrs. Riley demanded nervously, "what are you doing?"

"Shut up, you old bag," the girl shouted. "Always telling me what to do! Well, try and stop me now!"

She swung back toward Father Peter who was standing, his head cocked inquisitively, as though waiting for Susan to reveal what she wanted.

"You think you're a little god!" she cried. "Too good for me . . . and for them!"

"Tom, help her away," the Cardinal commanded Father Brinkley. He had heard enough. He could see why Mrs. Riley had said she was a handful.

"Susan!" Father Brinkley said, advancing.

"Don't touch me!" Susan squealed, eluding Father Brinkley. She squirmed away, staying out of reach of the crowd also. "I've got something to tell you about your wonderful monsignor!" she shrieked. "You think he's so good! He raped me!"

For an instant, Peter wanted to laugh. It was so absurd. But as a priest, he had to live by his reputation. A strange fear suddenly filled his soul. Would they believe her?

"Susan," he said quietly, "tell the truth."

"You did!" she accused. "You did it in the sacristy!" Her face was vicious, eyes bulging.

"Liar!" Mrs. Riley cried suddenly from the crowd. "God will punish you for such a lie!"

"We don't believe you either!" Lerda shouted. "You should apologize to Father Peter for such a thing!"

The mumble that ran through the crowd said the

farmers were in agreement. They were embarrassed by this girl's reckless slander.

"Susan," the Cardinal said, as gently as possible. "This is a very serious charge. Even if he's innocent, Father Peter would be involved in controversy. That alone might keep him from becoming a monsignor. Now, don't you want to take back what you said?"

"He *did* do it!" Susan screeched, her face flushed. She was glaring at Peter. "He raped me!"

"Father Peter?" the Cardinal asked, "is any of this true?"

Peter Stamp flicked his eyes above the Cardinal's head and he saw that the play on the field had stopped altogether. A boy dropped the black and white soccer ball and it rolled in front of where the strawberry blonde, the brunette and the black girl were standing motionless, abreast. They seemed to be watching him as he stood below in the center of the crowd.

"Father Stamp?" the Cardinal asked again. "Did you rape this girl?"

Peter tilted his head downward. Briefly, he gazed into Neil Wright's eyes, then he swiveled slightly until he was facing Susan.

"Her accusation is false," he said evenly.

"He did it!" Susan shrieked. "I swear before God he did it!"

"We'd better go inside," the Cardinal said resignedly to Peter. "This is serious. We've got to settle it before I go."

"I'll wring the truth out of her!" Mrs. Riley said, advancing toward Susan.

"He did it! He took off my nightgown!" Susan shrilled, dodging Mrs. Riley's grasp. And as she did, an object zoomed out of nowhere and smacked her hard in the chest. Susan flew backwards off the ground. Her right shoe soared over her head. A sound like a bat striking a softball echoed up between the buildings. It was distinct and awesome. Susan lay in a broken little heap.

"Jesus Christ Godalmighty!" Francisco swore, shaken at the explosion.

Doctor Jimmy Heim squatted beside Susan and began to examine her.

"What was it?" Neil Wright asked. "What hit her?"

"Soccer ball," Rick Hospeth, one of the schoolteachers, said. He held up a flattened piece of black and white rubber. The ragged hole where it had blown out on impact protruded in shreds. He handed the ball to Father Peter and nervously adjusted his round owlish glasses.

Peter looked up toward the field. But the three girls were gone. Several other school kids were there, staring down at the crowd.

"Who kicked it?" Father Brinkley yelled at them. Without waiting for an answer, he pushed his way toward the field.

Jimmy Heim stood up. "She's dead," he announced.

"Can't be," Peter said. "A ball doesn't do that!"

"Swallowed her tongue. I tried to dislodge it to give her resuscitation but it's stuck tight. I could perform a tracheotomy. But there are no life signs."

"*Madre de Dios!*" Lerda cried. "Truly a punishment from God!" She crossed herself.

A small child who had been on the soccer field turned away into her mother's arms and began to sob.

"Bring Susan inside," Cardinal Neil Wright said.

Several farmers picked up the girl and carried her into the rectory.

Peter, still clutching the ruined ball between his

hands, strode toward the field. Father Brinkley was interrogating the schoolkids who had been practicing soccer. A big boy was protesting his innocence.

"None of us did it!" he was saying as Peter approached.

"Who was it then?"

"We don't know!"

"All right, you can go," Brinkley told them. "But I'll want to talk to you later."

The children scattered toward their parents.

"A day to celebrate," Brinkley said in apology. "It's become a day to mourn." He shook his head and went down the gentle slope toward the rectory.

Peter walked across the soccer field to the far goal net, to the edge of the hill that fell away to Bethany. As far as he could see down the steep hill, though the road to the right was now filled with departing cars, there was no one on foot.

Squeezing the soccer ball between his hands, he stood there momentarily, feeling somehow disoriented, trying to dredge up an answer.

He had not seen those three girls kick the ball. Yet, he *knew* they had!

With a last hurried look for them, he strode back across the field, toward the rectory. As he passed the table on which sat his birthday cake, he noted absently that the wind had blown out all his candles.

NINE

When Peter entered the rectory, he heard voices upstairs and knew Susan's body had been taken to the guest room. He knocked on Father Brinkley's closed office door.

"Come!" the old priest said.

Peter entered and saw he was on the phone, making funeral arrangements. The closest mortuary was in Rusy.

"Susan." Father Brinkley spelled, "S-U-S-A-N. Riley. That's right. I'll notify her parents. They're in Ireland somewhere. But we'll want you to keep the body there until we know where it's to be sent. All right, Clay. Bye." He hung up and sighed, then stood wearily.

"I'll take the body down tomorrow morning first thing," he told his assistant.

Peter nodded.

Father Brinkley crossed to the door. "I'm going to talk to Mrs. Riley. She's wailing about the girl being punished. Thinks her soul's gone too."

"Have you ministered Extreme Unction?" Peter asked.

"Cardinal Wright's doing it now," Brinkley said, pulling the door open.

"Father," Peter said, catching him before he exited.

"Who are those three girls, the ones who stick close together. The redhead, brunette and black girl."

"Oh, the new ones," Brinkley said. "You been so busy in the fields, you probably didn't meet them. They're the Calendar sisters."

"Sisters?"

"Adopted orphans. They were born here awhile back, but moved away. They returned to Bethany 'bout a week ago. Live with a guardian, or somebody outside town on 57. Toward Rusy. Old Hall place."

"I haven't seen their guardian."

"No one has," Brinkley said. "Went out there myself but nobody answered the door. Town gossip says somebody rich adopted the kids, sends a monthly check to keep 'em fed and clothed. Are they the ones who kicked that ball?"

"I don't know yet," Peter demurred. "Thought I'd have a talk with them."

"Good idea," Brinkley said. "I'm going up now. See you in a little bit." And he shut the door.

Peter crossed to the bookcase behind the pastor's desk. Scanning the three shelves, he located the oversized gray ledger marked BAPTISMS. He pulled it down and sat back in Brinkley's swivel chair.

How old were they? he thought. Eighth grade, right?

He flipped the pages backward, watching the years recede. 1972-1970-1968-1965.

1964. Running his fingers across the page, he noticed names he had inked in himself. Zimmerman, Butley, Ramirez, Robinson, MacArthur. No, not here. He swung back another page. 1963. The year he had come to Bethany.

In blue, peacock ink, there were several names

written at the head of the page in Father Brinkley's careful, printed hand:

NOVEMBER 21 . . . CROWLEY, SALLY.
Posthumously named after mother who died in auto accident. (No last rites performed.)

NOVEMBER 21 . . . CRUZ, ROBERTA.
Performed baptism. Used name of mother. (Baby found near fire at Rusy oilfield.)

NOVEMBER 21 . . . PERKINS, NANCY.
Emergency, conditional baptism performed at Rusy. (Baby found at Pinedo Lake.)

Three girls. The Calendar sisters? And if so, when did they receive the adopted name of Calendar? He scanned the page. There were eight other entries that year. Some in his own handwriting. But every one was familiar, all of them family names of the valley. Just to be sure, he turned pages, checking 1962, 1965, 1966 and 1967. There were no other orphans.

He stood up, slid the heavy book back onto its shelf and searched for the companion ledger he knew so well: DEATHS.

He carried the black book with the red binding to the desk and flipped the pages to the year 1963. There were only four entries. Two in his own handwriting. None of them was a Crowley, Cruz or Perkins.

Peter leaned back in the swivel chair. What did all this mean? Three girls born in 1963, three women who must have died that same year. But there was no record of the mothers' deaths or burials. He ransacked his memory to recall any history of this. But there was not a clue.

The door opened and Cardinal Neil Wright, now in his black suit, poked himself inside. Hal crossed behind him, carrying the bags, and went out the front door.

"Oh, there you are," the Cardinal said. "I'm leaving. Got a meeting in San Francisco yet tonight. I'll see you in a week, ten days, huh?"

"Neil?" Father Peter asked, rising from the desk. "What about . . . ?"

"Her accusation?" the prelate asked, jerking his head toward the stairs behind him. "Poppycock! You didn't do anything, did you?"

"No," Peter said. "It's just. . . ."

"I know, I know," Neil Wright said, "it's the day. Terrible day. Don't let it bother you. Did I tell you? Livy's coming for your elevation!"

"He is?" Peter asked enthusiastically.

"It was supposed to be a surprise," Wright said. "But you look like you need cheering."

Peter managed a smile.

"Until then, Monsignor," Wright grinned. He waved and went out the door.

"See you!" a voice chimed and Father Thomas Brinkley hustled back into his office. He opened the top drawer of his desk and peered inside. "I forgot to fill out the death certificate. You seen the forms?" he asked Peter. "Never here when you need one." He rummaged in the drawer.

"Tom? What were the Calendar sisters' names before they were adopted?"

"In the parish book. Above you there," Brinkley said. "1963, I recollect rightly."

"Perkins, Cruz and Crowley?"

"That's them," Brinkley said. "Unusual cases. I

remember writing the babies' baptisms in the ledger. Mothers had all died, right?"

"Three of them."

"Yes," he said, straightening and stopping his search for the death certificates, "strange thing. It was like an epidemic. Three babies brought into the hospital up at Rusy on the same day. One of their mothers, I was told, was killed in a car accident. The second apparently died in a fire near the oilfields. Third drowned."

"I don't remember you mentioning all that," Peter said.

"No? What date did it happen?"

"November 21."

"That explains it. Must have been the last thing I did before heading for my once-a-year in Idaho. Probably didn't remember to tell you when I got back. Ah, here they are!" He pulled a blank sheet from the bottom drawer. "I've gotta straighten all this out. What are they doing under MARRIAGES anyway? Getting sloppy in my old age!"

"So all you saw were the babies?"

"That's right. No sign of the mothers. Somebody later figured they were strangers to these parts. Just passing through."

He picked up a pen from his desk and began to fill out a form.

"But if the mothers died around here," Peter went on, "wouldn't they be buried somewhere nearby?"

"Only one of two places possible," Brinkley said, signing the death certificate. "Rusy cemetery or Bethany. No others around."

"And Rusy's pretty filled up."

"True," Brinkley said, "but they're not buried in our

cemetery. I would have remembered them, believe me!"

The old priest closed the drawer, folded the certificate and slipped it into the breast pocket of his cassock. "Why all these questions?"

Peter shrugged. "I don't know. Something's wrong . . . those three girls. Something I can't quite put together."

"I didn't see who kicked the ball. But I will admit it was an unusual accident," Brinkley said thoughtfully. "The way that ball hit Susan. It was . . . unnatural!"

He shuffled toward the door. "I'm goin' back to comfort Mrs. Riley," he said. "Doc Heim's giving her something to relax. Be going early to Rusy tomorrow. Doc's coming up with me."

"While you're there, will you find out who adopted the girls?" Peter asked. "Papers should be there since it's the county seat."

"Sure," Brinkley said. "Judge Sanchez can let me into the courthouse files."

Brinkley started for the door. Suddenly, he swung toward Peter. "Father, if those three Calendar sisters did kick that ball . . . why? Why?"

"I don't know yet."

"It's too bizarre," Brinkley said. He stepped out of the room.

Peter put the DEATHS book back on its shelf. Emerging, he noted that the door to Mrs. Riley's room was open. He could hear Doc Heim and Father Brinkley speaking in soothing voices. Mrs. Riley was sobbing softly.

He went down the hallway and out the front door. From the front steps, he saw three peregrine hawks, predators in the sky, riding the breeze currents, searching the fields below.

He paused, thinking again of the miracle in the church and the terrible event outside. Then, nagging, came the oddness of the missing mothers.

His eyes shifted from the sky to the cemetery below. I've been there a hundred times, Peter thought. Father Brinkley was right. They were buried in Rusy.

Yet something pricked at him. That premonition he had when he passed the cemetery; the vision last night in his mirror. The three different sets of hands on the beast. The three differently complected, but matching girls!

As he stood in thought, the shrill sound of the water pumps starting up in the valley came to his ears. They switched on automatically to flood the fields toward evening. Was it that time already? Quickly, he checked the sun. It was setting behind the western Santa Marias. Because Bethany lay directly against them, the sun here went down early. Suddenly, he knew what he had to do. Impulsively, he dashed to the garage.

By the time he skidded the pickup to a halt and parked, shadows from the tombstones were reaching like eerie, dark fingers down the side of the hill. He got out and slammed the pickup door harder than he had to. At the white picket fence gate, he paused and muttered a silent prayer before pushing it. The top hinge, broken, let the gate snag in the browned grass. He squeezed through the narrow opening.

The upright stones were familiar, almost like old friends. His apprehensions vanished as he began to walk by them, reading again the quotations he knew: "GONE BUT NOT FORGOTTEN," "HE IS WITH THE ANGELS

NOW," "REST IN PEACE IN THE LORD." Names of parish-ioners, many of whom he had buried.

He walked the rows; no surprises. Father Brinkley had been correct. The three women were not buried here in Bethany. It had to be Rusy. And even if they were there, what did it matter? The girls, not their mothers, were the mystery. Why had he even wasted his time here?

With a last glance at the small graveyard, he made his way down the hill toward his pickup. He had to find his footing carefully. The sun had vanished behind the mountains and darkness was setting in, a misty fog building in the cemetery. As he cut across the open space between the last of the stones and a border of fence, his heel skidded on something.

He caught himself, turned and saw that he had stepped on a slippery, grass-covered chunk of marble. He bent to it and brushed away the mark his shoe had made and saw lettering of some sort. He straightened and in the bleak light could see that there were other stones in this area, fallen down and uncared for. A part of the cemetery he had never seen before.

Kneeling, he brought his face close to the lettering on the stone. But he could not make it out; the light was too dim. He made his way down the fog-shrouded hill as fast as his stumbling legs would take him, opened the truck's glove compartment and fumbled inside. His fingers found the stick matches. Good old Doc Heim! Like a pack rat, he always left behind some matches for his pipe.

He hurried back through the gate and up the hill. He knelt before the piece of marble.

He struck a match and pushed close to the stone.

"H-U-T-T-O-N," he spelled out loud. Then, brush-ing more of the tangle of weeds away, he saw the first

name was *William*. The man had been born in 1805
and died on the third of August, 1862. This part of
the cemetery was older than Bethany. The town had
been founded in the early 1900s. Who had been here
before? Explorers? Pioneers?

He snapped the match out, burning his fingers. Hurriedly, he lit another. In the burst of fire, he moved to
the next weathered stone. It was the wife of Hutton,
LAURA LEE. On his knees, he edged sideways, using
his hand to guard the small torch against the breeze
he made as he moved.

In the flickering light, he leaned close, a solitary
figure on a mist-covered darkening hill, and made out
the first three letters on a third, rain-worn tombstone.

"C-R-U-" he deciphered. And then the first name.
"*Roberta*. Roberta Cruz." Quickly, he scanned the
lines on the slimy-green stone. "Born 1801, Died
1827." The match burned his fingers and he flipped it
away.

Hurriedly, he lit his third and final match. Moving
to the next marker, he felt his heart leap into his
throat as he saw "CROWLEY, SALLY. B. 1857. D. 1888.
R.I.P." This site, like the other, was slightly depressed
as though the earth had settled. Or, Peter had the
crazy thought, as if the bodies had been removed.

He jerked to the third stone in the row. Frantically,
he clawed away the crabgrass and pushed the dying
match close. "N. PERKINS," the stone stated. And in
bleached letters. "B. 1870. D. 1900."

He sat back on his haunches, dumbstruck.

The heat from the flame scorched him and he
flipped the match away. The stub landed on the dried
grass at another stone's center, igniting it. The fire
spread quickly through the veins of the crabgrass, il-
luminating the name on the final tombstone. In

deeply etched, bold letters, the marker read: "PHILLIP CALENDAR. B. 1830. Hanged: 1865." That grave too had settled into a shallow declivity.

The circle of fire sputtered out. From nearby, he heard the sound of feet running through the grass. But he could see no one.

Peter stood. His knees were shaking. He backed down off the hill, his eyes transfixed by the glowing embers of the still smoldering grass. Then, turning, he fled, running blindly into the foggy night.

Missing the gate, he struck the low fence full force and flew over it. He landed on his belly.

Clambering into the pickup, he pushed impatiently on the starter rod. The old truck coughed into life, and he flicked on the headlights.

He paused, regaining control. His face was coated in cold sweat, he felt sick to his stomach. Out the window, he could see the darkened cemetery, the tombstones shrouded in the mist.

There was only one way to get to the bottom of it all. He threw the truck into gear. Wildly spinning the rear wheels, he fishtailed the pickup down the road, and through the main street of Bethany. At the end of the boulevard, he swerved left onto highway 57 and sped toward the farm Father Brinkley called the old Hall place.

TEN

The rattling pickup careened off the asphalt highway and stopped at a dirt road. Gray ground fog flowed like smoke across the beams of the headlights. KEEP OUT a large, black-lettered sign on a closed chicken wire gate advised. Peter set the emergency brake. Motor chugging, he alighted and walked through the thick fog. As he fumbled to unlatch the iron gate, a rustle in the tumbleweeds along the fenceline startled him.

A coyote, red-eyed in the headlights, stuck its head out. In its jaws was a struggling, soft-furred cottontail.

"Get away!" Peter shouted, trembling.

The coyote lurched from the brush and, tail between its legs, fled off into the night.

Peter collected himself and swung open the gate. The dirt road ahead did not look used. Weeds were growing over once-worn ruts, and rains had further eroded its surface.

He drove the truck through the gate and down a road covered by eucalyptus trees. His headlight beams refracted all around him from the fog. It was like driving through a lighted tunnel.

Tall milkweeds raked beneath the floorboard of the truck, and an occasional Russian thistle caught and scraped along, pinned beneath the frame and the dirt road. Several times, Peter had to slow, shift into first and drive off the road because the ruts were too keep to negotiate.

At last, he came to a curve and beyond it saw a sun-faded two-story farmhouse badly in need of fresh paint. There were no lights on in the house.

Parking, he left the engine running, headlights on to guide him across the yard. Mounting the two ce-ment porch steps, he rapped on the door.

As he waited for someone to answer, he turned toward the truck. He felt a presence nearby—as if someone were watching him.

He knocked again. Louder.

" 'Lo!" he shouted, expecting to see a light go on in-side. "It's me, Father Peter!"

The thick trees around the house muffled his words.

Impatiently, he twisted the door knob. It was locked.

Stepping down, he walked to the front window and tried to peer inside. But the curtains were drawn and he could not see through them.

"They've got to be here!" he reassured himself.

He rounded the corner, leaving the glow of his headlights behind. The side of the house was over-grown with vines. He had to bend low to pass under them. At the rear, he tried the door but heard a pad-lock rattle. Continuing his circle of the house, he turned another corner and near the ground spotted a light. The beams from the truck were filtering through a basement window.

He put his hand on the siding of the house and worked toward the light. In a few steps, his hand fell away; he had found an open passage. Carefully, with the lights from the truck as his guide, he felt his way down the steps. There was a sound of dripping water.

The walls of the basement were shining wet. It was like a cave.

The sound of water was louder now. He walked toward it.

In the truck lights, he saw drops forming, slowly building, then falling into an unseen pool on the floor. He reached up to the source of the drops and felt the metal coldness of a rusted pipe. A leak.

Suddenly, a rotting stench assaulted his nostrils. A foul smell like something had died. Then more light from the truck entered the basement. He spun around. A front door had opened. In the illumination, he could see several small, human forms dash up a stairway.

"Hey!" he yelled.

He ran toward the elevated door. His shoes sloshed through standing water. He stumbled at the bottom of the steps, skinning his shin, then found his footing and ascended toward the light.

Pounding up the steps, he arrived on a landing. He stepped forward and found himself in a large room. The stench was worse now.

"Hello?" he shouted. "Calendar sisters!"

He lurched toward the windows and threw open the curtains. Dust rained down on him. In the bright illumination from the pickup outside, Peter could see the room.

A stand-up piano stood against a far wall, one leg gone, tilting crazily to one side. In a corner, near the front door, was a pile of boxes, cans, rusted iron bedsprings, rotting rugs, shredded padding and filthy, stained blankets.

His flesh crawled. Suddenly a sour note shivered

from the piano and a hairy-tailed rat leapt from the inside. The rodent dashed across the littered floor and dove into the pile of rubbish in the corner.

Then from behind him came the sound of footsteps clattering on the bare floorboards and of stairs being climbed.

He picked his way carefully through the room's door and turned right into a darker expanse. The rays from the headlights outside lit this space only dimly, but he could see a long cabinet covered with peeling Formica and then a sink. A dust-coated table stood to one side. The kitchen.

He held his arms out before him to ward off any unseen obstacle. Beneath his shoes, the floor felt spongy as though it had been wet a long time, its very grains rotting and pulling apart.

Suddenly, a draft blew the foul smell directly into his nostrils. Nearly retching, he saw what looked like a dark tunnel. Then he realized the shaft held narrow steps leading to a second floor.

Now he faltered. What could he find up there in the dark? He had no right to be in here anyway. He was an intruder. He had come to talk to the girls' guardian, but he was obviously in the wrong place. No one could live here! The running figures, the footfalls he had heard were only imagined, he told himself.

Turning to go, he took several steps, then stopped. What was he running from? The unknown? The "unnatural"? Perhaps he was just jumpy after the graveyard; the filth and spooky noises of this house. Whatever he needed to know was up there, waiting for him. He would not finish a coward. He'd take a quick look upstairs and then leave.

With renewed determination, Peter forced himself

to face the flow of rotten air. He put a tentative foot out and found the first step. Pushing up, he ascended into the smothering darkness. He felt as though he were wrapped in black velvet.

He groped his way to the top step where the stench of decay enveloped him again. But at least up here there was more light. A broken window enabled him to see the truck outside, chugging, waiting.

His eyes sweeping the room, he had just picked out several piled trunks when a headless figure lurched against him. He gasped and stumbled back, but the round-shouldered thing kept after him. Pell-mell, he retreated to the stairway and was descending when he saw that the thing on the floor was a tattered mannequin.

He laughed out loud. "Good God! I've seen too many movies!"

From the corner came the sound of breathing.

As quickly as he had felt relieved, he now experienced an anger born from renewed fear.

"Who's here?" he demanded.

He scooped up the mannequin, and savagely rammed it through the window. The glass burst outward. The lights from his pickup streamed fully into the room.

Spinning, he saw the three sisters standing in the corner. In the heavily shadowed light, their faces looked even older, somehow ravaged. They looked at him warily, like trapped animals. So this *was* their home!

"I want to talk to you," Peter said advancing. "I'm not going to hurt you. I only want some answers. Who is your guardian? Where is she . . . or he?"

Still, they stared.

"Who were your mothers?" he asked. He was very close now, nearly within arm's reach.

The girls giggled.

Peter's eyes narrowed. "Who *are* you?" he asked.

The blond girl jerked up her hand. An arc of electricity exploded before Peter's eyes. He was hurled backwards into the pile of stacked trunks. As he scrambled to his feet, one of the trunks slid down and shattered in a heap of rotten boards. There, lying at his feet, was a withered mummy in a long, tattered dress, a ring of brittle strawberry-blond hair about her skull.

"The trunks . . ." he muttered, pointing to the two others stacked nearby. "They're coffins!"

The girls giggled again. The remaining stacked trunks shed their boards. Two other leathery corpses, hair brown and kinky, lay inside.

In horror, he backed away. Could they be the same women who were once buried in the cemetery? His mind would not hold the question.

"Follow us!" the black girl commanded. "This house is over!"

As they passed, he lunged to grab them.

In defense, the strawberry-blonde gestured again. A ball of fire burst onto the floor and rolled toward him. He leaped aside. But the floor, like wet cardboard, crumpled beneath him. In a rush of plaster, splinters and flying debris, Peter plummeted through.

Hitting the kitchen floor below, he was engulfed in a shroud of dust. For a moment, he lay still, expecting pain to wrack his body. But miraculously, he was not hurt. From far away, he heard footsteps on stairs. Rolling over, he dimly discerned shadows flit through the kitchen and race for the front room.

"Wait!" he yelled.

Throwing off the mess, he bounded toward the front room. Its door was already open. He saw the front yard was vacant.

Determined, he vaulted down the steps and dashed to the waiting pickup. He threw it into gear and swung out of the yard toward the road. Behind him, the roof of the house was shooting up bright flames.

In the headlights, down the long dirt driveway, he saw the escaping girls. They were jogging leisurely toward Highway 57. Turning the lights onto bright, he roared through the tunnel of overhanging eucalyptus and sped after them.

The sisters seemed to be loping along, as though teasing him. They were glancing over their shoulders to make sure he was following. He floored the gas pedal, closing fast.

Suddenly, the girls spun around and faced the oncoming truck.

In a panic, Peter hit the brakes. The pickup went into a sickening slide. In crazy slow motion, he rushed at them in certain collision, the glare of the lights brightening as he neared. Desperately, he cramped the wheel. He felt the truck shiver as it hit something.

For a moment he hung suspended, hurtling into the darkness. Then he landed heavily. Behind him there was the sound of limbs cracking, shattering. Then, it was quiet and the silence of the night resumed itself.

He felt the cold dampness of the ground beneath his buttocks. He thought he was under the pickup. The vehicle was on its side and the headlights were still burning.

He tried to push out but could not move. Yet, again, he was not in any pain.

As he looked up, he saw the three girls standing squarely in the headlight beams, in their usual abreast line. Together, they smiled down at him.

"Now, we can talk," they chanted.

"Get help," Peter begged.

"*We* will help," they said together in high, girlish voices. "We are for you."

"I don't understand," Peter said, grunting, trying to extricate himself. "I don't understand any of this, What are you trying to do?"

"We are helpers," the girls recited in singsong.

The strawberry-blonde marched forward, looked briefly at her two sisters and giggled. "I start fires! You really didn't think your match in the cemetery did that?" And she jerked up her hand. A flame exploded near the front tire of the truck. She lowered her hand and it died out.

The black girl stepped toward him. "I control things," she said. "Like that ball that hit the girl who lied about you."

"You killed her!"

"She tried to hurt your reputation. It was necessary."

"It was *not* necessary!" Peter screamed. And with renewed energy, he struggled to free himself.

"I find hidden things," the brown-skinned brunette announced. "Something important is near you now. Exactly under the tree."

"What . . . what are you talking about?" Peter demanded.

"Never mind, Father," the three said in their peculiar ominous rhythm. They turned toward the eucalyptus grove.

"Stop!" Peter shouted, trying to wriggle after them.

Helpless, he watched as their dark forms floated through the field of weeds. He struggled one last time but found himself still solidly pinned. Sensing he was only wasting his strength, he rested his head on the ground.

ELEVEN

The washed-out blue dawn shone up all around. Peter awakened and for a moment did not remember where he was. Then, as he had been doing periodically during the night, he put up his hands to shove against the body of the truck. To his surprise, his hands met nothing.

Looking down, he saw that his legs were no longer pinned. The pickup was upright. Wearily gaining his feet, he stood uncertainly. The truck's cab and bed had been crushed level to the wheels. It was as if the entire vehicle had been put into a huge vise and squeezed flat. A large eucalyptus tree lay just in back of the wreck, its roots awkwardly stretching toward the morning sky.

As he walked around the twisted mass of metal, he began to wonder if he was sane. How could something like this happen?

Tires squealed on nearby highway 57. Looking up, he saw the parish's '64 Chevy fishtail to a halt, back up, then turn down the dirt road. When the car was near him, Father Brinkley and Jimmy Heim climbed out.

"Hey!" Brinkley yelled. "You all right?"

Peter didn't know how to answer.

"We were coming home from Rusy," Brinkley went on, "Doc spotted you out here!"

"You okay?" Heim asked. He was puffing his ever-present pipe, studying his disheveled and begrimed friend.

"Fine," Peter said absently. He glanced down at himself then brushed off plaster dust and clinging humus from his jeans and cowboy shirt. But he was too dirty for it to make any noticeable difference. When he straightened, both men were staring over his shoulder.

"What happened?" Heim muttered. Without waiting for a reply, he strolled toward the devastated pickup.

"You come here to find the Calendar sisters?" Brinkley asked, staring at the shapeless wreck and wondering how Peter had survived.

"Found them," the young priest said, turning and seeing for the first time a black column spiraling into the sky.

Brinkley swung and studied the smoke.

"Came out here to get some answers. But now I don't even know who the Calendar sisters are."

"But they were there, inside the Hall place?"

"I chased them," Peter said. "They did that!" He gestured to the wreck. "Last night before coming here, I went to the Bethany cemetery. There're three women buried with the same names as the sisters. Plus a Phillip Calendar, coincidentally the last name of the person who adopted them!"

"Impossible! I know every marker in Bethany!"

"It's an old section. One I never knew existed. All of them were buried in the 1800s!"

"Hmmmmm," Brinkley said, scratching his unshaven chin, "Old Father Andrew, who was pastor here before, did mention a previous cemetery. But I could never find it. If I remember him right, this whole valley was some sort of outlaw's hideout. Roadmen who held up stagecoaches on the way to San Francisco." He brought up his hands in agitation and rubbed them together, appearing to warm himself in the morning cold. "Father," he said to his young assistant, "are you trying to tie all this together with Susan's death? I know you pretty well, having been your confessor for twelve years. Your imagination is a slippery thing! Remember the time you thought you saw a devil in your room? Or how about when we were fishing for bass in Pinedo Lake and you swore you'd seen a fish with the face of a man?"

"It was Halloween and there *was* somebody in my room. A kid with a mask, I think, from the school. And on Pinedo, I said I saw a fish that *resembled* a man."

"You know what I mean," Father Brinkley said, without wavering.

"So the gravestones were only my imagination?" Peter asked with a trace of anger.

"I don't know," Brinkley said. "Just don't jump to anything odd. By the way, speaking of odd things, I got Judge Sanchez to open up the courthouse this morning. We were walking into the file room when we smelled smoke. Seems we got there just in time. Another couple minutes and the whole courthouse could have burned down."

"There was a fire?"

"In the adoption files. Somebody left a cigarette or something. Unfortunate thing."

"Yes, wasn't it?" Peter said pointedly. He swung back to the pickup and the fallen tree and studied the scene carefully, reliving last night's event.

"What else happened here, Father?" Brinkley inquired.

"Things you wouldn't believe," he said. "The girls . . . one of them said something." And he started walking toward the trees. "Something. . . ."

Brinkley, unsettled by Peter's obsessiveness, followed silently, watching the young priest.

Peter strode past the wreckage to the smooth white trunk of the tree, stepping in between the branches with their scimitarlike leaves.

Doc Heim sauntered over.

Peter squatted.

"Under the tree," he muttered out loud. "She said . . . something important is near you now. Exactly under the tree."

Compulsively he crawled on hands and knees back through the foliage. The tree's outer branches and roots were supporting the trunk so it was raised off the ground. Working his way forward, Peter crept along the fallen tree, feeling beneath the trunk, scrambling over and through the downed branches. Finally, disappointed, he rose.

"Nothing," he said.

"Nothing what?" Heim asked good-naturedly.

"Yes, what is it you were looking for?" Brinkley asked.

"I don't know," Peter said. "Something important. Something . . . needed."

Doc Heim raised his eyebrows and shot a glance at

Father Brinkley. "Peter," he said solicitously, "how about some breakfast? I'm famished."

"That's a good idea," Brinkley agreed. "Food can solve a lot of things."

Peter turned once again to the tree. He stared at it, trying to figure the puzzle. His eyes were ringed with dark circles.

"I'll treat," Doc Heim offered. "C'mon, we can stop in Emma's. She's got coffee and doughnuts. Mrs. Riley won't feel like cooking your breakfast this morning anyway."

The three men walked toward the parish Chevy. Doc Heim climbed into the back seat and Father Brinkley drove. As the car rolled down the dirt road, Peter suddenly turned around in his seat and took one last glance at the truck and fallen tree. Behind the trees, the smoke had dwindled to a wispy white line. For some reason, it reminded him of the smoke from the pipe atop the Sistine chapel.

As they came down 57 and turned toward town, Father Brinkley stopped the car. The fields, as far as they could see, were vacated. There was no activity at all.

"Where is everyone?" Brinkley asked.

"Farmers are gone," Heim observed ominously.

Peter jacked open the door and stepped out, keeping one foot inside the car. He listened briefly, then slid back in.

"Pumps have stopped," he said.

"But they pump all night and into the early morning, don't they?" Brinkley wondered.

"Not if the water's gone," Peter said.

"Oh, Sweet Jesus!" Brinkley begged and threw the car into gear.

They found the farmers in Bethany. Most were standing on the sidewalks, talking in groups. Brinkley parked the car in the small lot on the side of Emma's bakery. Through the front glass windows, they could see her eating-room was filled.

"It's happened," Doc Heim said. He opened the old-style Dutch door.

The room was smoke-filled and hot. Emma Myer was busy behind the counter, popping doughnuts and roll twists into a boiling vat of oil. She waved to them.

"You may have to stand and eat!" she yelled, handing a metal tray of jelly rolls to a farmer.

"No problem!" Brinkley shouted back. "Just give us three cups of coffee and half a dozen iced doughnuts."

"Hey!" Lerda beckoned, seeing them. "Over here! We got room!"

Brinkley led the way to the table. Francisco stood at Lerda's insistence and offered his chair to the old priest. Several other farmers got up and stood and Doc Heim took one of the chairs but Peter politely refused.

"I'll just stand," he said.

"You better sit, Father," Brinkley said. "You look awful!"

Peter obeyed and slid into the waiting chair. Everyone at the table eyed him curiously.

"Father Peter was in an accident," Heim explained.

"Did he get hit on the head?" Ramirez, the old man who was one of Lerda and Francisco's partners, asked. "He *looks* like he got hit."

"He's okay," Heim said.

"What happened, Father Peter?" Lerda wanted to know.

"What?" he wondered, coming momentarily to her question.

"Did you get hurt in the accident?"

"Oh, no," he said slowly. "I wasn't hurt." And again, he lowered his head and his eyes became unfocused as he stared at something far off.

Emma brought the coffees. "Doughnuts'll be here in a minute," she said.

"Thank you," Brinkley said. And when she had gone, he asked Francisco, "The pumps?"

"Burned out," the Mexican stated heavily.

"The water, she is gone," Ramirez added.

"When did it happen?" Doc Heim wondered, lighting his pipe.

"Before dawn," Lerda said. "There was this high whining noise and Francisco leaped up from our bed and ran outside even without his pants. But the pump was smoking already."

"The water went quick," Francisco said bitterly. "All the other pumps in the valley burned up too. They smoked like dominos falling, as far as my eye could see. Little blue smokes. Then the motors froze and I could hear their hummings as they melted."

"Tell me one thing, Padre," Ramirez, the old man, said, turning to Father Brinkley. "Why is it God always picks on the poor?"

"Everyone suffers misfortunes in life," Father Brinkley answered him. "The poor seem more affected because they don't have as many alternatives as the wealthy. That's why the poor must have great faith in God."

"*Dios!*" Francisco cursed. "*Qué hace Dios para nosotros?*" What has God done for us?

"Francisco!" Lerda cautioned. "Do not doubt God!"

He said something under his breath, drowning the words as he took a sip from his coffee cup.

Father Brinkley, eager to avoid a dispute, changed the subject. "What will you do now?" he asked solicitously.

"Sell out," Ramirez said in despair. "What else is there?"

"Where will you go?"

"We are Mexicans, Father," Lerda said quietly. "We have family who will maybe help us."

"And the others?" Doc Heim asked them, surveying the room.

"There's talk of selling," Ramirez said. "Some will stay, plow under the crops, try again next year. Not us *bendejos*! We're finished!"

"This year broke our backs," Lerda explained unnecessarily.

Peter had not touched his coffee. He was gazing down at the worn surface of the plastic table as if looking right through its solidness.

"Drink your coffee, *Padre granjero*," Lerda reminded him. And with one of her big hands, she pushed it toward him.

He did not notice it. His brow furrowed, he only stared.

She shot a puzzled expression at Father Brinkley who shrugged.

"Anyway, it's over," Francisco spoke up. "Finally over. God has taken what he wanted."

"I told you, don't talk like that!" Lerda said.

"I will talk any way I want!" Francisco yelled, sloshing his coffee. "I am no longer a man! I have been cut off from my roots!"

Peter's head jerked up and his bloodshot eyes widened.

"What did you say?" he asked.

"He didn't mean to curse God," Lerda apologized.

"What did you *say*?" Peter shouted. His eyes looked slightly too bright.

"I said," Francisco growled, leaning forward pugnaciously, "I am no longer a man."

Conversations in the room stopped. The farmers looked toward the commotion.

"No!" Peter insisted. "What else? What else?" He jackknifed up, nearly knocking over the entire table as he faced Francisco.

"What's going on?" Brinkley asked.

"Say it!" Peter demanded, ignoring the pastor. He reached out to Francisco and caught his shirt front in his hands and jerked him close. "Say it again!"

"He didn't mean anything!" Lerda cried out in fright.

The room was totally quiet now. Every eye was on Peter as he held a subdued Francisco in his fists.

"I said . . ." Francisco stammered, "I said . . . I have been cut off . . . from my roots!"

"Roots!" Peter said in wonder. "Roots!" And everyone around the table, including Francisco, gazed at him as though he was mad.

"You!" Peter ordered Francisco. "Come with me." He caught his arm and yanked him through the crowd.

"What is happening?" Lerda asked, seeing her husband being towed after Father Peter.

Without answering, Father Brinkley stood up and pushed his way after him. Lerda, Ramirez, Doc Heim and several others who had been at the table followed.

Outside, Peter was already in Francisco's pickup.

"Everybody!" he ordered, hanging his head outside

the cab, "Come on. Get into your cars." Then he motioned Francisco to drive away.

As the orange pickup bounced down Main Street, Father Brinkley and the others ran toward the parish car. And many of the farmers who had been in Emma's with them came out and followed. Soon, Francisco's orange pickup was leading a line of twenty vehicles.

"Where's he going?" Lerda asked Father Brinkley as he drove fast to keep up with the truck.

"Wherever it is," Brinkley said, as he made the left onto Highway 57 and glanced up into his rearview mirror, "he's just put everyone's trust in him on the line."

Doc Heim turned to see the long row of undulating cars behind them.

"It would be a bad time to go crazy," Ramirez remarked, seeing the cars also.

"Father Peter is not crazy!" Lerda said. But when Father Brinkley looked over at her, she added uncertainly, "He knows what he's doing, doesn't he?"

No one in the speeding car answered.

TWELVE

Francisco's pickup ground to a halt, and Peter jumped out. He slammed the door and strode toward the fallen tree. Then, still in stride, he spun and yelled, "Francisco, you got a shovel?"

"No!" Francisco shouted back, standing at the door of the truck.

"Get one," Peter commanded. "Hurry!"

"I got a shovel," Willie MacArthur offered. "What you gonna do, Father, chop weeds?" He had swung out of his own vehicle and was waist high in the overgrown field.

Other farmers parked and climbed out of their trucks. "Only thing this valley grows decent is weeds," one said. "Better let 'em stand, Father."

Lerda pushed her way through the gathering farmers and took Francisco's arm. "*Trae herramienta!*" she said. "Bring the tool!"

"What for?" Francisco wanted to know. They could see the priest circling the bottom of the tree now, bending near the roots.

"To help him. Come on."

Ramirez thrust a shovel into Francisco's hands.

Francisco took it and led the pack of farmers toward the young priest who was now kneeling on the ground, looking as if he was about to begin pray-

ing. Father Brinkley hung back near the '64 Chevy
with Doc Heim, afraid that Peter had gone too far.

"Here," Francisco said, holding the shovel out.
"Here is what you wanted, priest."

Father Peter jumped up and took the shovel. "All
right," he said, "this is where we want to dig. Right
here. At the roots." He pointed to the cavity created
when the tree fell.

Peter poised the blade of the shovel, took a small
leap into the air and came down with both feet on its
back. The blade sliced into the earth and Peter lifted
the first scoop out and threw it to one side. Then, he
bent for another.

"Help him!" Lerda cried to the farmers. And then
to Francisco, "Please!"

"*Loco*," Francisco muttered. "What does he think
he is doing anyway?"

Willie MacArthur stepped forward to Peter's right
and sunk his shovel into the earth. Other farmers
grabbed up their tools. Several had only picks and
hoes, but they began digging.

"Over here," Peter instructed them. "Here, closer to
the roots."

The farmers dug in concentration now.

"Like to know what we're doin'," one mumbled.

"It's a waste of time," Francisco said, arms crossed
on his chest, still not pitching in.

"You got something better to do?" Ramirez asked
with good humor.

"There's another shovel in the back toolchest,"
Lerda said. "I'll get it." She scampered back toward
the orange pickup.

As she neared, Father Brinkley hailed her from his
vantage point near the Chevy. "What's he doing?"

"He is digging. Everyone is digging." She ran back toward the group with the spade.

"This is bad," Father Brinkley said. "In one single day, Peter will destroy all he's worked for."

Big Lerda handed Francisco the shovel and sternly pointed to the hole. Reluctantly, he joined the working group. Farmers who had no shovels ringed the workers, giving advice.

"Hey, Cal," one said, "that all you can pull up? Those shovelfuls ain't full."

"I'm a Baptist," the man kidded back. "We don't dig tunnels to Rome."

"Little faster, boys," another joked. "I'm bound for China."

Peter, sweat streaming from his face, jammed his spade into the earth and dug faster. The hole was knee-deep already.

He began to work more furiously, straining now, flailing away, spewing dirt over his shoulder as he tossed it. His face was gaunt and sweating, his eyes haunted.

One by one the others stopped and began to step warily away. They watched the priest, his face caked with dirt, stab at the ground. He began mumbling "Roots . . . roots!" Their faces filled with pity as Peter frantically scooped out the dirt. No one spoke. There was nothing humorous anymore about this terrible scene. Their feelings were common. All sensed they were watching the derangement of a once sensible man.

Father Brinkley, hearing the sudden silence, strode forward. Doc Heim followed, his pipe smoking.

Brinkley worked his way through the ring of silent farmers and approached the hip-deep hole. "Peter," he called.

The young priest did not hear. He kept digging, his lean body on the verge of collapse.

"Father," Brinkley said softly, "enough!"

Still, Peter jabbed at the dirt, his movements weakening.

"Peter," Brinkley pleaded, his eyes filling, "Peter, please!"

At last he stopped. He lowered his shovel and leaning on its long, straight wooden handle, brought his hand up and wiped his face. He closed his eyes and for a moment wavered as if he would faint. Then, he stepped back and sat on the dirt bank of the hole, his head lowered in defeat.

Lerda shielded her face and began to weep. The group began to disperse slowly, men trundling back toward their vehicles.

"Father," Brinkley said softly. "Come on home now. It's all right."

"It's not all right!" Peter choked. "You don't understand! Nobody understands!" His eyes were wild and tormented. "God damn!" he swore. "God *damn* all of you!"

He raised the shovel to hurl it up at the shocked group but caught himself. In a final burst of exasperation, he flung it instead into the ground. The blade sliced into the earth and the shovel stood upright, quivering.

From the hole came a rumble like an approaching freight train.

Everyone froze at the frightening sound.

"Stamp!" Heim yelled in warning.

Peter looked down at his feet. The ground beneath him was shaking.

"Get out!" Heim screamed. And he reached down to pull Peter from the hole.

At that moment the shovel catapulted into the air. A thirty-foot column of water rose beneath it.

Lerda cried out, *"Madre de Dios!"*

Francisco stood awestruck, his eyes filled with the glorious sight.

"It's an artesian!" Willie MacArthur screamed, watching it spurt up.

"What do you think of your assistant now?" Doc Heim asked with a smile.

Brinkley did not reply.

The hole was now a pond.

"Water witch!" Willie MacArthur shouted. "He's a witcher only he don't use a rod!"

Peter stood and watched. Unconsciously, he brought up his hand and clutched the stone face that hung around his neck beneath his shirt.

Several farmers began dancing. Francisco spun Lerda around. Ramirez bent to the pond and bathed his face in its coolness. He cupped a handful of water and threw it at Lerda. She retaliated and soon others, like unworried children, were playfully soaking one another with the miracle that had saved their valley.

As Peter watched them, a movement in the corner of his eye made him turn.

Hidden in the thick grove of eucalyptus stood the three sisters. They watched him a moment as though satisfying themselves at his pleasure. Then as one, they turned and slipped back into the heavy foliage.

Who *are* they? Peter wondered to himself. Who *sent* them?

THIRTEEN

Borne above by the *uscieri*, he waved to the thousands of people in St. Peter's square. Wearing the papal tiara, the ancient crown for all popes, Livingston Stamp gave his blessing again and again. In the background, as he bobbed along on the shoulders of the Vatican ushers, the boys' choir sang Mozart's Coronation in ineffably sweet voices. Red and gold banners hung from the Apostolic Palace and St. Peter's basilica balcony on which he had only yesterday received the initial accolades.

And now borne above their heads, tears streaming down his face, lifelong ambition finally realized, ex-cardinal Livingston Stamp remembered choosing a very old name for his papacy.

"What will you be called?" Cardinal Mazande, the black African cardinal, had asked him after his acceptance in the Sistine Chapel. Over a hundred cardinals eased forward in their chairs to hear his answer. The choice of a title would set the tone for Stamp's papacy.

"*Petrus*," Stamp had replied loudly. Peter.

Mazande had staggered back from him as the Conclave filled with whispers. No pope since Peter the Apostle had ever had that name.

Now, he descended the chair and walked toward the altar. He would say Solemn High Mass in thanksgiving for his coronation. At his feet in the piazza knelt the half million people. He began the Mass. The choir sang in the purest of lilting voices. He proceeded to the consecration, raising the white host to heaven as he made it the Body and Blood of Jesus Christ. He stretched, lifting It to Almighty God. And before he brought It down, he heard a strong voice say: "You are Peter and upon this stone I will build my Church."

He lowered the host.

"Rock," he whispered, correcting the voice. "Not this stone. Upon this rock!"

"Stone!" the voice laughed. "Stone! STONE!"

"Noooooooo!" Livingston Stamp cried.

"Lord Stamp?" a voice asked. "Eminence?"

He opened his eyes and saw that hot Mediterranean sunlight was falling across a ceramic tile floor.

"You dozed off," an old man in black, gauzy robes said. He was stroking a white Persian cat which sat on his lap. "I did not mean to bore you," he chuckled.

"I must be tired," Stamp said, sitting up.

"You travel too much," his host, Archbishop Moshe Malthustos, replied congenially. He stroked the cat, allowing the Cardinal to awaken totally.

Moshe, born a Hassidic Jew, had converted to Eastern Christianity as a young man. He had risen quickly after being ordained a priest, dedicating himself totally to fulfilling the mission God had created for him in life. But despite his spectacular rise in hierarchy, his mission had always eluded him. He had the insight that the Lord had never really used him in life. Now old, as fragile as an orange blossom in the wind, he felt passed over. Yet, outwardly, he was cheerful.

"More tea?" Moshe offered when he saw Stamp stretching and rubbing his eyes.

"No, thank you," Livingston said, realizing he yet held the empty teacup in his lap.

"Another cake then?"

"No, I'm fine. Just weary, as you guessed." He set his cup down on the still warm brazier and leaned his head back in the chair. "Please continue your conversation, Moshe."

"It was politics," the frail old man said, stroking his soft gray beard. "My point was simply that Greece and Turkey will never stop being enemies. We expect trouble on Cyprus shortly. Athanagoras is not popular."

"And the Church?"

"Like a sacred cow, she is revered and tolerated. Both countries do not desire to offend God."

The cat unsheathed its claws and dug them into the knees of the bearded Archbishop.

"Get down, Protea," he commanded. "I am too old for your rough play!" He shooed the cat off.

The long-haired cat leaped to the floor, took several steps toward Cardinal Stamp, but changed her mind. Suddenly turning tail, she scampered into the sunlight on the balcony, twisting in circles, playing with her tail.

"Many thanks to the Holy Father," Archbishop Moshe said, "for lending us his financial troubleshooter. It's a gracious thing to do, when we are not offically in the fold."

"It's my job," Stamp yawned.

"You traveled also when you were Prefect of Non-Christians?"

"Only then I never grew tired."

"That position was very powerful," Moshe smiled. Like most, he knew something of Cardinal Stamp's failed ambitions.

"We all must serve where we are placed," Stamp said, rising to go.

The Eastern Orthodox churchman arose also and bowed. "My diocesan accountant will keep you informed. His report will be on your desk by the end of the month."

Stamp nodded, picked up his briefcase, and turned toward the door. As he did, a swarthy, small-boned man in a fez entered and said, "Telephone for His Eminence."

"You can take it in my study," the Archbishop said.

"Do you have a phone here?"

"Of course. But if it is private. . . ."

"None of my life is private," Stamp said. And following the Archbishop's gesture, he crossed to the French telephone that sat on the unusually low table. Only when he lifted the receiver did he realize that the Archbishop, as was eastern custom, probably sat on the floor before this table to read and pray.

"Stamp here," he said. "Neil? What? He's doing what?!"

The Archbishop saw a new life suffuse the tired Cardinal's frame.

"But can Peter find water again? He has! But can he find it anyWHERE? Well, ask him. Do you know what this means?"

He listened a moment longer, then said, "Okay! Yes, I can catch a plane tonight. Yes. Wonderful news, Neil!"

He hung up thoughtfully.

"I could not help but hear," the Archbishop said. "You mentioned the name Peter."

"My adopted son," Stamp said, still savoring the news.

"It is only coincidental then," the Archbishop said, shrugging his shoulders.

"Coincidental?"

"Forgive me, Eminence," the Archbishop said, bowing slightly. "But when you slept briefly, you cried out the name 'Peter' in your sleep. You must love your son very much."

"Yes, I do," Stamp said. "He's a bright hope."

"Forgive me, also, and tell me to mind my business, but what does the word 'Stone' mean?"

"Stone?"

"Yes," the Archbishop said. "You were saying 'this rock. Not this stone!'"

"It had to do with Jesus founding his Church on a rock," Stamp said quickly. He walked toward the door, thinking to hurry through his next business appointment. A commuter flight to Ankara would lift off in a half hour. Then he could catch a Pan Am later from Athens for San Francisco.

"Forgive me," the Archbishop said. "you know how much import we Easterners put in dreams. No dream is accidental. I have also studied etymology extensively. The unconscious use of words has always fascinated me."

The Cardinal paused, only half-interested. Academic chatter annoyed him.

"I mean simply," the Archbishop apologized, "that the idea of a 'stone' is a perversion. Something we would etymologically call a corruption. In this case a mockery of a holy idea. Very subtle. But definitely an adulteration."

"What are you getting at?" Stamp asked, checking

his watch, barely able to contain his irritation at this whole rigamarole.

"In your dream, who was it who said 'stone'?"

"Jesus, I suppose," Stamp snapped.

"He would have used the correct word. Someone else was speaking to you."

The phone rang.

Stamp, seeing his chance, pulled the door open. "Good-bye, your Excellency," he said. "Talk to you when I get your report."

His thoughts distant, Archbishop Moshe Malthustos picked up the receiver. The Mayor of Istanbul's voice squeaked over the telephone.

"Rahmann!" the Archbishop-diplomat said brightly. "Supper? Of course. Seven. Delighted, delighted." He hung up.

As he sat before his low, knee-high table, his thoughts returned to Cardinal Livingston Stamp's dream. Why did it hang in his mind so? True, 'stone' was not the correct word. But why his concern?

He cracked open his missal and found the purple ribbon that marked Lauds. A late start today.

A church built on a rock would survive centuries, as it had, he thought. Peter the rock. But a church built on a stone? Impossible! Like setting a great house on a pebble. A stone, then, perhaps meant the downfall of the Church. Could it be? The beginning of the final era? The coming of the anti-Christ himself? What, if anything, did Cardinal Stamp know?

He sighed, catching himself.

Perhaps he was being senile. A hobby used all his life now an obsession. He would have to stop poking his nose into others' dreams. With renewed effort, he bent his face to his breviary.

Outside, from atop a minaret, a chanter-priest announced that evening prayers were beginning to Mohammed's God. And Moshe Malthustos put aside the odd thing that had struck him. Yet for no logical reason, it would continue to haunt him the rest of his days.

FOURTEEN

BETHANY, CALIFORNIA: *April 11, 1975*

In less than a week since he had found that first well, Peter had found four others. The task was simpler now. He would just walk with the farmers in tow until he saw, hidden behind a barn or in a ravine or a clump of trees, one of the sisters pointing.

The drought was over for Santa Maria, but the young priest was not happy about what was happening. He did not understand how the girls found water and he was worried about his growing acclaim. He was already being referred to as a "miracle worker."

How he wished he could talk the whole thing over with his father. But what would the Cardinal think of his adopted son? From the time they had met, Livingston seemed to have a revulsion for Peter's talisman. He'd never accept the idea of supernatural girls. Yet, he would have to hear. It was out of the question to approach Father Brinkley. In the meantime, the decision as to what to do remained on Peter's shoulders.

He had arrived at some sort of a workable, ethical conclusion. It boiled down to this: since what was happening was good, it had to be God-sent. He realized it was no more than a Band-Aid to the whole problem. But for now, until he could seek advice from Livingston, it would have to do. He was counting the days until he would meet the Cardinal in San Francisco.

Father Brinkley, knowing Peter's reluctance to talk about his new gift, became the young priest's protector as he searched. But he could not keep the news from spreading.

The farmers were having a picnic lunch, while helping Peter search for a sixth well. Brinkley looked around and noticed that Peter was not among them. Ramirez gestured to a plowed strip of land, a sloping outcrop of the Sierras. And Father Tom saw that his assistant was walking toward the finger, a solitary figure in the blowing dust.

A large, white panel truck with a microwave antenna on top and CBS logo on its side pulled near the group. A woman in a red blouse and tan pants stepped out and began speaking to the farmers. They motioned her to Father Brinkley.

The woman was blond and her bare nipples beneath her blouse were high and pointy. A cameraman and soundman plowed along after her.

"Hi," she said, her hand out for shaking. "I'm Mary Lou Rowen. You must be Father Brinkley?"

"How do you do," Brinkley said.

"Is that Father Peter out there?" she asked. "We would love an interview with him. How many wells has he brought in now? You know Cesar Chavez wants him to come down to the San Joaquin and Imperial valleys. Will he do it?"

Father Brinkley couldn't help smiling. He spread his fingers in exasperation and said, "You do ask questions, don't you?"

"I'm sorry," Mary Lou said. "But this is big stuff, Father. It's not every day we get a wonder worker. You would say that Father Peter is working miracles, wouldn't you?"

"Miracles?" the old priest mused. "No. But he is very talented."

"Where's he going now?" the newswoman asked, watching the small hill eclipse Peter as he circled it.

"To find another well, I suppose."

"And will he?"

"Probably."

"Father Brinkley," she said, "does he realize what power he controls? Half the world's a desert! He could have everyone at his feet!"

"I don't think that's what Peter wants," Brinkley said. "He's just a simple country priest."

"A simple country priest," Mary Lou repeated. "That's good. That's very good, Father!" And she flipped open a long, lined white pad and wrote: "Country priest works miracles!"

There was a cry. Peter had stepped back into view and was beckoning. The farmers ran across the open ground, whooping.

The ever-present water drill, its steel tower swaying precariously against the cloudless blue sky, clanked with them toward the hillock.

Peter retraced his steps, his gait slow, almost plodding. He was dressed in worn jeans and sweat-stained workshirt. Brinkley doubted he had even taken the time to change this morning. The young priest,

though always thin, had lost more weight, and his
eyes had sunk deep into his face from lack of rest.

As he approached, the newswoman smiled and
asked the cameraman, "Everything ready?"

"Working," the burly man shouted. "Take your
mike!"

The soundman handed her the microphone and she
swung to Peter as he neared, "Father, we're doing an
in-depth segment for the nightly San Francisco news.
Can I talk to you?"

Peter shrugged and kept on walking, forcing Father
Brinkley and the newspeople to keep up with him.
"The real story is the farmers," he said. "They're back
there."

"Hey!" she yelled, plodding beside him, her Gucci
loafers filling with dirt. "Father! I'm not the only person who's gonna bug you about this water thing."

At the parish Chevy, he paused. "Miss," he said. "I
don't mean to be unkind. It's just I'm tired and believe me I don't have very much to do with finding
water. It's just . . . just something that happens."

The drill motor suddenly shut down. The silence in
the air made both of them turn. There was a pause
and they saw the drill operator back hurriedly away
from the rig. Water blew up from the ground.

Peter climbed into the car. "Father Brinkley?" he
shouted.

"Coming!" the old pastor yelled, turning from the
sight of the water, and skittering across the broken
clods of earth.

Mary Lou Rowen leaned into the window. "Nobody'll leave you alone," she said, "your days of solitude are finished. You could give me your first
interview."

Peter shook his head. "I'm just an instrument of

God and that's what I want to remain. Nothing more."

Father Brinkley slid into the front seat. Mary Lou watched as Peter drove away.

"Want me to at least get his exit?" the cameraman asked.

"Never mind," she said. "We'll get farmers' reactions.

"Weird the way he found that water, huh?"

"Honey," the newswoman said, still gazing at the Chevy retreating down the dirt road, "he's better than Jesus Christ!"

As they came into Bethany, Peter slowed. He had driven the whole way in silence, mind distant, thinking of something. Brinkley in his wisdom let him alone.

Finally, as they passed Emma's bakery and started up toward the cemetery, Peter asked quietly, "Father, do you consider me a good priest?"

"You appear almost destined to be one," Brinkley said, bouncing along in the truck. "Ideally suited, you might say. Unlike normal people, you don't seem to mind having nothing; you never get lonely, in fact you seem to thrive on being alone. You seem to be perfectly happy. Yet. . . ."

"Yet?" Peter asked.

"Yet, lately," Brinkley went on, "I've sensed something happening inside you. A conflict surfacing. As though you are torn. Almost as though you did a great violence to yourself long ago. And only now you're starting to struggle with it." He turned to see the effect of his words. But Peter had not seemed to hear. His attention was riveted to the passing cemetery. The truck slowed.

"Father," Peter asked, "do you think it's possible for Satan to manifest himself in these times?"

"What a question!" Brinkley stated. "Your mind is certainly jumping around these days, Father."

"In the Bible, we knew him in various forms: a serpent, pigs, even a deranged man. Is it possible for him to come again in bodies of the dead?"

"It's not impossible," Brinkley allowed, studying Peter with misgiving, wondering if perhaps the strain of finding water was too much for him. Was he leaving his senses? Stress tended to bring out hidden facets of a man's personality.

"And would it be possible for their children to be possessed?"

"Sadly, yes," Brinkley said. "Children for some reason are very susceptible to a devil. Perhaps because they are so malleable and open."

"Even from infancy? Even if they have done nothing to deserve it?"

"Deserving has nothing to do with it, Father. Evil can grow where the ground is fertile, as in the soul of a child who cannot recognize good from evil. But in adults a possession usually does not take place unless there is something in a man's personality that invites it. Something strong, like pride or a lust for power."

"I feel," Peter said, turning from the cemetery, "as if there was a vast evil surrounding me. I sense it."

"Where does it come from?"

"A devil, maybe."

"You should never fear a devil," Brinkley said. "He's not omnipotent like God."

"But he's strong, isn't he?"

"Not by himself," the old priest stated with conviction. "God has seen to that. His only power is a negative, destructive one. And we humans are the only

ones who can give him that power. You see, he's like
a parasite. Nothing without us. So a man can fight
and win against devils. The only time he can't is
when he wants it all to happen."

Peter was gazing wide-eyed at Brinkley, pensive,
mulling over his words.

"You're thinking *you're* possessed," Brinkley said
with a half-smile.

"Oh, no!" Peter grinned. "I wasn't thinking about
myself at all. Just those children. . . ."

"Watch that imagination of yours, Father!" Brinkley scolded. "And don't worry about evil surrounding
you. It wouldn't stand a chance with you."

Peter turned for one last look at the tombstones.

Brinkley, watching him closely, said, "When you're
rested, we can go up to Rusy. My theory's those
women buried out there are distant relatives of the
real mothers."

"They're not buried out there," Peter said.

"No, not the mothers," Brinkley said, misunder-
standing.

Peter swung the Chevy into the garage. An unfa-
miliar Plymouth was parked nearby, a ruddy, porky-
faced man standing near it.

"Hello, Fathers," the man said. "I'm Jennings
Riley."

"Ah, Mrs. Riley's brother," Father Brinkley said.
And then to Peter, "She asked to spend a few days
with Susan's parents."

"We came home early from Ireland when we heard
. . ." Jennings trailed off.

"It was a terrible accident," Brinkley said, shooting
a "help me" look at Peter. But the young priest was
keeping a distance from Jennings Riley as though he
were ashamed to come closer.

An awkward silence fell between the men.

The back screen door of the rectory slammed, and Mrs. Riley emerged on the side of the garage. She was carrying a bulging leather suitcase. On her head was a straw hat with plastic cherries.

"Fathers," she said, "I'm glad you're here. Are you sure you can cook and everything?" Her eyes were red, a continuing symptom since Susan's death.

"We can take care of ourselves for a while," Brinkley said.

"We'll miss you, Mrs. Riley," Peter offered.

"Oh, don't you worry," she said, brightening a little, "I'll be back. Long as I have my priests, I've got a reason to live." She smiled bravely.

"Thanks for allowing her this time with us," Jennings said, taking her bag. "Time for a family to be together, you understand."

"We understand," Brinkley said.

The two of them went toward the Plymouth and as Riley opened the door, Mrs. Riley felt in her coat pockets. Pulling out a yellow piece of paper, she hastened back toward Peter.

"For you," she said, handing it to him. "Came this morning."

Peter took the telegram.

Jennings Riley drove off. Mrs. Riley stuck her head out and waved as they went down the hill.

Peter raised the missive in salute to her, noticed it in his hand, and ripped it open.

"It's from Cardinal Wright," he said. "Wants me in San Francisco tomorrow. I'm to become a monsignor." Absently, he folded it.

"Wonderful!" Brinkley said. "Shall I tell everybody?"

"Don't make a big thing of it, Father. I'll just go to San Francisco tomorrow, get it done quietly."

"The parishioners will be disappointed they won't get to see the Mass."

"They can hear all about it when I get back," Peter said and walked toward the church. "Think I'll just pray a bit."

"I'll call Doc Heim," Brinkley said. He can cheer you up. I'll cook supper too!"

Peter did not answer. He shuffled toward the little church and climbed its few steps into the front entrance.

Father Thomas Brinkley scrambled a dozen eggs and Doc Heim fried two pounds of bacon and brewed a pot of coffee. Peter sat absently at the table, his mind distant and wandering.

"Worn out?" Jimmy Heim asked, placing the bacon on a paper towel to soak off the grease.

"Haven't slept too well," Peter said. "Keep having dreams."

"Dreams?" Brinkley asked, shoveling portions of the eggs onto the plates. "You didn't tell me. What kind of dreams?"

"Obscene ones," Peter said.

"X-rated?" Heim asked with a grin. "In color?"

"I don't know. I always wake up when they start. I ... I don't remember them."

"Well, you'll sleep tonight," Doc Heim said. "I've got some horse pills in my bag. Effective on most everybody. But who knows about a miracle worker?"

The three men sat and ate in silence, shoveling in their eggs hungrily and washing them down with hot coffee.

"Peter," Heim said, waving a strip of bacon between two fingers, "How do you find water? Somebody touch you with a magic wand?"

"No magic wand," Peter said ."I . . . I just do it."

"Well, you've got what thousands will pay for. Only a matter of time before success catches up with you," Heim teased. "You'll be the most important man in the world. Think of it! Where will it all end? President of the United States? Maybe even Pope!"

Peter was startled. "I have no ambitions," he said fiercely.

"People who are gifted don't always make their own decisions, you know. Events, forces, even fate take a hand. You might wind up being something you never thought about."

"Oh, cut it out, Doc!" Brinkley said. "Enough!"

"Okay, okay!" Jimmy Heim said, seeing Peter's alarmed countenance. He tore off a corner of Mrs. Riley's homemade bread and leaned over to Peter.

"But I want ten percent," he whispered conspiratorially.

"You're hopeless!" Brinkley said, laughing. Even Peter managed to smile faintly at that.

In his bathroom, Peter Stamp downed the large blue capsule Doc Heim had given him. As he set his water glass back on the sink, he paused momentarily and checked the mirror. His own image was reassuringly reflected there.

He walked into his bedroom and arranged his cassock on the back of the chair near the bed so he would have it for Mass in the morning. Then he lay down. Outside, the sun was just beginning to set. Downstairs, he could hear Father Brinkley answering the telephone. More requests for finding water? Interest from TV and radio stations?

"God," Peter prayed, "let me sleep . . . don't let me dream those dreams . . . God. . . ."

His shoulders settled from their tensed position and his breathing deepened. His hand opened as his fingers relaxed and he unconsciously brought up his right palm and placed it protectively over the talisman which lay on his chest.

Around ten, Father Brinkley and Doc Heim peeked in on Peter. When they heard his easy, rhythmic breathing, they closed the door, satisfied, and bade each other good night.

Heim trundled down the stairs, climbed into his car and drove to his small house near the railroad station.

Father Brinkley took two teaspoons of milk of magnesia for his upset stomach. Eggs never agreed with him. But it was all he knew how to cook. Burping, he went to bed.

FIFTEEN

Asleep less than three hours, Peter began to dream of a naked man. The man in bed was covered only with a sheet, one leg sprawled out of the covers. A woman's shadow fell on the bed. A hand reached out, pulled down the sheet and knelt on the bed, straddling the man's belly.

In the dim light, the woman seemed black or sienna. She brought her long legs forward, then lifted until she was squatting over the man. Raising slightly, she tilted forward and reached behind her with both hands. The man's penis was abnormally long.

The woman, impaled by the erect cock, began to rock up and down, balancing on the balls of her feet. There was no sound from her, only the rocking and slippery noises of lovemaking. The man beneath her did not move at all. When she pulled off, two new forms crept onto the bed.

"Wake up!" they whispered, bouncing the bed. "Hello? Wake up!"

The man did not move. So the brown-haired one lifted, grunted audibly and defecated on his belly. The other two women guffawed.

The man stirred and sat up and Peter saw that it was himself!

Thunderstruck, he jackknifed up and looked around. There was no one else in the room. It was perfectly quiet. Suddenly, looking down at the sheets, he realized he had an erection. Ashamed, he pushed it down, forcing it to flatten between his legs.

A chorus of giggles came from the hallway. He spun. The door to his bedroom swung open. The three girls stepped into the moonlight streaming from his window.

"Father," they whispered together. "You have seen our mothers."

"Who?" he asked groggily, swinging his legs to the floor and not understanding.

"Succubi," they whispered. "You found their empty graves. You found the coffins."

"In the attic?"

"Yesssssssss. They were alive to help us in our work."

"What work?"

"Pooooor father," they consoled. "You will remember in spite of yourself. In your dreams."

"I am not your father," Peter said, suddenly shaking off his sleepiness.

"Ah, but you are," the girls said. They giggled in unison, mocking him.

Peter, realizing his nakedness, reached for his cassock on the chair and slipped it on. The girls edged back as he stood.

"Now," he said, "let's stop the riddles!" He lunged and managed to grab hold of the black girl's arm. Her eyes rolled in panic as she struggled to free herself.

"If you're so powerful," Peter growled, "why are you afraid of me?"

"We are mortal!" the girl confessed in terror. She struggled feebly in his grasp. The others backed away, fearful of Peter's anger.

"Tell me the truth about all this!" he demanded of her. "I don't believe anything I've heard so far!"

The two other girls suddenly giggled. Together they pointed. "Then believe them!"

"Come!" voices coaxed from behind him.

Appalled, he spun, releasing the black girl.

Three skeletons covered with wisps of hair and tattered clothing were sprawled on his bed. Their faces were blackened as though burned in a fire. Their stench filled the room.

In terror, Peter fought for his breath. He ran to the door. But it was locked.

The girls laughed louder.

The apparitions slithered off the bed and glided toward Peter. "Come closer," they requested.

He darted for the bathroom, slammed the door, and turned the key in the lock.

As he stepped away, seeking the recesses of the

cold-tiled bathroom, he noticed the face in the mirror. Sagging eyelids, sunken eyes and cheeks stared back at him, the grotesque face of an animal.

The bathroom door fell inward, slamming to the floor.

"Take us!" the hags moaned. "Take us *now!*"

Wide-eyed, Peter burst past them into his bedroom. The door was unlocked now. Without looking back, he flew down the corridor to Father Brinkley's room and began pounding.

"What?" the old priest asked, opening his door. "I thought you were sleeping."

"I was!" Peter blurted. "I shouldn't have!" He turned back toward his room, his eyes full of fear.

"What is it?" Brinkley asked. "You're shaking, Father!"

"They broke down my bathroom door! Do you smell anything? Like rot?"

The old priest sniffed. "Nothing," he said.

Again, Peter jerked his head over his shoulder.

"What is it, Father? What are you afraid of? What's there in your room?"

"Father Brinkley," Peter said, "I want to confess!"

"Now?" Brinkley opened the door wider, revealing his striped pajamas.

"Yes, now, please!"

"But it's one in the morning!"

"Please, Father! Oh, please!"

Brinkley assessed the young, worn-out priest standing pitifully in his bare feet, wearing only his cassock. Turning his gaze down the hallway to Peter's open door, he saw the moonlight playing softly through the lintel.

"Look," Brinkley said, "we'll go back to your room

and turn on the lights. You'll see there's nothing there."

"No!" Peter screamed so loudly it startled him. "Don't go in there!"

"Okay," Father Brinkley said. "What do you want me to do?"

"Confess me!"

"How did you sin?"

"I don't know." Peter brought his hand up and wiped the sweat off his face.

"If you don't know how you sinned, then you probably didn't."

"Confess me," Peter begged. "I . . . I feel I am unclean!"

"All right," Brinkley said, "go to the church. I'll get my robe and meet you there."

"Good! Good!" And as Father Brinkley watched, Peter hurried down the hallway, paused carefully beside his open door, then fled past it. The old priest shook his head and went back inside for his woolen robe.

"He's losing his mind," Brinkley told himself. "Not unexpected, the way he's driven himself."

Cinching the robe, he went down the hallway. As he passed Peter's room, he glanced inside and found all normal. The bathroom door was intact, standing open. He went down the stairs. To his dismay, he felt the gas in his stomach again.

"Darn, darn," he said, rubbing the center of his chest as he crossed the chilly, moonlit playground to the church. Entering the back door of the church, he snapped on one overhead light and saw that Peter was praying, preparing himself in the rear pew.

"Come in when you're ready, Father," Brinkley sighed. He genuflected before the flickering red sanctuary light signifying the Eucharist was present and slipped through the red velvet curtains into the confessional box. Inside, he switched on the small reading lamp, kissed the purple confessional stole and hung it around his neck.

Peter, his face drawn, his cassock raggedly open at his neck, bare feet slapping the floor, rushed toward the box to unburden his soul. Of what? He did not know. Yet, somehow he had to be cleansed of the filth that had touched him in his room. What was he guilty of? Again, he did not know. He would rely on the powers of penance to cleanse away what he could not understand.

Quickly, he pushed through the velvet drapes of the left wing of the confessional. Kneeling, he could see through the cloth partition the outline of old Father Brinkley, could see him raise his hand in familiar blessing and then brush back the wisp of white hair that always hung down on his forehead.

"Bless me, Father, for I have sinned," Peter recited rapidly. "It's been a week since my last confession."

He looked up to see the old priest turn his head slightly toward the window as though cocking his ear to hear better.

Peter bowed his head.

"I . . . I don't know exactly what is happening to me," he began.

"Are you *sure* you've sinned?" Father Brinkley asked through the curtain. "It's a false pride to try to be as perfect as God. That may be your only sin, Peter.

"No, no, I've sinned! Against my chastity!"

Father Brinkley uttered a small strangled cough and his head swung directly toward the screen. Peter hardly noticed the new angle. He was absorbed in trying to detail his feelings of the recent bizarre events.

"It . . . it began . . . with the girls," Peter went on disjointedly. No . . . I dreamed of three women who *looked* like the girls . . . but the women were the ones buried in our cemetery. . . ."

There was a series of small snapping sounds like twigs breaking. Father Brinkley gasped as if resisting and his shadow on the screen was jolted.

"Tonight I saw them . . . not just in my dreams . . . but actually in my bedroom. The girls accused me of siring them. I don't believe a word of it but. . . ."

Sighs of air wheezed out from the other side of the confessional.

Peter stopped, frowned and raised himself. Father Brinkley's head was bouncing up and down as though it were a jack in the box on a spring.

"Father?" Peter asked.

In answer, the head rose by some unseen force, the neck muscles stretching into a thin, straining cord.

"Nooool!" Peter screamed.

Stumbling outside the confessional, he lunged to the confessor's partition and threw back the central red curtains.

There, inside, sat old Father Brinkley. His head was high off his torso as if he were hanging by a rope. A guttural final grunt rattled from his open mouth. Then he collapsed, his broken neck lolling pitifully on the top of his right shoulder.

"Ah, no, no!" Peter begged.

"We can only tell *you*," three voices said from behind him.

He spun, tears streaming down his face. "Murderers!" he spat. "Why? Why!"

"It's not for others to know," they sang in unison.

"Everyone will know!"

"Tell no one," they warned. "They'll die too."

The black girl gestured to something behind him. Spinning, Peter saw old Father Brinkley's lifeless body rise in obedience. His head, however, did not lift from his shoulder nor did his eyes open.

"What are you doing?" Peter cried.

Upright, his feet scuffing the floor, Father Brinkley was being compelled forward by the black girl, dragged down the main aisle, toward the doors of the church.

"Stop!" Peter shouted, hysterical from what he was seeing.

The black girl, keeping one hand pointed at Brinkley, raised the other in a soft gesture toward Peter and his advance after them was halted. The girls and Brinkley disappeared through the door.

Try as he might, he could not seem to push through the invisible barrier. Only when the doors closed was he released. He fell to the floor. Then lifting himself up, Peter pushed through the doors and ran after them into the night.

Cassock skirts flying, he sprinted half-naked across the playground and down the fog-shrouded road. He ran, searching for the shadowy forms of the three girls and Father Brinkley. He was well off the hill when blinding headlights swept him, then approached head on. Only when the car horn blew did he lurch to a halt. The vehicle came alongside and Doc Heim rolled down his window.

"Out jogging early, aren't you?" he asked with a grin. "Forget your shoes?"

Peter looked over his shoulder toward the church on

the hill. Then, he scrambled to the other side of the and slid in.

"Take me to Bethany!" he gasped, his eyes still on the church.

"Sure," Heim said. "Can I get my pipe in the rectory first? I forgot it."

"No. I have to make a call."

"You can call from inside the rectory, can't you?"

"I don't want to go back there!" Peter said, tension filling his voice.

"Peter," Heim asked kindly, "what's happening?"

The young priest, remembering the girls' warning, only shook his head. "Please, take me to Bethany. Hurry!"

"Okay," Heim said.

The Dodge swung down off the hill, roared past the fog-filled cemetery and into the gathering mist around the town.

"Father Brinkley's dead," Peter said as Heim drove.

The doctor stared over at Peter. "Dead? How?"

"Can't tell you," Peter said. "You'll find him in the church."

They approached the lighted phone booth in front of the Frostee Freeze hamburger stand.

"Stop the car!" Peter shouted.

Heim wheeled in and shut off the engine. Peter slid out, then darted into the phone booth. Dipping in his cassock pocket, he frowned and returned to the car.

"You have a dime?" he asked.

"Sure," the doctor said and fumbled in his pocket. "Never met a priest yet didn't need a dime." He found two of them, handed them out of the car.

Again, Peter entered the lighted booth. He picked

up the receiver, inserted a coin, and dialed the operator. The coin returned.

"I want to call Rome, Italy. Collect to Cardinal Livingston Stamp. The routing is 011-39-6. His number is 61.40.61. Tell him his son is calling."

Peter saw that Doc Heim was walking toward the phone booth. He glanced at his wrist, but his arm was bare. "What time is it? I've forgotten my watch."

"Nearly two."

"Nine hours difference. Someone should be there. C'mon . . . C'mon!"

"Sir?" a different female voice said. "This is the international operator. You may go ahead. Your call has been accepted."

"Peter?" a faint voice asked. "This is Father Reddin. Your father's not here."

"Where is he?" Peter demanded. "I've got to talk to him."

"As far as we know," the garbled voice said on the other end of the line, "he left Athens this evening. He should be en route to San Francisco."

"Oh, thank God!"

"Got the jitters, huh?" Reddin commented. "Well, they won't last long. Congratulations!"

"For what?"

"Your elevation, of course."

"Oh, thanks," Peter said, and thought, How remote those festivities seem now.

He hung the phone in its metal sling. "Doc," he said, turning, "I have to go to San Francisco. Will you take care of St. Michael's until I get back?"

"Count on me," Heim said, "I've always wanted to run a parish."

"And . . . Father Brinkley?"

"Leave him to me too. Can you tell me what's happening?"

"Not yet," Peter said. "Too much danger. But I can tell you this much. There's an evil out to get me. Father Brinkley's death proves it."

"Strange," Heim said. "First Susan, now Father Brinkley."

"Yes," Peter concluded grimly. "Sometimes I wish I'd never decided to become a priest. Nothing but bad seems to happen to those around me."

"Nonsense!" Heim said in his defense. "You're just depressed."

"Train for San Francisco'll be in at dawn," Peter said, looking up at the starry sky. The moon was very high. From somewhere came the call of a nightbird.

"Why wait? Take my car."

"What will you do?"

"Everything around here is walkable, remember?" He reached inside his pocket and pulled out the keys. "Look," he said, "why not let me drive you back for some clothes first? You can't go to San Franciso without shoes."

"I don't want to go back up there!" Peter said, snatching the keys. "Besides, my godfather will take care of me."

"I've got a pair of shoes at my house," Doc Heim shouted after him as he strode in his long cassock toward the car. But Peter did not reply. He slipped inside and started up the Dodge and threw it into gear.

"Peter!" Heim called. "When you get back, come see me for a checkup, huh?"

The young priest drove off in a hurry toward Highway 57.

Doc Heim watched his car recede into the fog, tail

lights winking in the mist. When they had disappeared entirely, he shook his head in dismay.

"Oh boy," he said to himself. "I hope he makes San Francisco okay."

SIXTEEN

Through the night, Peter drove past Stockton and Clayton and Walnut Creek. Up through the lakes valley of Castro and across its cement bridges. Then through San Leandro, Alameda and Oakland. As dawn pushed up in the sky, he made his way over the Bay Bridge, the commuter traffic still light. The booth operator, demanding the usual seventy-five-cent toll, allowed him through for the twenty cents he had. It was clear the priest was in trouble.

Peter took Highway 101 to Franklin Street, skirted the gold-encrusted San Francisco Opera House with its ornate architecture, the War Memorial with its simpler lines, ran up four blocks and turned left. When he had crossed Geary, he saw a bright, white cathedral. He parked his car in an adjoining lot and walked toward the modern marble structure nicknamed "The Pope's Hat" because of its shape.

At a rear wall, he opened a wrought-iron gate and entered an enclosed garden. A rock-lined brook tumbled through California oaks and fruit trees. The path led to a pretentious, two-story, Spanish style house nestled cozily within the garden walls. Peter rang the bell.

A sour-looking man in a butler's tuxedo opened the door.

"Yes?" he asked unctuously, giving the once-over to the barefoot, open-collared priest.

"I'm here to see Cardinal Wright," Peter announced, self-consciously buttoning his collar and attempting to straighten himself.

"Are you a priest?" the butler sniffed.

"Who's there, Henry?" a voice asked. And Father Charles Kalki, one of the chancery priests, stepped into the doorway. "Peter!" he cried.

The butler, still not bothering to hide his disapproval, peered curiously.

"It's Father Stamp," Kalki said.

"Father *Stamp*?" the butler coughed. "I'm . . . I didn't recognize you. Come in, please." He flung open the door and Peter entered the dark-wooded, parquet foyer. A crystal chandelier hung overhead. To the right was a graceful winding stairway.

"The Cardinal is having breakfast just now," Father Kalki said. "Tell him Peter's here, Henry."

The butler, mortified, rushed off. "Right away," he muttered.

Peter spun slowly around, dazzled by what he saw. Early Picassos lined the foyer. Along the stairway, a solid row of Renaissance artists led the way to the second floor: Rembrandt, Botticelli, Fra Angelico.

"Pretty overwhelming, huh?" Father Kalki asked. "First time you've seen the new place?"

Peter nodded and gazed fully at the priest. Father Charles Kalki had been one of Peter's professors in Theology. He was a good-looking man but he had a nervous habit of flicking his eyes sideways as he spoke, almost as though to deny the truth of what he said. Several times during his Theologate, Father Kalki had approached Peter for favors from his powerful father. Peter had always refused, not liking to be used. But Father Kalki had remained friendly to him.

"How have you been?" Kalki asked. "And what's happened? How did you lose your shoes?"

Before he could answer, a big voice boomed out from the hallway, "You're early! I didn't expect you until this afternoon!"

Cardinal Neil Wright, dressed in black clerical suit with a red vest, approached Peter with open arms and enfolded him. Then he stepped back.

"You look like hell. And what are you doing without shoes? Will you ever take care of yourself? Kalki, get Father Stamp something to eat and see if you can find a pair of shoes to fit him."

Peter pulled loose of Cardinal Wright's grasp. He stood rooted in the foyer. The Cardinal, noting the frightened expression on his face, frowned.

"What is it, Peter?"

"I . . . I don't want anything to eat," the young priest said. He began shivering.

"Then come in, there's somebody here I want you to meet."

"I don't want to meet anybody!"

Neil Wright, sensing deep trouble, turned to Father Kalki and said, "Charley, find Peter some shoes . . . some clothes."

The priest nodded and left them.

"Lawrence Belconi, the Governor of California, is inside those doors," Neil Wright said, motioning. "He's come to watch that news report that woman reporter did on you. He wants you to find more water for California."

"I have to see my father," Peter muttered.

"Well, he's not here yet. Just come along inside and...."

"No!" Peter blurted. "I want to see my father! And I do not intend to find any more water! EVER!"

"I don't understand you at all, Peter," Neil Wright said. "How can you refuse to use such a gift?"

Peter, eyes wild, said, "And I've decided definitely not to become a monsignor!"

"What is it?" Neil Wright gasped. "What's causing all this? Will you tell me, for Godsakes?"

"I can't," Peter said, his face clouding with confusion.

"Livy will be on a ten o'clock plane," Wright said exasperated. "I'll go down with you to the airport. In the meantime...."

"No," Peter said. "I won't meet him there!" He thought a moment, mind working furiously. "Does the rapid transit run near the airport?"

"No, the closest BART tube is at San Bruno."

"I'll meet him there. Got to talk in secret. Just in case."

"In case what?"

"Just tell him I'll be inside the San Bruno station at ten-thirty."

Peter strode toward the front door. Father Charles Kalki arrived with a bundle of clothing, a pair of shoes. Peter grabbed them from him, opened the door.

"Anything I can do in the meantime?" Wright asked solicitously.

"Yes," Peter said, pausing momentarily. "Call Doc Heim. See how it is at Bethany. He's taking care of things."

"Where's Brinkley?"

"Father Brinkley was murdered last night," Peter said. And he exited, shutting the door behind him.

Wright, stunned, gazed at the closed doors. Then, clamping tie cigar between his teeth, he turned toward Father Kalki.

"Get me Bethany," he said curtly.

The priest hurried toward a phone.

The doors behind Neil Wright slid open and Lawrence Belconi, mop of silky black hair hanging boyishly in his eyes, pushed his head through.

"I heard voices," he said jovially. "Is the water-finder here?"

At the bottom of the escalator, Peter paced. Since Neil Wright was so much larger than he, he was wearing a short-sleeve blue shirt and black trousers that Father Kalki had loaned him. The black shoes belonged to Henry. He glanced anxiously at the clock over the stainless-steel ticket booth and saw in the false daylight glow of the subway's lights that it was ten-twenty.

"Excuse me," he said, leaning close to the glass-fronted booth, "is that time correct?"

" 'Zactly right," the gum-chewing woman announced. "Better be!" She went back to reading her love story in the bluish lights of her booth.

A gleaming white train flashed through the subway without slowing. The wind it created ruffled Peter's blond hair. He watched until the lights on the caboose blinked out of sight.

"Miss?" he asked. "What time is the next train?"

"Told you before," she sighed in bureaucratic exasperation. "One BART train goes into San Francisco at ten twenty-five. Other at ten-forty goes to Emeryville. You want that first train it'll be three bits."

"Yes, probably," Peter said, his eyes again checking the DOWN escalator. But there was only an overweight woman with a package.

"Then, that'll be seventy-five cents," the ticket woman said and she pushed a button and a blue ticket whirred up onto the counter.

"I can't pay," Peter said. "I don't have any money."

"Well, you should have told me that!" she snapped.

Embarrassed, Peter flicked his eyes again to the escalator. To his delight, he saw Cardinal Livingston Stamp on the landing. Neil Wright was behind him. They were searching the station below.

"Here!" Peter yelled, bolting toward the escalator.

Cardinal Stamp swung and saw him. He called out a farewell and thanks to Wright and stepped on the DOWN escalator. The woman with her brown paper package watched as father and son came together.

"Father, father!" Peter said, and clung to the Cardinal.

Even when the two men separated, they stood arm in arm. Peter saw that his father's hair was thinning and there were deep lines around his mouth.

For a moment, neither of them spoke. A BART train pulled into the station and stopped.

"C'mon," Peter said, "We'll take this one!"

Cardinal Stamp hesitated, watching as his son scurried toward the ticket booth. He had been shocked by Peter's moon-eyed appearance. Wright's warning that Peter looked tired was an understatement.

Well, the Cardinal thought, I'm here now, and I'll get rid of whatever it is that's bothering him. He was pleased he would be spending more time with his son.

A lot more time, he told himself. A great, great deal more time.

"Father!" Peter shouted. "Do you have money?"

"Certainly," Livingston said quickly. He fished into a pocket of his knee-length overcoat.

"Gimme the money first," the woman said suspiciously before handing out the stubs. She took the five-dollar bill and made change.

"Hurry!" Peter said, keeping an eye on the waiting train. Then, unable to wait any longer, he burst toward the first car and stood outside the door.

Livingston picked up the money and the tickets. "Where does this train go?"

"San Francisco!" the woman in the booth yelled.

At the door, Peter motioned to his father to wait. Then he peeked into the car. Satisfied, he tugged his father's sleeve and the door shut behind them automatically.

"Here!" Peter said motioning to a bench at the front of the car. It was empty except for one person. The woman with the brown paper bundle sat at the rear.

The train started smoothly out of the station.

"It's okay now," Peter said, "we're alone."

"What is it, son?" Stamp asked. "I've never seen you like this."

"Where do I start?" Peter asked, exhaustedly rubbing his eyes. Through the spacious windows, green and red lights were flashing by on the sides of the darkened tunnel. "So much has happened. So much." He took a deep breath and leaned his head back.

Outside the car, the tunnel finished abruptly and they shot up into the gray daylight of the morning. They were traveling fast now and the foggy wisps on the water of the bay zipped past dizzily.

"I don't want to be elevated," Peter said. "I don't want to be a monsignor."

"Yes, Cardinal Wright told me that. He also said you refused to find more water."

"How did you know I found water?" Peter asked amazed.

"Neil called me in Istanbul," Stamp said. "He's been following your exploits closely."

He reached out and laid a long-fingered hand on Peter's arm. "Son," he said, "You *must* find more water. There's a world out there that needs it desperately."

"But, Father," Peter objected, "that's what I have to talk to you about!"

"Hear me first," the Cardinal begged. "You have a chance to unite all the warring factions in our Church. Don't you see the possibilities?"

"I've told you before. I'm not interested in politics!"

"Son," the Cardinal said, "this isn't just politics. This is a chance to galvanize the entire world. To show others the power of God! People of all religions need someone to give them hope. Someone to believe in. Your miracles would offer them that."

"They're not miracles!"

"Call them what you want."

"Father," Peter said fiercely, "you don't understand. I'm confused."

"Nonsense," Stamp said sternly. "You're tired, that's all."

"Am I?" Peter half-shouted. "Father Brinkley was killed because of what I told him!"

"Peter," Stamp said, his voice mellowing to dulcet tones, "Cardinal Wright called Bethany. Father Brinkley was found in the hills. Dead from a heart attack."

"I saw him! His neck was broken!"

"Peter, he was *not* killed," Stamp insisted. "Your

own friend, Doctor Heim, diagnosed his death as heart failure!"

Dumbstruck, Peter stared at his father. Outside, the landscape eclipsed as the subway plunged into the darkness of its tunnel.

"Son," Livingston said, "do you know what possibilities lie ahead if you have the foresight?"

"What is it you have in mind, father?"

"Why," the Cardinal said, "what every father wants for his son. Success, happiness. And what you have now could take you all the way!"

"All *what* way?"

"Wherever you want to go," the Cardinal said vaguely. He reached down and twisted his sapphire ring on his finger. "Peter," he added, "there's one thing that is very, very important and I must know it now. Everything centers on it. Peter," he whispered throatily, "can you . . . is it possible to find more water?"

The car lurched slightly and braked to a halt. The woman with the package stood, clutching her possession, and shuffled through the open door.

Peter turned to face the Cardinal. But the doors in the train shut and he saw that three small figures in hooded parkas had taken the woman's seat. He could not see their faces.

"Is it possible?"

The three girls unzipped their nylon hoods and pulled them off. They smiled.

"Tell me, for God's sakes, Peter. Can you find water again?" The Cardinal was focused only on him, waiting for an answer.

The three girls nodded their heads affirmatively.

"Yes," the young priest said finally in a whisper. "It's possible to find water again."

The train began to move.

"Anywhere?"

The girls continued to nod.

"Anywhere."

The Cardinal took a deep breath and exhaled. "You have no idea how happy that makes me," he said. "Now, what was it you wanted to tell me?"

"Nothing."

"Wright said you drove through the night. That something was bothering you."

"It was nothing. Forget it, father."

From the other end of the car came a giggle, then another and finally a third. The Cardinal turned and saw the children.

"Cute kids," he said smiling.

"Yes, cute," Peter agreed, not taking his eyes from them.

"Son," the Cardinal said. "I know you need rest. This finding water must have taken a lot out of you. But I promise I'll get you back on your feet."

"Thank you," Peter mumbled without any inflection in his voice. The midnight tunnel was flashing by again.

"Now, let me tell you my plan. After you find water for California, I'm going to accompany you to the Rajasthan Desert in India, the Nubian, the Kordofan, Sahel in Africa, even the Sahara! We'll go all over. To every part of the Third and Fourth Worlds. I've already talked to the different Cardinals."

"Sure," Peter said as if in a daze.

"Then, when we finish, Cardinal Wright's going to hold a Theology of the World Conference here in San Francisco. A religious leaders' convention to decide how the Church should participate in underdeveloped countries. You'll be invited to give a speech."

Peter again nodded. He had not taken his eyes from the girls. It was all happening too fast and there was nothing he could do to stop it. As though everything was predestined! He had no choices to make. What was his father's part in all this? What, indeed?

"I have something for you, son. A very special gift." The Cardinal dug into his pocket and withdrew a worn, velvet box. "Open it," he said.

Peter broke his trance and looked down at the purple velvet container. He flipped open the lid. Nestled inside was a ring with a large amethyst gem.

"My bishop's stone," Stamp said proudly. "Yours now. The Pope himself approved you by phone."

"Father, I don't . . ." Peter mumbled, gazing at the ring.

"I called the Holy Father from Athens," Livingston Stamp continued enthusiastically. "Once I convinced him you could find water, he agreed it would be all the more impressive if a bishop of the Church did it!"

"But," Peter protested, stunned, "how were you so certain I *could* find more water?"

"I had faith in you," Stamp said quickly. He pulled the ring out of its box and slipped it on Peter's annular finger. "Perfect fit," he said. "I'll consecrate you myself tonight. Wright can assist. So you see, you won't have to be a Monsignor after all!"

The train came up out of its tunnel and the occasional light from the sun through the clouds glinted on the purple-velvet gem. The stone looked to Peter like a tiny, trapped star. It reminded him of himself.

The train slowed and stopped once more. The doors opened and Peter looked up. The girls were gone, their seats empty already.

"We're here!" the Cardinal said, seeing the Gough

Street sign on the station wall outside. "Neil assured me it would be a short walk to the cathedral. Come on."

Peter dutifully rose with his father and left the BART car.

But as he did an option occurred to him. He could simply go away. Go away and hide somewhere. Anywhere!

The street escalator was out of order, its steps motionless. He began to climb. Above, he could see the street, and beyond, the clearing blue sky of the day. He suddenly felt a surging elation. He was in control of his own destiny once again! Lightly, he bounced up the steps. From behind, he heard the BART pull away.

"Not so fast, son!" he heard his father pant. "I can't keep up!"

Unheeding, he ran faster up the escalator. The blue sky was so near he could practically reach out and touch it.

With a ragged breath, he grabbed hold of the rubber railing, and propelled himself out onto the sidewalk. Quickly, he spun to seek his direction. It did not matter!

But as he turned to dash blindly away, he felt powerful arms enfold him.

"Surprise!" Cardinal Wright said, bearhugging him. "We've been waiting for you!"

Peter sagged.

"Car's right here," Hal the chauffeur said. He was standing nearby, grinning. "Thought we'd save you a walk."

Cardinal Stamp puffed up. "Good thought, Neil," he said.

Peter felt himself bundled into the rear seat of the limousine. He sat listening to the voices around him as the car sped toward St. Mary's Cathedral.

SEVENTEEN

After the eight doors to the cathedral had been locked by the custodian for the night, Cardinal Neil Wright of San Francisco and His Eminence Livingston Stamp of the Vatican opened a sacristy door and entered.

Beneath the towering roof, beneath the fifty-five-foot baldachino of shivering light rods, beneath the simple gold cross that hung over the altar, they laid out the vials of holy oils. All the lights in St. Mary's except those over the sanctuary had been turned off. Outside, the wind was coming off the bay, blowing in heavy gusts. Seagulls had gathered in downtown earlier, signifying a coming storm.

On the bottom step of the altar, Peter Stamp knelt in prayer, waiting to be consecrated a bishop of the Roman Catholic Church. He wore white vestments symbolizing purity.

The two Cardinals mounted the altar steps, clad only in white alb robes. Speaking together, their voices small, echoing out into the cavelike structure, they recited the timeless, ancient words that levied the unseen mantle of spiritual power onto Peter.

"Come, Holy Spirit and do ordain and invest in Peter Stamp, the potency of Almighty God. Whom He will ordain as priest so be it done! Whom He does condemn as anathema to the fires of hell so be it done also!"

Together, they descended the steps. Livingston Stamp laid his hands on Peter's head.

A sound rattled up from the rear of the church near the raised organ high on its pedestal. It was as though the outside doors had been tried.

Cardinal Stamp looked toward his cohort. Wright turned, listened a moment then shouted, "Who's there?" When there was no answer, he said, "Wind's up. Probably just shook the doors."

Stamp, satisfied, proceeded. "I, representative and Senator, Lord and Cardinal of the Holy Mother Church of Rome, now ask you, Peter Stamp, do you swear fealty to Jesus Christ, Lord and God of Heaven?"

"I do."

"And do you renounce Satan and all his wiles?"

"I do!"

The huge building shuddered. A ground wave undulated through the floor and rolled past the altar. The four tall, high mass candles bounced, their flames flickered at the sudden movement.

"Earthquake," Wright whispered.

Cardinal Stamp hesitated. Then, feeling no renewed shaking, he turned to the altar behind him and picked up the tall, white miter and placed it carefully on Peter's head.

"I, then, do here ordain in the name of Jesus Christ, you, Peter Stamp, Lord Bishop, Excellency, forever! Peter, receive the Holy Spirit!"

Immediately, a new rumble began at the darkened

rear of the cathedral. The altar shook as if in an angry grip. The glasses of holy vials fell against one another and shattered. Oil stained the linens in seeping patterns. Several vases of roses tipped and broke, water spreading onto the altar.

Above the altar, the large, gold cross swung precariously. The crystal rods of the baldachino tinkled like wind chimes. Suddenly, the air was filled with a vile odor.

Both Stamp and Wright were looking up at the swaying cross.

"Strong one," Wright commented. "Smells like it might have broken a sewer outside."

Livingston Stamp nodded, but he did not take his eyes from the swinging cross. It jangled at him angrily. Christ seemed to be accusing him.

"Congratulations," he heard Neil Wright say. Stamp turned and saw that Peter was shaking his godfather's hand. But the young man was staring directly at his father.

"Father," Peter said. "Why did you do this?"

"So the world will know when you find water," Livingston said.

"Oh, tell him," Neil Wright said. "Tell him about the overall goal."

"Yes, tell me, father," Peter said, his teeth clenched.

"Go on, go on," Wright urged. "He's got to know."

Cardinal Livingston Stamp dropped his eyes.

"The fact is," Neil Wright announced proudly, "we now have a worthy candidate! You, Peter, with God willing and a little luck, could become a future pope!"

For a moment, the three men stood silently on the altar steps. The wind whistled up into a gale and skirled the walls outside, moaning loudly.

"Is this what you want, father?" Peter asked.

"I . . ." Cardinal Stamp said quickly, "I . . . I am not a candidate anymore. I've made too many enemies. And . . . we've been looking all over creation and. . . ."

"You found me," Peter finished.

"Yes," Stamp said. "We found you."

"Then this is what you want, father?" Peter asked, his brown eyes widening.

"More than you can ever know," Cardinal Livingston Stamp said.

Peter nodded his head slowly, as if taking it all in.

"You'll get used to the idea," Wright pointed out quickly. "Give it a chance."

Peter turned down the center aisle. The bobbing white miter atop his head reminded Livingston Stamp once again of the cross. Obsessively, he turned and raised his eyes to a reproving God.

"To think of it," Neil Wright said admiringly. "We may have found a candidate in your own son! But will he be on our side, Livy? He's not conservative at heart."

"He trusts me, doesn't he?"

"Yes, but. . . ."

"Peter can be brought over," Stamp said. "As of tonight, we have a candidate."

Peter continued through the gloom of the cathedral. When he was near the presbytery, he roughly plucked off the tall bishop's miter and collapsed it between his hands. Then, he pushed open the doors. The wind outside rushed into him. His hair swirled in its currents; vestments flew up around him. For a moment, he wavered at its force. Then he thrust himself out the doors. They slammed with an explosion that rocked the cathedral.

Immediately, there came a high wailing sound, a scream like a child in terrible pain.

"The wind?" Neil Wright asked.

Both men held briefly. Then together, shaken at the sound, they hurried down the aisle toward the rear doors.

Down the thirty-two steps Peter rolled, his vestments clinging to him like Christmas wrapping-paper. And on the bottom landing, he lay unconscious.

The men rushed outside into the wind, down the travertine steps. Both knelt, eyes stinging in the hurricane force.

"He's out cold," Neil Wright said.

Cardinal Stamp, seeing Peter's right hand clutched at his throat, reached up and pried apart his fingers. Dark red blood seeped out. Imbedded in his palm were shards of stone. The Cardinal removed a large piece. In the dim light from the cathedral windows, he saw the head of the beast.

"Cut himself too!" Neil Wright cried, noticing.

The blood was flowing freely down Peter's wrist dripping onto the smooth, gray marble of the church steps.

"We better get help," Neil Wright said. And slipping his arms beneath his godson, he lifted him and started up the steps.

Cardinal Livingston Stamp followed, alb pulsating in the wind. Halfway up the steps, he spun toward the clouds that were flying across the face of the full moon. He flung the broken beast's face into the night.

Wright carried Peter through the cathedral and into the coziness of the sacristy. He lay him on the floor, propping his head on a folded chasuble. Outside, the wind pushed against the building and whirred around the walls of the sacristy.

*   *   *

Because the call came from Archbishop Neil Wright himself, the ambulance arrived at the rear of the sacristy in less than five minutes with two paramedics. One of the attendants gave Peter oxygen immediately and checked his blood pressure.

"Will he be all right?" Cardinal Stamp asked nervously.

"He's just unconscious," the attendant who was in charge said. He was about forty with acne scars on his thin face. The other one, the driver, mid-twenties, was staunching the flow of blood from Peter's hand, picking out more pieces of stone.

"What was going on here?" he asked amiably. "Late Mass, fathers?"

"Something like that," Neil Wright said.

They carefully picked Peter up then and placed him on the stretcher with wheels. But as they did, his teeth began to chatter and his arms and legs thrashed about.

"He's going into a convulsion," the older attendant remarked. He forced a piece of rubber tubing between Peter's teeth. The driver fumbled for the oxygen mask and replaced it on Peter's face. But as soon as he did so, Peter's convulsions ceased.

The two attendants looked at one another. The older one, without saying anything, bent to Peter's purplish lips and put his mouth on them. Steadily, he blew. Peter's chest filled but he did not respond. The attendant listened with a stethoscope.

"Cardiac!" he said, gasping suddenly.

The driver found a syringe and filled it with six cc's of clear fluid. He helped open up the sacred robes, then unbutton Peter's cassock and finally pull up his T-shirt. The older attendant stabbed the long needle directly into Peter's heart and emptied it. Cardinals Wright and Stamp, stunned by the suddenness of what was happening, could only watch helplessly.

Peter's face, the color now of a deep bruise, remained immobile.

The attendant stood and began to thump Peter, smacking his fist down hard above the solar plexus. But he could get no reaction. He kept at it, pounding the chest cavity. Finally, breathing heavily, he slumped.

"Don't stop! Do something else!" Neil Wright cried.

"Did all we could," the sweating attendant said. "We only got so much equipment on these things, you know." He checked his watch. "His brain's been without oxygen for at least five minutes."

Cardinal Neil Wright staggered against the vestment table. "How? How?" he murmured. He dropped his head and began to weep.

Stamp, still in shock, squatted beside Peter's body. He took his son's lifeless hand and squeezed it tightly, refusing, yet forced to believe what had happened.

God has punished me, he thought. Punished me heavily for the sin I committed.

Neil Wright pulled out his handkerchief and was wadding it against his nose to stifle his sobs. In the quiet of the sacristy, the pitiful noises of the big man crying were terrible.

The young attendant, shaken by what had happened, slipped outside to the waiting ambulance. He reappeared momentarily with a blue hospital sheet. He shook it out and laid it over Peter's body and covered his face.

"There'll be papers to sign," the older attendant said in a sigh, rising from where he had rested.

"I'll come down to the hospital," Cardinal Stamp said quietly.

They rolled the stretcher from the sacristy, out the door into the wind which was still strong. The rubber wheels thumped across the aluminum door frame.

Outside, the two attendants aimed the stretcher toward the back door of the ambulance. Beneath the canvas sheet, a tremor coursed through Peter's body and his right leg kicked. The driver jumped back.

"It's okay," the attendant in charge said. "Stiffs do that."

"Jeez, they give me the creeps sometimes," the driver said.

As the two men bent to pick up the stretcher to dolly it into the amublance, Peter pulled the sheet off his face.

Both men dropped the stretcher. Fortunately, it was only inches off the ground. Peter groaned and sat up. In the flashing, twirling light of the ambulance, his grayish face looked very dead.

The two Cardinals, supporting one another in their grief, pushed through the sacristy door. They saw the two attendants staring, paralyzed. Peter was fumbling with the straps on the stretcher, trying to undo the one which bound his feet.

Neil Wright, simple in his approach to life, immediately knew it had all been a mistake. His godson had not died. He rushed to Peter and helped him off the stretcher, saying, "I knew you were okay. Look, Livy!"

Peter stood up stiffly. He was rubbing his chest, wincing at the pain.

Cardinal Stamp had not been able to move toward his adopted son. He had *seen* him dead. Only when the thought came that this was a direct sign from Almighty God that Peter had been saved for greatness could he make himself approach.

"Are you all right?" Cardinal Stamp asked, his voice quaking.

Neil Wright was hugging Peter in relief. "We thought you were dead!" he guffawed.

"He *was* dead," the young driver said wholeheartedly. "Jeez, was he dead!"

The older attendant who was watching Peter could not bring himself to believe it. Damn odd, he thought. Goddamned odd. His brain should be a vegetable by now. He approached Peter and took hold of his hand. "Better let me dress that," he offered.

Peter looked down at his wounded hand. He suddenly remembered part of what had happened while he had been dead. Someone had taken him by his hand and led him to a place. In that place, he had witnessed the present Holy Father, Pope Paul VI, collapse and die. On August 7, 1978, more than three years from now, Paul VI, alone, would try to cry out for help. But he would choke to death on his own vomit.

Why had he been shown that? And by whom? And why couldn't he remember anything else of what had happened while he was dead?

"You'll need stitches too," the attendant in charge said. "Otherwise it'll scar."

Peter raised his eyes to the attendant. For the first time, he seemed to focus. The pupils in his eyes contracted to small points. With a power and verve Wright and Stamp had never seen before, he commanded, "Let my hand scar! Let it always be there!"

The attendant as though bowing to a new and powerful presence, unconsciously backed away.

Peter closed his hand, making a fist. "Now," he said. He spun toward Livingston Stamp and smiled grimly in the moonlight. "Now, father, you wanted water? Well, I'll find it!"

PART THREE

ACTS AND CONVERTS

EIGHTEEN

The car sped down the mountain road toward the distant lower plain of Adrar. After an additional train ride to Fort Gouraud, an army jet would be waiting to whisk Bishop Peter Stamp to yet another location in the desert so he could find more water.

In the rear seat of the ancient black Packard, Peter bounced along, head lolling. He was weary and yet somehow elated. Distantly, he remembered himself as an assistant parish priest. It seemed so long ago. Almost like thinking of someone else. Perhaps that was what he had become. Someone else.

Yet, he was happy. Already he had found thirty-nine good wells here in this region. He would find others before he reached the French fort. And then? More and more wells somewhere else, he smiled to himself. And more and more allegiances from the people he would help.

It shamed him a little to think of it. The truth was

he had begun to enjoy his acclaim. And for such a simple thing as finding water. Lately, he had begun to wonder what other miracles he was capable of.

Enjoying himself, he chuckled inwardly at the memories of his start. At Governor Larry Belconi's request, he had journeyed with his father to California's Imperial Valley. The first day, the beginning of it all, he could find no water. The girls had not shown themselves since the subway in San Francisco. He had stood around nervously, walking off by himself, hoping to spy them. But they were nowhere to be found.

By the third day, the farmers of the Imperial Valley had grown antagonistic and Cardinal Stamp was worried. He was convinced that if Peter had done it before, he could locate more water. And he had pleaded with his son to try harder. But Peter had responded that he could not, that he seemed to have lost the power. He made the excuse that he was too exhausted to continue. So the Cardinal, learning of his friendship with Doc Heim, had sent for him, hoping his presence would in some way help.

Jimmy Heim flew down to the Imperial Valley. "Why not just point like you used to?" he had asked.

"I don't know where to point," Peter had whispered, his hands jammed in his pockets, the farmers and his father standing eagerly nearby in a tomato shed.

"Well, they're all watching and waiting," Heim had grinned. "Here, take this." And he had bent down and held a clod of dirt to Peter. "Just throw it!"

"What?"

"Throw it! Trust yourself!"

Peter in desperation had flung it as far as he could. And the Cardinal had convinced the farmers to dig.

In amazement, Peter had watched as water spurted from the earth.

"See?" Heim had said. "You're just as good as you used to be!"

In the following three years, Peter had uncovered the hiding places of six hundred and eighty-four sources of water. Since that distant day in the Imperial Valley, he had slept long and well. The terrible dreams seemed to have vanished with the three girls. And he realized he had been attributing the power to them when it was really his.

After the Imperial Valley, the San Joaquin had yielded eighty good wells. The Mojave desert had been totally disappointing at first. Geologists said that sea water had been seeping into existing pockets deep in the earth. They told him fresh water was simply not available. But after a week of walking, he detected an entire underground river flowing less than a hundred feet below the surface!

Far-flung areas that his father had suggested had yielded water also. The Kalahari with its bush people; Sahel, caught in the midst of a civil war; Bahrain, where the water was more precious than oil. The Rajasthan, arid wasteland of India, now to be revitalized thanks to the water he had found. It made him feel very, very good. And more and more, it was dawning on the young bishop that it was he, not Cardinal Livingston Stamp, who was running the show.

The car braked suddenly. Peter opened his eyes and heard the driver curse in Arabic, then swerve at the last moment to avoid a man leading three shaggy camels down the mountain road. Peter turned and looked out at the immense desert of Erg Iguidi below.

"Boy," Doc Heim said, stretching his long legs. "Am I sick of seeing those deformed horses."

"We'll be finished here soon," Peter said. "Couple more wells. I want them to remember how good God is."

"Not to mention Bishop Peter Stamp," Heim kidded.

Peter, ignoring the remark, leaned forward and tapped the gaunt, sweating driver. "Next town?" he asked.

"Atar!" the driver yelled over the sound of whining brakes and gears.

"How long?"

"Two, three, maybe four hours."

"Maybe, maybe," Heim said. "Most important word they got." He brought out his pipe and tamped in fresh tobacco.

Peter, reached out and laid an affectionate hand on the doctor's knee.

"You homesick, Jimmy?" he asked.

"I'm okay. I guess I do miss Bethany though."

"We haven't seen the old town in a while. Wonder what it'll be like when we get back?"

"The same," Heim said. "Only for you, smaller. Maybe too small." He struck a sulphur stick match and lit his pipe.

Peter did not answer. He removed his hand.

"Well, Pope Paul's funeral is over," Heim said to make conversation. "He ruled your church a long time, didn't he?"

"More than fifteen years."

The view from the mountain extended a hundred miles. In the far distance, above the horizon, a shadow was forming on the desert, indicating the coming sunset. Peter thought of how he had felt that morning of August 7, 1978, the day Pope Paul had died. He had been in El Fasher on the way to Bilma with a contingent of African churchmen. The news had arrived by messenger at breakfast.

"Paul's dead," Cardinal Stamp had announced.

There had been consternation among the Africans. Peter had continued eating.

"Did you hear what I said, son?" Stamp had inquired, seeing his son calmly sip his thick coffee.

"Yes," Peter had said. "I heard. He died of a heart attack."

And several present, including Cardinal Stamp, had thought: the message never mentioned a heart attack. But in the excitement, making plans to leave the Sahara and journey to the conclave in Rome, they had forgotten it.

Now, Peter, sitting in the car with Doc Heim and peering out across the expanse of desert, said, "He died horribly."

"Who?" Heim wondered, puffing his pipe.

"Paul the Sixth."

"How would you know? You psychic or something?"

"I saw him die," Peter said. "I even knew the date."

"You didn't say anything about it."

"No."

"But you knew?"

"From that night I died."

"But if you *knew*, why didn't you say something?"

"There was no reason to tell anyone," Peter said. "It wouldn't have done any good. Anyway, it's just part of my new power. I don't want to go into it." He squirmed down in his seat and changed the subject. "They should be in conclave about now," he said.

And Doc Heim who had grown accustomed to not

prying into this new and mysterious side of Peter asked, "Think your father will win this time?"

"No, he's finished."

"He's listed as a candidate in the newspapers."

"They don't know Vatican politics. Those names are passed out to take the heat off the real ones."

"Well, that could be right," Heim grinned. "You're a real candidate and your name wasn't mentioned."

"Let my father have his ambitions for me," Peter said, ignoring the humor. "An American can never be pope. Italians have controlled the Vatican for four hundred years."

"I wouldn't underestimate him," Heim counseled. "He's a powerful man, capable of a lot. Anyway, you can't say you're not enjoying this whole thing. Your newfound importance seems to agree with you. And maybe your father is pretty wise. Maybe he sees who you really are."

"It's a game with him," Peter said. "An unrealistic one. Besides, you know I hate the whole idea of politics."

"You know what they say. Sometimes the thing we hate most is precisely what we want."

The car continued downward, propelling them from side to side as the driver negotiated the hairpin turns. Doc Heim studied Peter thoughtfully, the gray smoke from his pipe gathering beneath the felt roof of the car.

"Ever since Rajasthan," Heim said, puffing on his pipe, "there's been a tenseness between you two." He was referring to the time in India when Peter had decided to relax a few days, wishing to shop in the outdoor bazaars, drink warm beer and simply loaf. Cardinal Stamp, had vetoed the whole thing, saying it would upset his carefully planned schedule and had added that if Peter took vacations, he would never amount to anything.

Peter had disappeared. When he showed up at the Courtier hotel two days later, he was polite to his father, but the warmth and ease between them had lessened.

"I think there's a chasm growing between you two," Heim finished.

"Ever since he's started managing my life, things have changed . . ." Peter said, averting his eyes. And he thought to himself how much the Cardinal was like those three girls trying to control him.

"I don't like him ordering me around!" he said fiercely, turning toward Heim. "After all, who's finding the water anyway?"

"You, pal," Heim said, grinning.

Peter relaxed and smiled also. "Sometimes," he said, "I think you're my only friend, Jimmy. And I'll tell you something, this is the way I like it. Just you and me finding water. Him off in Rome."

For the next seventy miles, they rode in silence.

At evening, when the sun had nearly set and the light was ambient and soft on the desert, the Packard entered the town of Atar with its single ziggurat and striped moorish train station. The driver said, "Curious ones!" He motioned to a crowd gathered beneath the soot-covered arches at the station entrance. Several policemen in faded red jackets were holding them back. The train puffed patiently, waiting on the nearby tracks.

The purple-garbed bishops and a passel of priests pushed toward their car. It had been this way all across northern Africa. Each region they passed through, they were met by local prelates. It was the way Cardinal Stamp had wanted it. Peter's renown, he said, would be firmly founded in the voices of lower churchmen. The "grass roots" campaign, he had deigned to call it.

"Bishop, Bishop," a man who introduced himself as Excellency Abdul Fahmi, said, "have you heard the news?"

"News?" Peter asked, shaking hands all around and trying to catch the strange-sounding names that twisted his tongue as he tried to repeat them.

"Yes! Yes!" Bishop Abdul cried. "We have a pope! We have a *new* pope!"

"Who?" Peter asked.

"Cardinal Albino Luciani!" Abdul announced proudly, the Italian name trilling on his tongue. The group of churchmen, recognizing the name, chattered like fat hens.

Peter grinned and turned to Doc Heim who was just getting out of the car. "Another Italian," he said. "See? No danger."

"He is to be called Pope John Paul the First!" Bishop Abdul Fahmi explained proudly. "And it is said his reign will be long and difficult."

An impatient cry exploded from the crowd. The police looked anxious.

"Ah," Abdul said unctuously, noticing them, "they wish only to kiss your hands!" And taking Peter by the elbow, he guided him toward them.

The crowd surged forward a few feet and Peter held out his hands. The sun-blackened desert dwellers pressed his fingers to their lips, murmuring in awe. The legend of the Water Finder had preceded him.

As he made his way through the crowd, Peter saw two boys carrying a sack between them.

"What is that?" he asked Bishop Fahmi who had stayed at his side.

The Bishop leaned in and asked one of the boys. When he pulled back to Peter, he wrinkled his nose and said, "Their dog has died."

"Ask them," Peter instructed Bishop Fahmi, "if they would like to have their dog back."

Fahmi, thinking he had misunderstood, asked Peter to repeat what he wanted. Doc Heim, hearing Peter say it again, said, "Hey, pal, you don't want to go too far."

Fahmi pushed toward the boys, spreading apart the crowd which did not understand the actions of the Water Finder. He sheepishly rattled off what Peter had told him. The boys looked at Peter not understanding what he meant. "A new dog?" one of them asked, puzzled.

Peter motioned them to bring the gunny sack and its burden to him. The dog had obviously been dead awhile. Its stench was apparent.

"Take it out," Peter said. "Out! Out!"

The boys, terrified by his gestures and still not understanding, dropped the bundle and backed off. Peter, looking at the crowd assembled around him, lifted the toe of his boot and tapped the bag.

An odd growling came from the bag.

"Come out!" Peter commanded.

There was a tearing sound as teeth snapped savagely at the burlap. An emaciated tan dog stuck its skull-like head through the hole, its eyes covered yet with the milky glaze of death. The dog ripped at the bag, forcing its body through the rent. Then leaping free, it charged howling up the street toward the open desert. The boys, paralyzed by what they had seen, could not follow.

Several women fell to their knees. Christians crossed themselves. Moslems stared in disbelief.

A woman in a black burnoose rushed from a hidden niche of the train station. She threw herself at Peter's feet. A local priest tried to drag her away.

"She has inside devils!" he warned in broken English.

But the woman clung to Peter's trousers. She grabbed hold of his hand and forced it open. Her eyes softened in pleasure when she saw the brilliant red scar that ran from the bottom of his fingers nearly to his wrist.

"*Eiiiiii lomma!*" she screamed. "*Ei lomma tuoi!*" And she kissed his feet.

The crowd broke rank. One of the policemen was trampled. Bishop Abdul pulled Peter toward the train station. Heim waded after them, knocking down a man who tried to rip the clothing from Peter's back. Priests tripped, enveloped. Like insects, the faithful of Atar swarmed insanely for Peter.

Bishop Abdul pushed him onto the train. Then blocking its doorway, he shouted to the engineer who swung up into his engine. The train began to move. Several priests pried off screaming women.

In the square, Peter could see the woman in black cowering. Villagers were flinging gravel and bricks at her. She lurched forward, arms up, then, turning, fled down the main street of Atar, pursued by the angered mob.

Wanting to see her again, Peter pushed down the inside aisle of the car and out to its rear platform. Several town children were pursuing the train, running along the tracks. Bishop Abdul and Doc Heim joined him on the platform. The town, growing smaller, was being covered by darkness.

"What did she say?" Doc Heim asked.

"Nothing important," Bishop Abdul denied quickly.

"Nothing important?" Heim snorted. "They tried to kill him!"

"One can never tell. These villagers are superstitious."

Peter turned from the vanishing town. "Tell me," he ordered. "What was it she said?"

Bishop Abdul raised his hands to protest but saw the uselessness of it. "She said, 'My Master.'"

"What else?"

The Bishop sighed in embarrassment at having to relate such a thing to a godly man. "She said, 'My Master, you are here!'"

Peter swiveled back to the town. Even though he could see nothing now, he stared.

"A case of mistaken identity," Bishop Abdul Fahmi apologized. "How could evil and good mix?"

Peter smiled at that. "Yes," he said. "Mistaken identity."

NINETEEN

ATACAMA DESERT, PROXIMITY ANTOFAGASTA, CHILE: *September 28, 1978*

The sixteen-vehicle caravan of drab, greenish-yellow trucks wound its way through the dry lake bed of the Domeyk. The wasteland crunched in protest beneath the fat tires of the trucks. Nothing grew there. Not

even cactus. It was the driest desert in the world, un-
fit even for lizards. No rain had fallen in forty-seven
years.

The Llullaillaco Volcano hovered above the desert
at more than twenty-two thousand feet. In the harsh
noon sunlight, even its snow-capped peak looked mis-
shapen and surreal.

The soldiers from the Chilean army drove slowly
and did not speak to one another. Their eyes swept
the horizon nervously for attackers. Their cargoes
were precious.

Inside each of the trucks were dignitaries: high-
ranking army officers; Cabinet members of Chile; visiting officials from the neighboring countries of
Bolivia, Peru, Argentina and Ecuador; and cardinals
and archbishops of the Catholic Church. They had
come at Cardinal Livingston Stamp's invitation to
watch the "Water-Finder," Bishop Peter Stamp.

In the lead truck, Peter swiveled and checked the
caravan behind him. Eight in all. Through the front
windshield of the truck directly following, he could
see that Doc Heim was speaking with his father. The
Cardinal had expressly asked Heim to ride with him.
As Peter watched, he had a strange feeling of jeal-
ousy.

A soldier in the rear of his truck rapped on the window. Reverently, he waved to Peter. But in his foul
mood, Peter sullenly swung forward.

"*Como tienes miedo?*" he sourly asked the driver.
Why do you fear?

"*No tengo miedo, Excelencia,*" the soldier denied.
"*Multas guardias para nada.*" So many guards for
nothing.

The driver shrugged and concentrated on his
driving.

It simply did not make sense. There had been bandits in the Kalahari, Sahara, Sahel. Marauders in Biafra and Rajasthan. No one had bothered him on those treks. Why now?

Reaching to the space on the seat between the driver and himself, Peter idly picked up the map. He gazed at it momentarily.

"*Halto,*" he said.

"*Agua?*" the driver asked, excitedly. He cut the wheels hard to the right. They had stopped on the edge of a deep ravine.

"*Donde, donde?*"

Peter studied the maps unperturbed.

Doc Heim ran up outside. "Got something?" he asked.

"I feel," Peter said, "we're near water now."

"Longest way we've ever come," Heim said. "This one's really dry, huh?"

Cardinal Stamp, dressed in fatigues like Peter and Heim, walked up to the window.

"Well, son," he asked. "Where is it?"

Peter, ignoring him, gazed out across the dunes. A red-capped army general pushed up to the window.

"*Agua?*" he asked.

"*Abajo la colina,*" Peter said quietly. Over the next hill.

The General gave a cry and one of the trucks broke out of the lineup and sped forward. The General catapulted his bulk into its open cockpit and urged his driver to race ahead.

Peter saw the officer doff his braided cap in quick tribute as he disappeared. The other trucks followed.

"*Vamos?*" Peter's driver asked excitedly. Shall we go?

"No! Get on," Peter said to Heim and Cardinal Stamp who were still standing outside the truck.

"What's up?" Heim asked.

"I'm taking a break," Peter said.

"But the water!" Cardinal Stamp cried. He always liked to be there when it was found.

"They don't need any help," Peter said. He turned to the driver and told him to stop at the bottom of the ravine.

Disappointed at being kept from the action, the Lieutenant yelled up to his men in the rear to hang on. Then he skidded down to the flat shelter of the draw.

Peter opened his door and stepped out onto the packed sand. The driver slumped in his seat and cursed quietly in disappointment.

The truck Heim and the Cardinal had been in had followed them. A lieutenant-general with oversized red epaulets on his rounded shoulders jumped down from it. He was followed by a Chilean archbishop who had insisted on wearing his silk purple robes.

"*Que pasa?*" The Lieutenant-General asked the Lieutenant.

The junior officer explained the "Water-Finder" wanted to rest. The Lieutenant-General did not look happy. He surveyed the small gorge.

"*Es necesario para ir!*" he remonstrated. He moved off to reconnoiter this strategically awkward place.

"Maybe we *should* get out of here," Cardinal Stamp said to Peter.

In answer, Peter lay down in the shade of the truck. "I feel tired today," he said petulantly. "I think maybe it's time for a change."

"A change?" Stamp asked. He squatted down beside him in the meager shade.

"From finding water."

"Needs a vacation," Heim said, grinning. "Man's getting rusty. One well in thirty miles."

"It's time anyway," Cardinal Stamp said to Peter. "Neil Wright's meet in San Francisco is due to start. We can continue your appearance there."

"When are you going to give up your silly dream?" Peter suddenly sat up, his words tumbling from a locked-away place. "It's *your* ambition! Not mine! I never wanted it! Don't you understand? I never wanted to be anything but a simple priest!"

A shot rang out and the Lieutenant-General, a few yards off, fell dead.

Small arms fire erupted from the rear of the ravine. The three guards atop the truck whipped around the large machinegun. But they were hit instantly. Two of them toppled lifeless over the side of the truck and landed in the sand. The third flopped like a fish against the barrel of the fifty millimeter.

Peter rolled onto his belly, flattening himself. Beneath the truck, he saw his driver, the Lieutenant, loading an M-16. Crouched beneath the other truck were two remaining soldiers. The Lieutenant barked something at them and they peered uncertainly toward him. Then, he sprang to his feet and bolted toward the curve of the ravine. The two soldiers hesitated momentarily, waiting for the officer to draw the fire. When none came, they followed him.

As the three neared the more advantageous cover, the explosion of a mortar blew them off their feet. The Lieutenant began to cry for help.

Peter jumped up and sprinted toward the smoking crater.

"No!" Doc Heim warned him. "Stay down!"

From over the hill appeared men on horseback.

They were dressed in rags, had rifles on their backs. One of the riders, a black-bearded man in a tattered officer's uniform, galloped ahead of them.

Peter knelt down beside the Lieutenant. He was dead.

The leader on his mottled gray horse drew up.

Peter stood up straight. "Who are you?" he asked boldly. "Bandits?"

The man threw his head back and began to laugh. He said something quickly in a local dialect and the others with him laughed also. Finally, when the joke was over, he turned back to Peter.

"I am Rodriguez," he said in perfect English. "I am the leader of the peasants of Chile. My men are guerillas. We wage war against this corrupt government."

"Violence is wrong!" Peter objected.

"The only way the Third World will ever right its social evils is by war and revolt. 'The Kingdom of God is taken by violence and the violent bear it away,'" the man quoted softly.

Stunned at the quotation from Jesus, Peter raised his hand, shading his eyes to study the man.

Behind him, near the truck, Heim and Cardinal Stamp rose to their feet. The Chilean Archbishop also stood up and began straightening his ecclesiastical garments. Furtively, he scanned the horizon. Then, reaching unseen into his voluminous purple robes, he switched on a small electronic beeper attached to his cincture.

Atop the hill, the other army general was standing up in his truck. He was watching his soldiers dig in the unusually moist arroyo. When he heard the signal from the beeper on his belt, he reacted at once. Motioning to a truckload of soldiers, he ordered them to follow him.

"Are you Peter Stamp, the Water-Finder?" the guerilla asked.

"I'm Stamp."

"Then, you are my hostage." He grinned. "The ransom will buy us ammunition, clothing and food for our cause."

"I can't go with you," Peter said.

The guerilla withdrew his police revolver. He cocked it.

"Please, come," he said. "It would be a waste to shoot you."

The sound of approaching engines cut through the air. The band of guerillas nervously scanned the hill.

Rodriguez kicked his horse forward and leaned down to grab the Water-Finder. Peter dove to the sand. As the guerilla wheeled for another try, machinegun fire whizzed over his head. His men broke for the top of the dune.

Turning his face sideways, his cheek to the hot sand, Peter saw Rodriguez make a dash up the hill. Bullets pocked the sand behind him. Then bright red spots appeared on the flank of his gray steed. Near the top of the rise, the horse collapsed. The animal and Rodriguez tumbled downward.

Peter picked himself up and ran toward Rodriguez. The guerilla's legs were bent contortedly beneath him. He looked around and saw that his horse was dead.

The Chilean soldiers were jumping from their trucks, running toward them.

"Kill me!" Rodriguez begged. He pointed to his pistol lying out of reach.

"I can't! It would be murder!"

"They will . . . torture me," the guerilla said. "I will name others!"

"Are you Catholic?" Peter whispered. "I can confess you!" The soldiers were very near now.

"Brother," Rodriguez said, raising his torso painfully, "I'm a Jesuit priest! Kill me!"

Peter shot him in the chest. He was holding the gun when the General arrived.

"Too bad he is dead," the General said. Out of spite, and to impress his men who were gathering, he shot the man four more times. "Rodriguez," he explained and walked away pridefully with his soldiers, exclaiming happily, "*Que dia! Que dia!*" What a day!

Alone momentarily with the priest he had killed, Peter knelt. "I'm sorry," he whispered to him. "I could bring you back to life but it wouldn't do any good. They would just capture and torture you." In disgust at his dilemma, he picked up a handful of sand and threw it down.

From the crest of the dune, two trucks appeared. There were soldiers in the rear, all of them soaking wet. They were waving buckets of water.

"*Un poquito lago!*" they were shouting. A small lake!

A soldier ran up to Peter and took one of his hands and began to smother it with kisses. Peter slapped him away and strode toward the trucks.

"Get in!" he yelled to Doc Heim and his father. He got behind the wheel and started a truck. Heim and Stamp scrambled for the rolling vehicle.

One of the soldiers jumped on the running board. Peter pushed him off. The General was waving happily, shooting his .45 in the air. And as the other trucks began to follow, Peter could hear their amazed shouts behind him, "*Milagro! Milagro!*"

"Why in heaven's name," his father asked as Peter drove the truck, "did you have to shoot that bandit?"

"You of all people wouldn't understand," Peter cried angrily. "It's over! I did it! Let's drop it!" He swung his face back toward the old tiretracks in the desert, pushing the truck to its limit.

In a few hours, the outskirts of Antofagasta abruptly appeared. Moments before, there had been only desert; suddenly there were cobblestone streets. The town lay on the downslope of a hill.

As Peter crested the small rise and started downhill, he saw not only the town but hundreds of Chilean Indians. They were lining the sides of the road. When they saw his truck, they swarmed down the road to him, waving and shouting like happy children.

"*Salvador!*" they chanted. Savior!

"Now I know what Palm Sunday felt like," Doc Heim quipped.

Women ran alongside as Peter drove, begging for blessings on their babies they held up in their hands. Children loped in a zigzag before the truck like welcoming porpoises.

"How fast they heard," Cardinal Stamp said, smiling, pleased. "The soldiers probably radioed. Look at how happy they are!"

I wonder if they would be so happy, Peter thought, if they knew their hero Rodriguez was dead.

He inched the truck through the adoring throng. Many reached into the window and tugged his hand out and kissed it. Embarrassed, he began to blow the truck's horn.

A boy squeezed into the window, jamming his upper body inside.

"*Porfabor!*" he pleaded, grabbing at Peter.

"Tell me something first!"

"*Besar, besar,*" the boy continued, not understanding.

"*Aeropuerto!*"

The boy looked up puzzled, then comprehended.

"*Al direcho!*" he said.

Peter gave the boy a quick blessing and let him kiss his hand. Beaming, the ruddy-cheeked mestizo scrambled up across the hood and straddled it. He began to wave his arms, opening a path for the truck.

TWENTY

Still in his army fatigues, Peter stared out the airplane window into the night. Doc Heim was sitting in the aisle seat and the Cardinal had walked back down the aisle where one row in front of the tail, he lay down in his house cassock and slept.

Peter opened his breviary.

"Aren't you going to sleep?" Heim asked, yawning. "You might as well. It's a ten-hour flight."

"Tonight," Peter said, lowering his missal, "I have this bad feeling. I'll just stay awake."

"But you look pretty tired," Heim said. "Want something to help you sleep?"

Peter shook his head and went back to his book. "I'll be okay," he said.

Heim fluffed his pillow and eased the reclining seat back. A stewardess came by, snapping out unused lights in the 707, leaving the plane in near darkness.

As he began the second part of Vespers, Peter's

eyes closed to slits. The book in his hands lowered to the rhythmic drone of the four engines. His head eased back on the seat rest.

Instantly, he was in a dark place. There was a movement to his right. As he spun, several rotted corpses tumbled from a shelf of rock.

"The wish is made," a voice rasped. "Blasphemy done! Another dies soon!"

Peter found himself transported to a long, marble-lined room filled with statuaries and ancient busts of Roman Emperors. A priest in a black cassock approached from the far end, his heels clicking on the marble floor. In his hands, he carried a silver tray on which sat a crystal glass filled with red wine.

The priest knocked on the door and entered when a voice said, "*Avanti!*"

Through the open door, Peter saw the gentle and much loved Italian, Pope John Paul I, look up at the priest, smile, then take the glass from the tray and swallow a mouthful of the liquid.

The priest bowed and started for the open door. Before he reached it, Pope John Paul's head bounced on the small desk as he slipped to the floor. The priest paused, observing a moment. Then, he closed the door.

"Hey, pal!" Jimmy Heim was saying.

Peter opened his eyes and gradually located the source.

"You okay?"

"Yes," Peter mumbled, sitting up straight. "Fine. . . ."

"You were moaning."

"Was I?" He was gazing at his open hand which lay in his lap.

"Want me to stay awake with you?" Heim asked.

"No! I'll . . . I'll be all right. Go to sleep, Jimmy. I'll be right back."

Peter eased out past Heim. Working his way toward the rear, he checked the rows. Near the back, he found his father, stretched across three vacant seats, his long legs bent at the knees. The entire section was dark.

"Father?" Peter asked, bending and slipping in toward the window.

The Cardinal had his hands clasped on his chest. "What is it?" he asked, startled. "Something wrong?"

"I need to know," Peter said, "did you ever wish anything for me?"

The Cardinal pushed up on his elbow. "Can we talk about this tomorrow?"

"Now!" Peter said, his voice breaking.

"Peter, I . . . ."

"Now!"

Several passengers stirred. A woman peered over the back of her seat and said, "Shhh!"

"What exactly did you wish for, father? Tell me!"

"Peter," the Cardinal said soothingly, "everybody makes wishes. Why can't I?"

"Something specific, father! Something . . . blasphemous. Like wishing a pope would die! Maybe even doing something about it!"

The Cardinal sat up, still groggy from sleep. "Son," he said, "all popes die. When they do, a new one must be elected. The climate for us is very good now. Africans, Latins and Asians are willing to unite behind you, give us the majority we need."

"I know you've been collecting votes," Peter accused him. "Your ambition for me is embarrassing enough. But why would you kill Pope John Paul?"

The Cardinal swept his hair back with both hands

and tried to address himself to what Peter was talking about. "The world needs an American pope," he protested, only half-awake.

"Sure!" Peter said, lips quivering with the effort. "The world needs an American pope all right! Someone to fulfill the ambitions of an old man!"

Two stewardesses who had heard the commotion and seen the call lights from annoyed passengers, arrived.

"Please," one begged. "There are many trying to sleep."

"It's all right, Miss," the Cardinal soothed. He stood up and took hold of Peter's arm. "Everything's okay."

With his open hand, Peter slapped his father's face.

The onlookers were shocked into silence.

"You're my father no longer," he choked, tears flooding his eyes. "And when we get to San Francisco, I'll tell them Peter Stamp is not, and never will be, a candidate for anything! I'm tired of being manipulated. First by these girls and then by you."

"What girls?"

"It doesn't matter. You've manipulated my whole life. I hereby declare my independence."

"You must go after the papacy," the Cardinal said, realizing how serious his son was. "It's our only chance to save the Church! And you know I can get it for you!"

"Whatever I do from now on will be on my own terms," Peter said and he spun on his heel, violently shoving aside the passengers who had stood for a better view.

The Cardinal sat down and stared at the floor.

"Are you hurt?" one of the stewardesses asked.

"Yes," he said. "Please leave me alone."

The aging angular Cardinal in the black cassock with red buttons sat absently rubbing his left cheek.

Then, he stopped. And looking up, he muttered in stubborn obsession, "He can't do this. I won't let him!"

TWENTY-ONE

SAN FRANCISCO, CALIFORNIA: 9:20 A.M., *September 29, 1978*

In the gleaming reflections of the bay, the 707 whined in over the water and slammed its wheels down on the runway. As it taxied to the terminal, Peter Stamp stood and silently put on an ordinary black cassock, sash and collar. He had never exchanged his priestly garb for a bishop's.

As he stepped off the portable stairs, a black limousine pulled up. The left rear window whirred down and Cardinal Neil Wright stuck his head out and said, "Boy, am I glad you're here!" He was wearing his scarlet red robes and beanie.

Hal, the chauffeur, jumped out and took Peter's small bag and then Doc Heim's and Cardinal Stamp's suitcases. Cardinal Stamp swung dejectedly into the back seat. Heim sat in the middle. Peter took the folding metal chair so he was facing the three men.

"Been a madhouse," Cardinal Wright explained

hurriedly. "Everybody wants to talk to Peter. Look at them hanging on the fence there!"

As Peter turned to face them, the crowd reacted and forced the gates open. They began to stampede toward the limousine. Hal accelerated and the car shot off.

"Fans, newspeople, converts to Catholicism. You name it! Livy, this is bigger than we expected!" There was a tone both of misery and of glee in his voice.

Through the back window, Peter saw a woman nearly touch the car. The TV newsmen stopped running but the fans did not give up. Many clutched autograph books as they scampered between parked jets and security guards.

"Who's here?" Cardinal Stamp asked Wright.

"Everybody except the Italians," Wright said, smiling. "John Paul the First has sent Nuncio Alvarez from Spain to observe. Notice his choice of a neutral country? All the Third World cardinals are coming. Even the Comunist countries are represented. You can't get a room anywhere in San Francisco!"

He turned excitedly toward Stamp. "Lopez, Ni Kand, Mazande and Duala are at the St. Francis. Thought we should have them together. Oceanians and Europeans are at the Mark Hopkins and the Fairmont just across the street."

He noticed for the first time the glumness shared by father and son.

"Peter wants none of it," Cardinal Stamp explained.

"Peter, Peter," Wright admonished. "Consider it. All of this is bigger than you, me or your father now. You possess a gift from God. To deny who you are or your potential would be a grave sin." He reached to a leather side-pocket and took out a bundle of magazines. "Look at what's happening!"

Staring up at Peter from the cover of the *Time* magazine was a portrait of himself. At his cassocked feet, water burbled from a desert floor. "The new Messiah?" the cover asked.

Newsweek carried a three-page color spread on Bishop Peter Stamp, "Water-Finder." There were articles clipped open in *U.S. News and World Report; Playboy; Fortune; Forbes* and *People* magazines. Riffling through a stack of newspapers, he spotted stories about himself in *The New York* and *Los Angeles Times; San Francisco Chronicle; The Washington Post; Osservatore Romano; Paris Match, El Tiempo,* and *Amsterdam Flagge.*

"Some people from Hollywood called," Hal said, turning, eager to add more information. "They want to do a movie on your life!"

"Told you a long time ago!" Heim said, peering at an article. "No one can fight events, forces and fate!"

As they came along the front of the bustling airport, Livingston Stamp whistled. Peter turned to where he was gazing. Ahead, two short, rotund men in wide-brimmed red hats and cassocks with red buttons and piping stood uneasily on the curb, trying to flag a taxi.

"Casselli and Barbolino," Wright said in amazement. "*They* weren't invited!"

"They don't need invitations," Stamp replied. "They go where they want!"

"Should we give them a lift?"

"It would be a courtesy between brothers," Stamp sniffed.

"Slow down and stop, Hal," Wright said and pushing his window button, lowered the glass.

"Dear Brothers in Christ. Cardinals Casselli and

Barbolino," Cardinal Wright said in a modulated voice. "May we give you a ride into town?"

"Brother Cardinal Wright!" Barbolino, a cherubic, fleshy-faced man, exclaimed. His gregarious manner marked a master diplomat's heart of ice. He reached in and shook Wright's hand, then Stamp's. "Thank you both," he smiled, "but I'm sure we'll find a taxi to take us to our suites at the Sir Francis Drake."

"What has lured you away from the Curia?" Stamp asked pointedly.

"Oh, we are only passing through," the other Cardinal wheezed, interrupting Barbolino in a high whiny voice. Cardinal Casselli was a chain smoker with a mild case of emphysema. In Rome, he was the Dean of the Roman Curia, the second most powerful Catholic in the world. He was known as the "butcher" because of his habit of killing careers and exiling the troublemakers.

"Did you come for the conference?" Stamp asked bluntly. "It should prove to be very interesting."

"Well . . . if we have time." Cardinal Casselli whined. "We are most busy."

"Is this the Water-Finder?" Cardinal Barbolino asked, thrusting his chubby hand in to Peter. "Bishop Coadjutor, is it not?" The "coadjutor meant "without a parish." It was a subtle insult for Barbolino to refer to the full title.

Peter uncertainly shook Barbolino's short, dimpled fingers.

"Well, well, well!" Casselli smiled, carefully appraising the young man. Then, he turned quickly toward Stamp and Wright. "He is very popular. I see you are doing everything correctly. His debut will be most impressive!"

Cardinal Stamp blanched but recovered quickly.

"My years should produce some small wisdom," he smiled back, cordially.

The two Italian cardinals straightened and bowed. The audience was over. Wright pressed the window up and the limousine drove off.

The Italian cardinals watched the limousine depart through the airport traffic.

"Piu pericoloso," the angular Casselli said. *"Grosso rivoluzione!"* A big revolution. More dangerous than we thought!

"Telefona il Papa?"

"Subito!" Casselli agreed. Then he added: *"Piu pre-occupazione per debole cuore!"* More worry for the Pope's weak heart!

He shouted at and successfully halted a passing taxi.

"Who were they?" Peter asked, watching the short men scamper toward a waiting cab.

"Either one could be John Paul's successor," Wright said, turning for one last look. "Cardinals Castillo Casselli and Emilio Barbolino, two of the highest-ranking churchmen in the world."

Peter understood. Other Cardinals like his father and Wright were only cardinal-priests. The two Curial men slipping into the taxi were cardinal-bishops.

Once on the freeway, the four men sat in tense silence. When they were near downtown, Stamp leaned forward and said to Hal, "Drop me off at the Fairmont."

Hal stopped at the corner of Stockton and Mason. The Fairmont sat like an elegant white toad squatted across the street from the towering Mark Hopkins.

A man in green tails snapped open the limo door.

"I'm going to caucus the Africans and Asians,"

Stamp said to Wright. "Regardless of what happens today, they must start talking to one another."

He looked toward Peter.

"Son," he said, "your welcoming speech opens the conference at eleven this morning. I'm not going to say anything to anybody until I hear what you've finally decided."

He hesitated a moment longer as though wanting to say more. Instead, he pushed away from the car and strode quickly under the carport and into the opulence of the Fairmont.

The doorman closed the car door. Hal pulled away, swung the luxurious automobile precisely ten blocks down California, made a left on Gough and through the parking lot of St. Mary's Cathedral.

"Hard to believe you were consecrated a bishop here three years ago," Wright said, making small talk. "Seems like only yesterday. So much has happened since then."

Hal parked in front of the rectory's white, ten-foot wall, swung out and opened the back door.

"You know," Wright said, "I'm proud of you. Very proud."

Wordless, Peter lifted off the jump seat and walked straight ahead through the gate and garden. Doc Heim followed.

Henry the butler opened the door. "Welcome back, Excellency," he greeted. "I'll have your things taken upstairs."

Jimmy Heim came through the front door with Cardinal Neil Wright. Peter said, "Doc, in here!" And he stepped inside the library.

"Close the door," Peter commanded.

"It's dark in here," Heim said.

Peter snapped on a pharmacy lamp and sat wearily.

"Doc," he said in the quietness of the room, his voice muffled by thousands of tomes, "my father has done something wicked. I need to get away from him."

"Your father has done more for you than any man could."

Peter shook his head. "He's no good. I see that now."

Doc Heim sat beside him and put a comforting arm on his shoulders. "Well, if you're decided, there *is* one way to escape him permanently," he said.

The black, inlaid pearl telephone tinkled in soft tones on Neil Wright's desk. He picked it up. The butler announced, "Governor calling, Your Eminence."

"Put him on."

There was a pause and Lawrence Belconi said, "Neil, I hear Peter's back!"

"Returned today."

"Sorry I couldn't make it to the airport," Belconi said. "Getting my yearly budget together. Gotta stand up before the legislature in Sacramento Tuesday. Tell you why I'm calling, Eminence. Wondered if Bishop Stamp would do me a favor. It'd be great if he found a couple of new wells in the Imperial Valley."

"I don't think so, Larry," Wright said. "He's awfully tired. He just got back from a long trip."

"I heard, I heard. And I know it's tough. But I'd see you got that parking lot at St. Mary's taken off the tax rolls."

There was a moment's silence and Cardinal Wright said, "Well, let me see, Larry. I'll give it a try. You wanna hold?"

"Sure," the Governor said, "I'll just wait."

The Cardinal laid the ornate phone on his leather-top desk and went toward the back door of the library. He was about to enter when he heard Doc Heim say, "Go for it, Peter. Give them their pope. But not the one they want. You're no conservative!"

"You're right," Peter said. "I do want change. You remember that bandit in the desert? Well, he was no bandit. He was a priest, trying to overthrow an oppressive government. There are hundreds like him in the Latin Americas, all trying to make a better life for poor people. That's who I identify with. And I killed him!"

"You could keep his work alive. Be as radical as he was in your own way! I don't know much about the Theology of Liberation, but doesn't it advocate changing exactly the thing your father stands for?"

"The established system," Peter said, agreeing. "I have a debt to the Third World people . . . to free them. I could do that if I were pope."

"You *can* be pope! You've got the world at your feet!"

For a long moment, Peter did not move. Then he turned quizzically to Heim. "You've never gotten this excited about church politics, Doc," he said. "Why the sudden interest?"

Heim laughed. "Maybe I like friends in high places."

Peter shook his head. "Your idea about my wanting change is right," he said. "But I still don't want to become pope. I could do *something* though. I could throw my weight behind Cardinals Barbolino and Casselli!"

Heim looked crestfallen. "They're not as liberal as you are."

"But what's important for right now is that with them I'd be out from under my father's thumb!" He went to the louvered blinds and opened them. Outside, in the garden, the rock-lined stream ran its endlessly circuitous route as pumps recycled the water.

"What if those two Italian Cardinals were not in the running?" Heim asked.

"But they are."

"But if they weren't?"

"Then, I suppose I'd throw my hat in the ring."

Wright backed away from the door. What did it mean? Would Peter carry out his threat to ally himself with Barbolino and Casselli? Despite Livingston Stamp's assurances that Peter could be brought over to their way of thinking. Neil Wright had always feared something like this might happen.

Suddenly, he knew that Peter should make no more public appearances until he was brought back to his senses. And Doc Heim must be sent away!

As Wright crossed to his desk, he caught a glimpse of the garden through the unshaded window. The acacia trees were billowing like sails in the San Francisco breeze. Beneath them, the brook bubbled along through ferns and flowers. And, near some white lilies and begonias, there stood three teen-age girls. They were watching him.

Mesmerized, he groped for the telephone.

"Larry?" the Cardinal said, "I'm sorry, but I can't reach him. I'll try later." He hung up.

He would have to report to Livingston Stamp. He picked up the phone again and began to call the Fairmont. He stopped. What he had to tell Livy, he should do in person. He dialed "1."

"Henry, here, your Eminence."

"Where's Hal?" Wright asked. The girls were gazing steadily at him.

"Took his car to fetch some supplies, your Eminence. Did you want the limo?"

"Never mind," the Cardinal said "I'll get it myself. Oh, Henry, we've got some young trespassers in our garden."

He hung up a second time. Through the library doors, he could hear Doc Heim urging something in a high, almost compulsive voice. He went out of the study and down the hallway. The car would be in the garage at the rear. Quickly, he turned and walked through the kitchen, noticing a leg of lamb thawing on the butcher block. The sight of the meat made him suddenly nauseous. He reached inside his vest pocket for a cigar. But he had smoked the last.

"Never when you need one," he muttered. He pushed through the back door. The three girls stood in the patch blocking his way to the rear gate.

The Cardinal had worked as a youth on the Embarcadero. He was known as a brave fighter; even bigger dockworkers feared him. But now, as he faced the girls, he felt his legs go soft.

Henry came down the side path. When he rounded the corner of the house, he saw Cardinal Wright standing before a black, brown and red-haired girl.

"These the ones?" Henry asked.

The Cardinal nodded in relief to his butler.

"Scat!" Henry said.

The red-haired girl turned. She flipped up her wrist and Henry burst into a crackling torch. He screamed in a long, high-pitched wail as he beat at the flames that consumed him. Then he collapsed to the ground silent.

Stupefied, unable to help, the Cardinal watched. The girls advanced on him. He had to move. And he did—in such terror that he did not feel his legs begin to pump.

Inside the library, Peter was standing at the window. "I've made up my mind. The first thing is to go to Cardinals Casselli and Barbolino," he said. "After that. . . ."

Cardinal Neil Wright, glancing desperately over his shoulder, hurtled by the window. He rushed toward the front gate and yanked on its handle. But it was apparently locked.

"What's going on?" Peter asked, confused. Then he saw the three girls. "They're back! Older, but it's them!"

"Who's back?" Heim wanted to know, coming to the window.

"The girls from Bethany! I never mentioned them to you because of their threat. They're the ones who killed Susan and Father Brinkley! O God, I thought that was all over!"

"What are they doing here?" Heim asked, watching them circle the Cardinal.

"If we don't stop them, they'll kill my godfather!" Peter shouted and he turned and darted through the library door.

The girls took their time closing the gap. The Cardinal, the locked gate at his back, seemed trapped. But summoning all his strength, he levered up onto the gate, balanced precariously atop it on his oversized stomach, and then flopped over. The black girl closed her fist. The wooden portal blew itself into splinters.

Peter ran down the path past the ruins of the front gate. As he reached the driveway, Neil Wright backed the limo violently out of the garage, hitting the outdoor statue of St. Theresa. Then, roaring ahead, he fishtailed crazily onto Gough.

"C'mon!" Heim said. "We can take my Dodge. If it's still running!"

They piled into his old car which was parked back of the rectory garage. It had been at St. Mary's nearly three years. Fortunately, Hal had driven it occasionally. Heim threw it into gear and lurched without looking onto the street.

"There!" Peter pointed, seeing the limo careen toward Ellis.

As they approached the intersection at Jones, Heim made a left turn. It took only a moment to realize he had turned the wrong way. A solid wave of automobiles was barreling toward them. Breathlessly, Heim cut the wheel and slid into an alley.

"You took a one way!" Peter complained.

"Thought it was a short cut."

"Go up the alley, then turn left. We can still help him."

Heim put the car into drive.

"Wait a minute," Peter said, "*Wait* a minute!"

"What?"

"Why didn't I think? Those girls are on my father's side, right?"

"If you say so. I can't believe they did what you said."

"They did it all right. But Neil will be all right! He's in this with my father! Must be a trick to get me to follow!"

"Even if they were after him," Heim said, "they're on foot and he's got a car."

Peter checked his watch. "You know where the Opera House is?"

"Somewhere on Franklin. I can find it!" And they shot up the alley.

In the Lincoln, the Cardinal sped further down Ellis, ran a yellow light and swung up Taylor. Repeatedly, Wright searched his rearview mirror. Then, realizing how foolish he was being, he took his foot off the accelerator and rolled the window down. Those girls could not follow him now! He breathed deeply, pulling the outside air into his lungs, forcing himself to be calm.

At the corner of Taylor and Post, less than four blocks from his destination, he obeyed a red light and stopped. The painted walk filled with San Franciscans crossing the street.

Wright rubbed his hand across his eyes and bushy brows and tried to shake off the jarring experience. When he looked up, he was facing a short, brown-haired girl. She was standing just outside his window, grinning at him.

"I can find you anywhere!" she said to him.

He floored the car and flew through the red light. Pedestrians scattered as the Lincoln sped across. Only two long streaks of blue smoke from the squealing tires hung in the intersection.

There were three steep grades ahead of him yet. He roared up the first hill, vaulted the intersection of Sutter and felt the rear bumper of the car crash down on the cable car tracks. Two more. He kept the Lincoln floored, screaming at over seventy miles per hours.

As he neared the level of Bush Street, he saw the light above change for him. Thanking his lucky stars, he sped toward it. It was only when he had gained the intersection that he saw the three girls. They were standing directly in front of his hurtling Lincoln!

He hit the brakes. But it was not necessary. As the huge car bore down on them, the black girl raised her hand in a "halt" position. As though it had struck a cement wall, the Lincoln slammed to a total stop. The bumper folded, the hood and fenders accordioned inwards, pushing the motor through the fire wall and onto the front seat. Cardinal Neil Wright broke off the top half of the steering wheel and smashed through the windshield. Thousands of square pieces of safety glass spewed outward with his body, trailing him in a spray as he rocketed across the ruined hood, then slid face down across the street. When he rested finally at the base of Nob Hill, several pedestrians were shocked to see that only the back part of his head remained.

No one noticed three smiling girls slip away in the confusion.

TWENTY-TWO

The Opera House nestled securely in the westernmost half of the War Memorial block. Separating the House and the larger War Memorial building was a small, tree-lined park with a circular driveway, designed for chauffeurs dropping off their important passengers. Spearlike, black wrought-iron fences tipped with gold surrounded the park and lent both buildings a feeling of grandeur.

By ten-thirty, a half hour before the conference was scheduled to start, lines of limos waited in the courtyard. One by one, they deposited red-robed cardinals, purple-gowned archbishops and bishops, monsignors and priests who were ministerial assistants and secretaries, world dignitaries. As they stepped from their automobiles and hurried up the granite steps into the cavernous foyer of the famed Opera House, TV cameras from three networks recorded their arrival.

Skirting the line of cars, a light blue Mercedes-Benz drove onto the median lawn itself. The chauffeur hopped out and opened the door. Cardinal Livingston Stamp stepped from the car. Nuncio Alvarez followed. Stamp surveyed the gathering, then picked out Cardinal Mazande.

"Have you seen Neil?" he asked him.

"No," the tall Swahili said. "But you know we wish to speak with Peter."

"I know, I know," Stamp whispered. "I'll have him here."

With Alvarez in tow, he joined Mazande and went up the steps.

Upon entering, Stamp again peered around. The foyer was filled with churchmen greeting one another and gathering gossip from far-flung parts of the world.

Father Kalki, the nervous-eyed priest who was acting as a guide, looked up and spied the Cardinal.

"Where's his Eminence?" Stamp asked.

"We don't know," Kalki said. His eyes flicked from side to side.

"When Bishop Stamp enters," Livingston said, "I hold you personally responsible to bring him to me."

"Where?" the priest asked conspiratorially, glad to be taken into confidence.

"The salon room," the Cardinal said. "We'll be waiting."

"I'll do that, of course," the priest said. "And you won't forget my name, Eminence? Father Charles Kalki. I was one of Peter's professors in theology."

The Cardinal nodded, agreeing to a favor owed, and went into the main section of the theater. There, he beckoned to Mazande who was talking to Cardinals Collier and Buff from Britain. All three nodded, turned. Discreetly, slowly, so as not to attract undue attention, a red, ribbon-like thread of cardinals eased past the plushly padded seats toward a hallway. There, they flowed into the salon with one hundred crystal chandeliers.

Outside, Doc Heim swung the Dodge past the gathering limos and whistled out loud. "Never seen so many fancy cars!"

"They should be arriving in Chevrolets," Peter said, looking at the line-up with open disapproval. "One of the things wrong with the Church."

Heim found a meter space by the side of the building, away from the commotion. When they got out, he popped a quarter into the timer.

"Half-hour for a quarter?" he asked. "Boy, inflation!"

Peter was already heading for the stage exit. Heim joined him as he trundled up the steps and opened the door.

A security guard, hired for the occasion, halted them.

"You can't come in here," he said, thrusting out his big belly pugnaciously.

"I'm with Cardinal Neil Wright," Peter said.

The guard frowned, checking his clipboard.

"He's on the *Committee!*" Heim winked. "Bishop Peter Stamp!"

"Oh, okay," the guard said. "How 'bout you?"

"I'm a doctor," Heim whispered with great confidentiality. He brought out his wallet and showed an AMA card.

"Okay," the guard said. He sat back down on his chair.

They worked past an alley of hoists and pulleys. They stepped into the side wing, then out onto the apron, and stopped, both men taken by the massive stage, the huge red and gold velvet curtain, the three tiers of individual velvet-lined private opera boxes rising to the gold bas-relief ceiling.

It was easy for Peter to see why Cardinal Wright had picked the Opera House as the site of this meeting. There was an implicit drama to the room.

Dignitaries and cardinals were filling the private boxes on the three tiers. Peter spied Cardinals Barbolino and Casselli entering a private box on the first level. Barbolino sat and arranged his robes, then Casselli glided across the purple velvet enclosure and took the other seat.

On the stage stood a polished mahogany podium and six attached microphones. A single spotlight shone on the podium, demanding that all eyes focus there.

"What are you going to do?" Heim asked.

"Before I give my speech," Peter said, "I'm going up to Barbolino and Casselli to tell them that I'll throw my support behind them!"

"You're sure?" Heim wondered.

In answer, Peter moved down the side aisle, keeping to the shadows between the columns to avoid being recognized. Pushing through the ornate bronze doors at the rear of the theater, he walked down the inner steps to the foyer. As they crossed the gas-lit front entrance, Peter heard his name called and froze. He sidled close to a marble-veined pillar. Heim stood nearby.

"You seen Peter Stamp?" a voice snapped.

Slowly, Peter edged around the pillar. It was Father Kalki questioning another priest, obviously an assistant.

"We're to bring Bishop Stamp to the salon," he said. "Don't let him get by!"

The assistant nodded and walked away. The priest searched the area, then padded off, a worried look on his face.

Now Peter saw a metal plaque that had been obscured by the priest's presence. It read simply: "In gratitude for the use of the San Francisco Opera House. The newborn United Nations. April 25 to July 26, 1945." Again, Peter had to admire Neil Wright's choice of locations. A great movement had started here before. Obviously, these participants thought another was beginning.

"Bishop Stamp, isn't it?" a squeaky voice asked. And startled, Peter swung to see a small Filipino cardinal, his frame overwhelmed by the multitudinous folds of red silk.

"No," Peter said, backing away. "I'm. . . ."

"It's Stamp!" the Filipino announced.

Heads swung.

"*Peter* Stamp?" someone cried.

Quickly Peter turned, put his head down and strode toward the marble stairway that led up to Barbolino and Casselli's viewing boxes. Doc Heim stayed by his side.

As Peter rounded a last pillar, a priest stepped in front of him and thrust out his hand.

"Hello, Excellency," the priest said. "How's my old student?"

"Father Kalki," Peter said. He turned his tired eyes from the darting ones of the priest. All around, bishops, monsignors and cardinals were looking up at him with fascination. Some men from the press snapped photos.

"Will you come with me?" Kalki asked. "Your father is waiting. He wants a last word with you before you open the conference."

As the priest spun and led the way, hands were shoved out to Peter.

"Kretchum, Germany," a voice said, pumping his hand.

"Duala, Senegal!"

"Cardinal Rotei. India. Where you found water in Rajasthan!"

"Hoolenbeeck!"

"*San Francisco Chronicle!*" a starstruck reporter who was half Indian said, then shouted a question never answered.

"Caliagua! Peru!" a sweating face announced.

"Champalaux. Faoud! Rampart!" The faces blurred.

Peter was propelled along by the crush of bodies. He saw Doc Heim struggling to keep up, then held back with the reporters and photographers who had been barred from the inner proceedings.

As the mass of churchmen shoved into the theater, Father Kalki took hold of Peter's cassock and pulled him sharply to the right. He led him down a short hallway, opened the door and thrust him inside. Then, he turned and held up his hands.

"Bishop Stamp will be right out!" he screamed to the assemblage. "Be patient, gentlemen! Remember who and what you are!"

Some of the seniors, mostly cardinals and archbishops, realized they had become carried away.
They cleared their throats, avoided one another's eyes
and drifted off to wait for Bishop Stamp's message. It
had been a long time since they had reacted so
openly, but every one of them had been pulled by the
same magnetic power. For all the gifts Bishop Peter
Stamp possessed, he seemed mysteriously, almost un-
bearably, humble. And to men such as they, brokers
of vast power, his was a humility that made them feel
vulnerable, almost childlike in his presence.

While news of his arrival circulated outside, Peter
stood inside the salon room. More than twenty cardinals were gathered here. They stood silently. Livingston Stamp, sensing that the pitch of the drama was
right, stepped to the forefront and said, "Bishop, we
are pleased you could come."

Peter remained mute, his head slightly bowed, his
hands folded before him.

Cardinal Mazande, the African, said, "Hello, Peter.
It's been a very long time."

Peter did not look up.

"I remember you as a boy," the Cardinal said in his
deep, resonant tones. "You used to stutter then. Now
you've lost your stutter and can find water!"

Several cardinals chuckled at the small joke.

"What we want to know," Mazande went on.
"What all of us here want to know, Peter, my brother
. . . is . . . will you help us? Change is in the air. It
is time for a new, renewed Church!"

The majority of the cardinals nodded in deep ap-
proval.

"We know who you are, Bishop Peter Stamp,"
Mazande went on. "We know you are not self-seek-
ing. We know, too, as your father has told us, that

you do not wish to be considered 'Papabile.' But you know that our Church is divided."

"You can unite us now!" Cardinal Bonkowski of Poland spoke out. "Catholics everywhere will listen to your words. Muslims, Christians, Jews, atheists and agnostics respect you!"

It is in your hands to bring a dead Church back to life!" Cardinal Tobey of England announced.

"Peter," Cardinal Kaszus from East Germany pleaded, "I am 'Papabile' in my own right. Eastern Europeans will vote for me. But not Africans or Asians. Unite us! Save our Church! She languishes. She floats without sail!"

"Make the Church the center of people's lives again!" Douala of Zaire begged. "Resurrect it!"

Then, they stopped. All were quiet and all watched the stoop-shouldered, blond-haired man as he turned and walked quickly across the hardwood floor toward the door. He pushed through it and for a moment, the buzz of the excitement outside filled the room. Then, it was quiet again.

Without saying anything, without looking at one another, the cardinals filed after him. Cardinal Stamp was the last to exit through the doors into the main section of the Opera House.

By now the word had spread everywhere. Not only did all in the House know that Bishop Peter Stamp had arrived, but each and every churchman had memorized his exact description. Very tall. An angelic quality to him. Clad only in rumpled black cassock, plain cincture. Tired, harried-looking. And from the moment he emerged from the salon, the applause started.

He walked down the side aisle, the posh wine-colored carpet springy under his feet. Hands stretched out as before. The churchmen began to cheer openly. The Opera House thundered with their acclaim.

When he reached the stage, Father Charles Kalki momentarily blocked his way. Only when he received Cardinal Livingston Stamp's nod did he allow Peter to ascend the steps.

"Water-Finder!" the assembled began to chant. "Miracle Worker!"

The applause quickened. Hopeful faces stared up at him. At the podium, he listened a moment longer. Then, he raised his hands. Immediately, the House quieted. The clapping trailed off.

Peter turned, surveying the scene. The lower section of seats was jammed. Three tiers to the roof, filled with cardinals of every country.

Someone backstage dimmed the lights. And Peter stood alone, the focal point of total attention in the single spot.

He bent forward to the six microphones and said, "I am honored to be here but. . . ."

"Mikes!" someone in the audience below whispered.

Confused, Peter raised his head slightly. He looked toward the curtain and saw the shadowy figure of a man he assumed was the stage manager. He was fiddling with something.

Again, Peter bent close to the microphones. This time, he said simply, "I want to tell you . . . all of you . . . I am not a candidate. . . ."

But there was no sound coming out. The public address system was not working. Someone in the audience shouted, "Houselights! Houselights, please!"

The lights raised slightly and Peter saw the short figure of Nuncio Alvarez hustle down the aisle. He was waving a telegram in his hand.

Quickly, he ascended the stage. "Excuse me, Excellency," he begged. He stepped in front of Peter Stamp, bent to the microphones and tapped them.

They were working perfectly.

"Brothers in Jesus Christ! Respected observers!" he said solemnly. "I have two sad announcements to make. A short while ago Cardinal Neil Wright, the organizer of this conference, was killed in a traffic accident."

Peter went numb. A buzz ran through the audience.

The Nuncio now raised the yellow piece of paper. "And this from Secretary of State Cardinal Jean Villot at Rome:

> "With deep anguish, I must
> announce the end of the
> brief, thirty-four-day
> reign of Pope John Paul
> the First. He died at
> 21.40 hours. May God
> grant him his eternal
> reward.
> *Requiescat!*"

"*Requiescat in Pace!*" rumbling baritones answered.

Briefly there was no more reaction, then conversations started, churchmen and dignitaries began to move toward the aisles. The conference was, in effect, over before it had begun. A duty born of ages lay before them now. The complicated machinery of a conclave waited to be assembled.

Above, the three tiers of boxes were emptying. To his dismay, Peter saw that Cardinals Barbolino and Casselli had already gone!

"Where?" he asked himself. "The Mark Hopkins? No, no."

"The Drake! Sir Francis Drake!" he muttered to himself. He turned and found an opening in the curtain. Sprinting past the backstage machinery he lurched out the stage door.

TWENTY-THREE

Dashing down the steps of the stage exit, Peter swung onto the sidewalk and froze. Diagonally across the intersection stood the three girls, shoulder to shoulder, idly observing him. He spun toward the parked Dodge. Inside, smoking his pipe, was Doc Heim.

Peter walked quickly up to him. "Move over—I'll drive."

"What's the matter?" Heim asked. "Don't trust me anymore?" But he slid over to the passenger seat.

Peter swung directly in front of the girls and sped down Grove, then took a hard right onto Franklin.

"Take off your jacket," he commanded.

"What?"

"Give me your jacket!" The speedometer was edging up to fifty. As he held the wheel with one hand, Peter began to undo the front of his cassock.

"We were wrong about my godfather," he said.

"What happened?" Heim grunted, bending forward to squirm out of his coat.

"They said he died in a traffic accident. But the girls killed him!"

"You don't know that! Maybe it really was an accident."

"Maybe," Peter said, pulling the hem of his cassock past his buttocks and slipping it over his head. "But I think he was murdered. If he was, you know what that means."

"That he wasn't involved?"

"Right," Peter said, sliding the car around California.

At Powell and Sutter, Peter turned the Dodge into an alley behind the brick facade of the Sir Francis Drake and stopped.

"Do you see the girls?" Peter asked.

"No!" Heim said. He twisted in the seat, searching the rear window.

"Act as a decoy for me so I can get to the cardinals. If you see the girls, make sure they follow you away from here, then make sure they see who you really are. I don't want you ending up like my godfather."

Peter snapped open the door and jumped out. Heim, dressed in the cassock, slid into the driver's seat, clutched the car into gear and screeched down the alley.

Peter ran into the delivery entrance of the hotel. At the front desk, he laid sweaty palms on the copper-plated top.

"Cardinal Casselli," he demanded.

The clerk looked at the man in black slacks, worn corduroy jacket and T-shirt. His face looked strangely distraught.

"Cardinal Casselli has gone directly to the airport."

"Did Cardinal Barbolino go with him?"

"No, he came back to check them both out."

"I must see him!"

"That's impossible," the clerk said. "He left word he

did not wish to be disturbed." He bowed slightly and said, "Excuse me, *sir*." Then he walked toward the cashier's desk and spoke to two bellhops.

Peter backed away. As casually as he could, he sidled toward the elevators, loitering a moment until the two bellhops arrived. When the "Up" elevator opened, he glanced about, then stepped on with them.

The operator shut the doors. He turned and asked, "Floors?"

"Sixteen. Fourteen," the bellhops said.

"Fourteen also," Peter said, taking a gamble.

One hop wheeled the luggage rack off the elevator. Peter smiled at the operator and stepped out to the left. The doors closed. In the corridor, Peter paused and watched the bellhop make his way to room 1422. When the bellhop entered the room, Peter hurried after him. Cardinal Barbolino, arms crossed on his chest, was watching the boy load his luggage.

"Eminence," Peter said, pushing in on the surprised Cardinal. "I have to speak to you. It's urgent!"

Barbolino's eyes widened in recognition.

"What can I do for you?" he asked, raising his eyebrows. He was dressed as he had been at the Opera House, in full cardinalate regalia.

"I came to tell you that I'm not your opposition. I will support you or Cardinal Casselli's candidacy."

Cardinal Barbolino appeared speechless.

"Sir?" the boy asked. "Is this all your luggage?"

"I have some things in the closet I will carry," Barbolino said. "Go get Casselli's luggage next door. 1423."

When the boy had gone, Peter said, "I am a liberal. I want a great deal of change in the Church."

"I'm a moderate," the Cardinal said. "But compared to your father, I, too, would be called a liberal."

"That will have to do," Peter said.

"Ready, sir," the bellboy piped.

"Goodbye, Eminence," Peter said. And he bent and kissed the Cardinal's deep blue ring. Then, he turned and walked down the corridor to the elevator. In a moment, he was on his way down to the first floor.

On the fourteenth floor, the Cardinal handed the bellboy a quarter. The boy frowned.

"There are prayers that go with that," the Cardinal mentioned.

It did not seem to placate the bellboy. Sullenly, he pushed the clothes rack piled with luggage down the corridor.

Barbolino turned toward the room, surveyed it one last time to see if he had left anything. Unconsciously, he rubbed his chubby hands.

It was really too bad that John Paul was dead, he thought. But the hand of God was very, very visible. Of all the "Papabili" only two Italians really counted. Casselli and himself. Because now that this anti-Italian affair had been snuffed, the Third World would get back into line again. There was no one they could all unite behind.

He clapped his hands in happy anticipation. Then, remembering his toiletries bag and fresh soutane, he stepped to the closet. Not bothering to turn on the light, he lifted down the cassock on its hanger, then groped for the black silk pouch that contained his toiletries. Finding its white drawstring, he pulled it off the hook. It took him a moment to realize there was something moving around inside the bag.

Carefully, he held it away from himself and carried

it to the polished writing table near the window. He set the bag down and watched it.

"Che cosa e?" he asked aloud.

Whatever it was, suddenly stopped squirming. Sucking in his breath, the Cardinal gamely reached out and tugged apart the drawstrings. Peering from a cautious distance, Barbolino could make out only his Gillette razor and the Valentino label on the deodorant bottle.

He leaned forward so that his face was over the bag. Still not touching it, he brought his eye close to the small opening and peered inside.

Two baby rattlers buried their fangs on either side of Barbolino's nose. A third struck his Adam's apple to pump its venom. Neck and face covered with the writhing serpents, Barbolino vainly tore at them, screaming, stumbling and thrashing about the hotel room.

From the lobby, Peter pushed through the revolving front doors. The sun was wonderfully bright, it seemed to him. He would go directly to St. Mary's and say a funeral Mass for his godfather. Then he would go home to Bethany. That thought alone pleased him.

He signaled to the doorman who clapped smartly to the line-up of cabs on the street. A green and white one at the front immediately pulled toward the entrance.

The cab parked just outside the overhang of the Drake's tearsail awning. The doorman had his fingers on the rear handle when a woman who was walking into the hotel screamed. A shower of glass rained down on her.

Peter whirled. A heavy bundle plummeted near the

bleeding, prostrate woman. Admist the shards of broken window glass lay the corpse of Cardinal Barbolino.

Above, white crinoline curtains fluttered outside a fourteenth-floor window.

A dark cloud passed over Peter's face. It was his fault. The decoy maneuver had not worked. He vaulted up the Drake's steps, past the gathering crowd of onlookers and into the foyer.

There were four elevators altogether. Two were immobile at the restaurant on the seventeenth floor. A third hovered momentarily at the eleventh floor, then it ascended. The fourth, descending, stopped at the fourteenth. If the girls were not on the fire stairs already, then he could expect to find them in that car! Unless, he thought, they had taken some supernatural way out altogether!

Racing to the nearby stairway, he pounded up its cement steps, madly clambering to the third floor, then out into the hotel's corridor. Car number four was continuing its descent, the only elevator moving toward him. Anxiously reaching out, he pressed the "Down" call button and waited, his breathing rapid as he gulped for air.

The door opened. A stocky western-attired couple were on the left side of the car. A Chicana elevator operator sat on her wooden stool. And in the rear, dressed in Peter's cassock, stood Doc Jimmy Heim!

"You!" Peter said. "I don't believe it!"

"Floor, sir?" the operator queried. "We're going down."

"Same floor as him!" Peter said and he boarded.

The doors closed. Heim had a silly grin on his face and was shaking his head.

"You really still haven't figured me out, have you?" he asked.

The burly husband was holding a Moose River stetson in his hands. Suddenly, he put his hat on his head. He turned and eyed the bedraggled man who had just got on, then turned toward Doc Heim and asked, "He bothering you, Reverend?"

"He's all right," Heim said, grinning. "Just confused."

The elevator dropped slowly. Peter, his eyes hardened to small points, stared as the numbered floors floated past.

"One," the operator announced.

Peter whipped around as the doors opened and grabbed hold of Heim's arm. "We're getting off here!"

Heim pulled away. The cassock sleeve ripped.

"Hey, we don't want no trouble!" the operator said.

"George, do something!" the wife commanded.

The man in the Moose River hat reached for Peter. "Mister," he said, "you oughta find your manners!"

Heim, seeing his chance, darted from the elevator while Peter fought the iron grip of the cowboy.

"Now, just steady down, son," he said.

In the struggle, Peter knocked off the man's Moose River with his shoulder. Dismayed, the man released him to pick up his hat.

The registration clerk who was outside watching stretcher-bearers load the waiting ambulance swung around at the new disturbance. A cassocked priest had burst through the front doors of the hotel. Hot behind was the disreputable young man.

"He's still here!" he cried. "Officer, it's him! The one who was asking for his Eminence!"

The cop who was taking a deposition from a woman onlooker glanced up. He folded his book and joined the pursuit, unlatching his leather holster as he ran.

An acid-rock band with accompanying Moog Synthesizer was playing in the open Union Square. Ringed by the cement and glass of high-rise towers on all four sides, the band's piercing electrical sounds were like fingernails scratching on glass.

Heim crossed Powell to the Square and fled over the open lawn.

Behind him, Peter pounded, sweat stinging his eyes, his stomach churning from the blow of his betrayal. Across the open cement fascia he ran, his long legs pumping, desperate to catch Heim, to force him to tell everything.

The cop, gun drawn, crossed Powell but ran into a group of Japanese tourists unloading from a bus. He cut around the outside of the bus into the street. A car slammed on its brakes as it narrowly avoided him. He circled the taillights and headed up the sidewalk again. But he had lost sight of his suspect.

In the trees, grouped at the upper end of the Square, Heim spun around, out of breath, and faced Peter. "Okay, okay," he said, "Enough!" He had his arms outstretched in a sort of supplication. "No reason to run anyway. We're both on the same team!"

Heim reached and jerked down the black collar of the cassock. Deep-etched rope burns scarred his flesh. "Long before I became Heim, I was known as Calendar. I took care of the sisters."

"You're dead," Peter muttered. "Hanged a hundred years ago! I saw your grave!"

"You saw the women's graves too. You also thought you found water."

"I *did* find water!"

Heim chuckled at that. "With my help," he taunted.

"But you sure took credit for it. Saviour, Miracle Worker, Water-Finder! Resurrecter of dogs! You might have known the truth if you'd let yourself dream. Would have told you myself, but you'd have thought it was a joke!"

"Told me what!"

"It was you who blasphemed! You who wished all this!"

"It was my father!"

"No, we only used him," Heim cried gleefully. "He capitalized on our plan because of his ambitions!"

"Liar!"

"Am I?" Heim asked. "That woman in the desert recognized the truth."

Peter stepped back, suddenly afraid.

"Who are you?" he asked. "Who are all of you?"

"Us?" Heim chortled. "Damned beings. Reincarnated for a chore. In this case, yours."

"'Evil has no power unless we give it,'" Peter quoted Father Brinkley.

"You gave us the power a hundred, a thousand times," Heim laughed. "Your whole life has been one long, blasphemous wish!"

"That's insane," Peter said, shaken. "I didn't do anything. I'm a good man."

"Course you are," Heim chuckled. "It's always the 'good' men who are the most wicked. Hasn't history taught you that?"

"I am *good!*"

"You're *our* candidate," Heim guffawed. "You said yourself you'd be Pope if Barbolino and Casselli weren't around. I merely granted you another wish."

Peter lunged forward to seize Heim.

"Freeze motha!" a voice commanded.

The cop was standing, legs planted, gun on Peter. "Move, I drop you!"

Peter hesitated, then raised his hands.

"You okay, Father?" the cop asked.

"I think so," Doc Heim said. "But I'm very glad you showed up." He straightened his cassock, adjusting the Roman collar.

Peter bolted for the trees.

The cop raised his gun and sighted. But Doc Heim stepped in his line of fire.

"Father!" the cop screamed, pulling off.

"Sorry," Heim said.

The cop lurched off after Peter.

Doc Heim quickly checked his watch. Then he sprinted back toward the Fairmont and his waiting car.

TWENTY-FOUR

He fled through the trees, the eerie spiraling wails of the electric band hounding him. Branches whipped at his clothes and face. Stumbling finally from the growth, he spotted a round reflecting pool. He ran to it and quickly crouched behind its wall.

The cop appeared, gun drawn, and scanned the open area. The small gathering of people near the band caught his eye. He pushed on.

Peter stood and braced himself wearily on the pool's wall. Leaning forward, he dipped his hands in its coolness. But before his fingers could disturb the mirrored image in the water, he froze. It was not his face staring up at him in the glassy surface. The eyes were small, the nose a snout, lips thick, the forehead folds of flesh. It was the beast from his mirror!

A tingle began in his extremities. Never taking his eyes from the image in the water, he screamed. And his scream joined the oscillating whine of the band's music.

The cop, searching among the listeners, saw a figure rush across the open lawn and dart toward Stockton. He wheeled after him.

Peter jaywalked through traffic. When he was on the sidewalk, he stopped, weaving, uncertain.

"Hold it!" the cop screamed from across Stockton.

Coming to his senses, Peter lurched through the doors of Woolworth's. He pushed past busy shoppers. The cop descended the steps behind him. Taking the DOWN escalator, Peter raced through the Gardening section. The cop followed. Feet flying, Peter rounded Hand Tools, then hopped on the UP escalator. Ignoring the people's reactions around him, he squatted down. The cop, riding the DOWN escalator, passed directly by, eyes seeking, but never seeing Peter as the escalator rose to the top.

On Stockton Street again, Peter forced his way through the strolling lunch crowd. The air held a chill now; a cooler north wind had begun to blow.

"Me," he began to say. "Me! It couldn't have been. No, not possible."

People skirted him at arms' length, giving the frenzied man plenty of room. In the Square across the street, the electric synthesizer was working itself into a new frenzy. Peter rounded the corner of Macy's and scurried toward the safety of a show window.

A blind man, his white stick leaning against his outstretched arm, was staring unseeing at the darkening sky above. He held a chipped enamel cup out to passers-by. His clothes were ragged, oil stained from sleeping in the street. Incongruously, around his neck, he wore an ostentatious, white pearl rosary with an oversized crucifix.

"I am to be the only candidate!" Peter blurted. "How will they get rid of the others?"

The beggar cocked an ear at the unusual monologue and listened. A crew-cut man in a seersucker suit passed and dropped a dime into his cup.

"Obliged," the blind man intoned.

"Five altogether," Peter raced on. "Casselli; Kaszus for the eastern Europeans; Ni Kand, the Asians; Mazande, Africa; and Reatequi, South America!"

The blind man continued to listen.

"All in one place!" Peter shouted to himself. "Taxi!" he cried and leaped across the sidewalk.

A yellow cab slowed. The driver leaned over to the window and surveyed the bedraggled young man.

"Where to?" he asked.

"Airport!" Peter shouted.

"Just a minute," the cabbie said looking him over. "You got the fare?"

Peter dug into his pants pockets. "I did have it. . . ." he said. "Must've been in my cassock!"

The cabbie swung back into traffic. Frustrated, Peter stepped up onto the sidewalk again.

"Sounds to me like he don't like the way you dress," the beggar said.

Peter started up the street, frantically searching for another cab.

"Hey, sinner man?" the beggar asked. "You need to get to the airport?" He reached into his pocket, pulled out some bills and peeled off a single dollar.

"Thanks," Peter said, "but that's not enough."

"That's a buck, ain't it?" He glanced up at the sky, searching for the heat of the sun. "And it's time. You see a bus?"

Up the street, a city bus was loading at the corner. The black and white sign above the driver's seat said: AIRPORT.

"I'll never make it in a bus!" Peter cried.

The blind man waved the bill in the air. "Faster'n a taxi this time a' day. Got its own freeway lane!"

Peter grabbed the dollar and fled toward the bus. "Bless you!" he cried.

"You too, brother," the man smiled. "Us sinners gotta stick together!"

After booking themselves on Pan Am flight 501, the cardinals and their assistants had assembled in the VIP lounge for a leisurely drink before boarding their plane.

All of the cardinals who headed the splinter factions—Kaszus, Ni Kand, Mazande and Reatequi—were there. They looked out at the Vatican's private white Lear Jet waiting to carry the Italian cardinals: the luxurious jet was a symbol of the power they did not possess—and never would, unless they united behind a single candidate.

In silence, they sat in the vinyl-stuffed chairs and sipped their drinks. Cardinal Livingston Stamp was at the bank of pay telephones, still trying to reach his son.

"The Holy Father *would* have to die during our conference," Kaszus said in his thick, Germanic accent.

"A proper revenge," Reatequi nodded, brown face wreathed in disappointment.

"His *influence* is not dead yet, brothers," the practical Ni Kand added. The Chinese was known for his no-nonsense attitudes.

The speakers in the VIP room cracked gently. "Ladies and Gentlemen," a syrupy female voice announced. "Pan Am flight 501, non-stop to Rome, and continuing onward to Athens, Cairo and Teheran is now ready for boarding at Gate 4."

The Cardinals rose. Cardinal Stamp was hurrying toward them from the telephones.

"Any news from your son?" Kaszus asked hopefully.

"No one knows where he is," Stamp said.

"He's beyond convincing anyway," Ni Kand concluded.

"Maybe this time," Mazande said. "But he is young and made of flesh like us!" And picking up his two bags, he led the way down the red-carpeted hallway and out the double doors toward the waiting plane.

As the bus passed Candlestick Park, Peter spotted in the distance a jumbo jet sluggishly rising into the sky. The wings wavered momentarily until they found rising currents, then the plane shot upward faster.

Anxiously, he glanced at his watch.

Standing in a north wing lobby reserved for private planes, Cardinal Casselli crumpled an empty package of cigarettes and reached for another. He had tried repeatedly to contact Barbolino. The hotel switchboard was constantly busy, and when he finally got through, there was no one in his room to answer.

The white Lear stood waiting out on the macadam. For the very last time, he told himself, he would call. And if he could not get through, Barbolino would have to take a commercial flight to Rome.

He lit another cigarette and hurried to a phone. He dialed the now familiar number of the Sir Francis Drake hotel. It rang twice. A rattled high voice came on the line. After a moment's pause, the woman connected him.

"Cardinal Casselli's room," a voice answered.

"This *is* his Eminence, Cardinal Casselli. Let me talk with Barbolino!"

"Eminence . . ." a voice stuttered. "This is Father Kalki . . . I work at the chancery."

"I'm waiting at the airport," Casselli spat in the receiver, "I *have* been waiting for a long time. Where is Barbolino?"

"Eminence," Kalki said, his voice straining, "Cardinal Barbolino is dead!"

"How can that be?"

"He fell out a window, we think," Kalki said.

To Casselli, who had recently lost his close friend Aldo Moro to terrorists, it was obviously a plot. He had heard about the new campaign of shooting random targets with pistols. Now had they picked Barbolino?

"What is happening?" He gasped into the mouthpiece. "Did the terrorists get him? Are they here too?"

"Eminence, I would suggest you go back to Rome. We are handling everything now." Kalki spoke the "We" with a great deal of pride.

"That is precisely what I will do," Casselli said, chilled. And he flung the phone back on its hook and hurried out of the private waiting room. Several assistants followed.

The bus signaled across four freeway lanes and cut through the heavy traffic. Turning off onto the airport exit, it slowed to a creep. A solid line of cars stood unmoving, all attempting to enter the San Francisco Airport.

Peter canvassed the situation. Why was the traffic so heavy? Forcing himself to remember, he realized today was Friday. The weekend was beginning. No wonder! He would never make it if he stayed on the bus.

He pushed forward, stepping over several suitcases.

"Open the doors," he said to the driver.

"Can't do that," the driver said, "we're still on the freeway!"

"I have to get off!"

"Now, look," the driver said. "Just take it easy. You miss your plane, there'll be another. . . ."

Eyes crazed, Peter slammed down the pressure lock. The doors sprang open.

Before the driver could call out, he was sprinting between the cars. He leaped down the steep incline of ice plant and squeezed through a row of oleander.

Livingston Stamp and the four cardinal candidates trooped down the long corridor, toward the elevator that would take them up to the Pan Am boarding ramp. Several noted with delight the children waving to them as they passed. Cardinal Stamp thought the brunette, black and red-haired girls looked vaguely familiar.

When the prelates and their entourages had passed,

the girls stepped out from the corridor wall and quietly trailed them.

Dashing into the International terminal, Peter forced his way to the TWA desk.

"You'll have to get in line, sir," a young woman said, motioning to the people waiting to buy tickets.

"I'm looking for a plane," he gasped. "One that goes to Rome."

"We have one this afternoon," she snapped, hurrying back to the ticket line with a fresh batch of tickets. "There are several other foreign flights tonight."

"Anything NOW?"

"Pan Am's got a flight at one," she said. "But that's all!"

Peter picked his way through the gathering lines. At the Pan Am counter, he glanced at the television monitor. Beside 501, the word "boarding" was flashing. Gate 4.

Doc Jimmy Heim parked his Dodge in the short-term parking lot. Gathering the skirts of his cassock about him, he walked swiftly toward the special boarding area for private planes. When he was near the cyclone fence, he saw Cardinal Casselli with his retinue, heading toward the waiting Lear jet.

"*Momento!*" Heim shouted. "Hey *momento!*"

Puzzled, several of the priests stopped.

"*Eminencia!*" one of them called to the Cardinal.

Annoyed, he turned, then stopped.

Doc Heim climbed the fence and made for the Cardinal. Impatiently, Casselli waited as he approached. He was thinking it was, perhaps, some last-minute message for him.

* * *

Peter sped through the security station, flinging himself past its electronic detector. Though its beeper did not sound, the woman guard yelled, "Hold it a minute!"

"I'm in a hurry!" Peter shouted.

"Come here," she said. She picked up a hand-searcher which had a horseshoelike chrome ring on its top and turned it on. She ran it around his body, then up under his arms, and the inside of his legs.

"You can go," she said with obvious disappointment. "Next time don't run."

Peter took off again.

"Slow down!" the guard yelled.

Peter raced to the boarding area. He quickly located gate 4 and cut toward it. The international boarding zone was partitioned off by a wall of glass.

Peter spun toward the counter. A muscular young man stood behind it counting boarding passes.

"Flight 501?" he gasped.

"Do you have a ticket?"

"No! I need to see someone!"

"I'm afraid you're too late for that."

"Late?"

"They're all aboard," the young man said, trying not to react to Peter's appearance. "See?"

On the apron, the boarding ramp had retracted. A tractor was pushing out the huge jet.

Peter pressed splayed fingers against the restraining glass.

As he watched, the big jet swiveled its nose wheel and rolled free across the asphalt, huge body bouncing on its shock absorbers. Turning right, it coasted toward a line-up of other planes waiting for take off.

Acting carefully so as not to attract any further attention, Peter watched as the man behind 4 continued tabulating the passes. He put one hand on top of the plastic separation and valuted over it. He hit the EMERGENCY door at full tilt and was through it when the alarm system sounded.

The man from counter 4 cried, "Stop him!" and ran hurriedly to unlock the door that led through the plastic separator.

Ahead, Peter thumped down the corrugated boarding ramp. At its end, he threw himself out, hit the pavement twelve feet below and was up and running again toward the Pan Am DC-10. It had moved up to third in line.

As he ran, he spotted Cardinal Casselli and three assistants waiting on a nearby tarmac. A fourth priest was approaching the group.

Peter slowed to a jog. He was less than two hundred feet from the DC-10. Who should he warn first? His father and the candidates were on that plane. But Casselli was his ally.

The fourth priest was at the Cardinal's side now. He appeared to be coaxing him away, or trying to. The Cardinal was shaking his head, resisting. As Peter watched, the priest grew more determined. He grabbed hold of Casselli's arm and bent it behind him.

"Heim," Peter muttered, recognizing him. "Heim!" he yelled.

The doctor spun. He saw Peter. In desperation, he grabbed the Cardinal by the throat and squeezed mightily. Casselli's face bulged in terror. He slipped to the pavement. Several of the priests were trying to pull Heim off. But they could not pry away his hands. The doctor seemed to possess superhuman strength.

Peter, running at full tilt, slammed into Heim. The

force of the blow freed Casselli. When Heim got to his feet, Peter hit him. The doctor's jaw snapped back and he fell to the pavement. Scrambling on all fours, he retreated toward the grassy median beyond the boarding area. Peter rushed after him. In a diving tackle he brought him down, falling on top of him. Heim lay motionless.

"Get up!" Peter commanded.

He rolled him over—and nearly lost his stomach. Jimmy Heim had landed on an upright airstrip light. The bulb atop the light had shattered. The remaining shaft had pierced the bottom of Heim's mouth and emerged through an eye.

"Oh, merciful Jesus," Peter said, shuddering.

"Can't . . . stop us," Heim rasped. "Pact . . . made." The flesh around the bones of his face seemed to droop inward. "No escape . . . like me . . . lost your soul . . . ."

Mesmerized, Peter watched as Heim managed a weak smile. His lips split open and oozed yellow liquid; his eyebrows and lashes fell out; the skin on his face wilted into dust. Peter backed away in horror.

The priests were helping the Cardinal to his feet. Peter hurried back toward their group. But as he neared, a voice called from behind, "You!"

He spun to see two ticket-counter men speeding toward him.

The Cardinal, still shaken and hearing the new commotion, looked up. *"Terroristas!"* he cried in panic and ran.

Several of the Italian priests turned and, alarmed, scattered also.

The ticket men lunged for Peter and caught his arms. From behind came the sound of a plane. They turned and to their amazement saw a red and white single engine Cessna rolling toward them. There was no one behind the wheel.

"What the hell?" the muscular ticket man asked.

The airplane, its propeller revving, swung across the boarding area, and aimed itself at the fleeing Cardinal. The tail of the Cessna rose with increased speed and the nose lowered closer to the ground.

Peter broke loose from the two attendants and cut across the taxiway. In long-legged strides, he gained on the Cessna. When he was beside it, he belly-flopped onto the left wing.

Ahead, the Cardinal zigzagged in terror, trying to avoid the slicing blade. With surprising speed, he broke completely away from the macadam, toward a grass-lined drainage ditch.

With his right elbow, Peter smashed open the small ventilation window. He thrust his hand inside. Shards of plastic along the edges of the window cut into his palm, tearing the old scar. He reached to the ignition and turned the key. The Cessna choked, died and rolled to a stop.

Peter glanced up. The Cardinal was cutting across the grass. The Pan Am DC-10 began to gather speed. In blind panic, Cardinal Casselli fled onto the number one runway.

"Noooooooooo!" Peter screamed to him.

The monstrous jet traveling at take-off speed, loomed like a giant buzzard as its wings covered the Cardinal. The undercarriage struck him squarely. As the plane lifted off the ground, Peter saw that Casselli's body had wedged between four mammoth tires.

The DC-10 turned hard to the right and circled for an emergency landing. Casselli's red-robed remains flopped grotesquely in the wind.

Two ambulances and fire trucks sped along the apron, then screeched to a halt on the taxiway.

The wide-bodied jet swooped down to less than a hundred feet from the ground, and gyrated into a steep right angle to gain landing attitude. The pilot gunned the jets repeatedly. The right wing wavered awkwardly and dipped low, nearly touching the ground. The desperate throttling whistle of the jets cut through the air.

For the first time, Peter noticed the three girls. They were standing on the far side of the runway. The black girl was slightly in front of the other two. She had her fist clenched at the approaching DC-10.

Scrambling off the Cessna wing, Peter burst across the taxiway.

"Stop!" he began to screaming at the girls. "StoooooOOOOOOPPPPP!"

The big plane, wobbling in the air currents, bounced down on the runway. Casselli's body jarred loose from the wheels. The pilot reversed the engines to brake.

Running, Peter saw the black girl now flip her wrist. The cadaver obeyed and leaped from the ground and was sucked up into the left outboard jet.

The motor tore loose from its mount and flew off. The aircraft's right set of tires skidded sideways off the runway. Two on the outside blew and the plane tilted. The right wing smacked the meridian grass and the fuel tank within ruptured.

Wrenching steel grated on the concrete, sending up showers of sparks. The front nose carriage collapsed. The cockpit scraped along the runway, gouging a shallow trench.

Then, brilliantly and unexpectedly, the pilot threw on the right brakes. The plane left the runway completely and began its slide on the softer surface of the outer grass.

The girls, totally surprised, began to run.

The first class section on the left side of the fuselage split open under the pressure of the dragging right wing The plane shuddered as though dying, and came to a stop. Immediately, passengers began pushing their way through the fuselage. In the middle and rear sections of the DC-10, emergency doors opened and plastic chutes inflated. They were quickly filled with escaping men and women.

The fire trucks and ambulances roared toward the stricken jumbo jet.

One of the Cardinals emerged on the left wing and without hesitation jumped down to the grass.

Peter arrived as Kaszus, ankle broken, hobbled up onto the cement runway.

"My father?" Peter yelled at him.

"There wasn't space in first class." Kaszus said. "He's somewhere in the middle of the plane!"

Glancing up, Peter noted dark swirls of smoke spewing from the plane's doors. Passengers were crowding onto the wing, jumping. A pool of burning kerosene was widening, spreading beneath the plane under the right wing. Soon, all escape would be cut off!

Circling the wing, Peter saw that near the inflated slides were emergency ropes, dangling unused. He ran to one, caught ahold and swung out over the flaming kerosene. Then, despite the hurt in his bleeding hand, he pulled himself up the rope and levered onto the jammed wing. Cardinal Ni Kand was sitting, legs dangling, preparing to jump.

Peter shoved his way through hysterical passengers,

grabbed hold of a ragged edge of the fuselage and swung himself inside the plane.

For a moment, he could see nothing in the roiling smoke.

"Father!" Peter shouted, searching desperately. He stepped over the wounded lying helpless on the floor. Plastic windows began popping from the intense fire. Eyes burning from the heat and fumes, he could hardly see. A tall, angular man lay face down on two seats. Peter rolled him over. The dead man was not his father.

Coughing, pushing deeper into the noxious air, Peter turned the corner into the third cabin. An Arab woman in veils ran full tilt into him and knocked him down, then, screaming at the top of her lungs, raced on toward the back cabin

Peter sat up groggily. Passengers were stumbling over him. Through darting legs, he caught a glimpse of a figure, belted in his seat, slumped over unconscious.

He fought to his feet.

"Father!" Peter said. There was a nasty cut on the Cardinal's forehead as though his head had struck the seat in front of him.

Peter swung Livingston Stamp over his shoulder and pushed back toward the first class cabin. An explosion somewhere beneath the plane rocked the floor.

"We're going up!" the plane's navigator cried. "Get out! Get out!"

At the second cabin, Peter stepped over the trampled body of a stewardess just as another blast, larger than the first, erupted. Scorching heat blew through the glassless windows.

Stumbling toward the hole, he plunged through the

heat and smoke until he had his father outside on the wing. Five firemen were shooting foam onto the plane, while passengers leapt off the wing. But the fiery pool had spread completely beneath it. Many were landing in the kerosene.

Pulling his father's limp body from his shoulder, Peter gathered him like a child in front of him, cradling his legs and chest. Then, running straight to the tip of the wing, Peter leaped!

End over end, they rolled on the cement runway.

Stunned, Peter rose. His father lay face down, black coat and pants clothed in flame. Crawling to him on all fours, Peter fell on top of him and beat out the fire on his father's back and legs.

"Get away!" a fireman warned and helped drag the Cardinal.

The spreading jet fuel blistered into a fire storm. The heat made the left wing tank bulge. Then with a thundering blast, the entire plane went up.

Peter knelt, shielding his father. The Cardinal coughed and took shallow breaths.

"What did I do? Forgive me, father!" Peter whispered into his ear. "Forgive me! Forgive me, please!" And lowering his head, he began to sob.

TWENTY-FIVE

The curtains had been drawn and the room was nearly dark. Only a table lamp was lighted near the couch. In the shadows, the forms of three men were visible. The fourth lay on the armless, backless sofa in what appeared to be a deep, consuming sleep.

Dr. Rollo Kinninger, official psychiatrist for the clergy of the diocese of San Francisco, peered carefully through his tortoise-rimmed glasses and observed the patient for the classic signs of having succumbed to hypnosis. Eyelids were still; fingers uncurled; breathing easy and rhythmic; feet pointing outward and relaxed. He turned to the two other men in the room. "Peter's under now," he whispered.

Seated in a chrome wheelchair, Cardinal Stamp, much of his face and the back of his neck in bandages, leaned forward into the light of the lamp. He could not speak; his vocal cords had been seared in the fire. He brought up a white pad and pencil and wrote: "Doctor, why did it take so long to put Peter under hypnosis?"

"He was very disturbed that you got out of the hospital to come here. He felt you shouldn't be out of bed."

"I could not lie in my bed one minute longer," the Cardinal wrote, "knowing the possibility that Peter, my son, might be inhabited."

The doctor read the note and passed it without comment to the third figure who sat nearby. He wore the black headdress of the Eastern Church. Archbishop Moshe Malthustos had been asked by Cardinal Livingston Stamp to come to San Francisco from Turkey.

At first, when Peter explained to his father what he thought he had done, Livingston had been heartbroken. The son he had so desperately wanted to become pope had been claimed by a devil? Unable to even to speak his sorrow, Cardinal Stamp, in those first days in his hospital bed, could only listen and clutch at the hope that something, someone would prove this whole thing false!

Peter couldn't be possessed, he had told himself repeatedly. Would a possessed man have risked his life to save his father? Could a man who was capable of so much good really be under the influence of a demon? It just didn't make sense. And each time he had awakened to see Peter sitting at the foot of his bed, calmly praying or merely sleeping in a chair, he had wondered about the story Peter had told him.

Yet, Cardinal Stamp knew he could not live with any doubt about his son. And so, from the time he was able to sit up and feed himself, he busily examined the possibilities. If Peter were now possessed or on his way to *being* possessed, then his soul must be exorcised, and the demon driven out. If he were not possessed, then Peter's fears were in his mind, a result, perhaps, of his striving too hard for perfection. Scruples, that state was called, seeing sin where it did not exist. The only way to get to the bottom of all this, Stamp had decided, was to perform an exorcism. But who was qualified to play the role of exorcist for his son?

After ransacking his memory of holy men he had known and met, he chose Archbishop Moshe Malthustos. He was scholarly, holy and as he had proven that afternoon in Istanbul, insightful. Livingston sent him a long letter, reminding him of that afternoon when the Archbishop had pointed out the odd use of the word "stone." But Malthustos needed no reminding. The memory of that afternoon had continued to haunt him even in his dreams.

Yesterday, after he had arrived and been briefed by Cardinal Stamp, he had considered the whole matter carefully. "We must look for a sign," Moshe deduced, "something that will signify a devil controls your son."

He had continued, "If and only if there is a sign, I will perform an exorcism."

Stamp had agreed on the strategy.

The psychiatrist reached across the foot table at the end of the couch and snapped on a Panasonic tape recorder.

"Now, Peter," Dr. Kinninger said. "We are ready. Let's find the truth."

"But . . . I have no clear memory of . . . anything."

"It's been suppressed. Your condition is called 'paramnesia.' Sometimes we do things we think so terrible we cannot admit them. Even to ourselves!"

Peter did not reply.

"You *do* want to remember?" Kinninger asked.

"Yes!" Peter said firmly.

"Good, then," the psychiatrist said. "You are sleeping. But now, you will drop into a deeper slumber. As deep and dark as the cave in which you were found. It is *very* dark . . . *very* quiet . . . *deep* dark. How old are you, Peter?"

"I don't know."

"How old are you now, Peter?"

"How old do you want me to be?"

"You don't have to do what I want," the psychiatrist said. "You're free to choose anywhere, anytime."

Peter squirmed on the couch as though that burden were difficult.

"How old, Peter?"

"Sixteen."

"And where are you?"

"In . . . Rome."

"And what are you doing there?"

"I have just decided to become a priest."

"Oh? Why did you do that."

"So I wouldn't have to live with another housekeeper."

"Is that the only reason?"

"No," Peter said.

"Why else did you decide to become a priest?"

"I . . . so I could become Cardinal Stamp's son."

"And is that the real reason you became a priest?"

"Yes."

"You wished to please Cardinal Stamp?"

"Yes."

Livingston Stamp leaned back in his wheelchair so that he was sitting now out of the light. Moshe Malthustos noted his reaction but did not embarrass him by showing it.

"What's happening now, Peter? Where are you?"

"In that cave."

"The one you were found in?"

"Yes. But I don't want to stay here."

"Why? What are you afraid of?"

"My friend Starbright."

"If he's your friend, you shouldn't be afraid."

"I want out of here!" Peter squealed in a high childlike voice.

"Don't you like your friend?"

"I shouldn't!"

"Did you try to please your friend?"

"Only . . . for my father!"

"The man who took you from the cave?"

"The best father in the whole world," Peter chimed in a six-year-old's voice.

"You'd do anything for your father, is that right, Peter?"

"I love him."

"Did you, in your view, commit sins for him?"

Peter frowned. He licked his lips and seemed to retreat into a deeper sleep.

"It has to come out," Doctor Kinninger whispered softly to him. "You can't hold it back anymore. It's okay to reveal everything. There is nothing you can't tell me."

"I hated the way I talked!" Peter suddenly blurted. "I stuttered all the time. I wanted to be perfect for my father. He's so strong and wise. He wouldn't want to have a weak son!" He began to cry in a childlike way.

"It's all right. All right," the psychiatrist said, taking out some Kleenex from a box and putting it into Peter's hand. "Blow your nose."

Peter lay back, blew his nose, then wadded the soiled tissue tight in his fist.

"How old are you, Peter?"

"Thirty-three," he said after a pause. "I'm in Bethany. I like it here."

"It's very peaceful, isn't it?"

"Yes, peaceful. But we need water. The farmers need me to get water for them. I asked God for it again and again."

"And?"

"He never helped me!"

"Who did help you, Peter?"

The young priest bit his lips. "Nobody," he murmured.

"Are you angry with God for not hearing your prayers?" Kinninger probed.

"Yes!"

"Do you resent Him?"

"He knew we needed water! I prayed and prayed! He should have answered my prayers! I hate Him!"

A sound as if someone had been struck in the stomach came from the direction of Cardinal Stamp.

"And what did you do when you found that God would not answer your prayers?"

"The only thing I could do!" Peter exclaimed, his eyes clamped tight.

"What was that?"

"I don't want to talk about it!"

"You must!"

"Please, I don't want to see it again!"

"You want to get well, don't you? You must tell me!"

"No, I . . . what else could I do?" Peter stammered suddenly, tears flooding his eyes. "I couldn't let the farmers down! What would they think of their priest? And if my father heard. . . ." He began to sob, holding the Kleenex hard against his mouth as if trying to stifle his sounds.

"Let it out, Peter," the psychiatrist said gently. "Was it Starbright you turned to? Was it him?"

"Yes!" Peter screamed, chest convulsing.

"Was that the first time you asked him for anything?"

"No! I .. I made lots of wishes!"

"And did you make specific wishes about those three girls and that girl, Susan, who died, everything that began on your thirty-third birthday?"

"No! But I should have . . . recognized what was happening. It was Starbright's plan for me!"

"So, Starbright took care of everything? All the details?"

"Yes."

"That's good, very good work, Peter." The psychiatrist handed him more tissues, pressing them into his hand. Peter smeared at his closed eyes.

"Now," Kinninger said. "Let's keep going. How old are you, now?"

"The same age."

"*Where* are you?"

Outside St. Mary's Cathedral. On the steps. It's nighttime. A storm is coming."

"What are you doing there?"

"I'm going to please my father," Peter said. "Please him once and for all. Make him proud of me! He wants me to be pope!"

"And how are you going to do that?"

"By giving myself to Starbright."

"What about God?"

"He doesn't count."

The exorcist, Moshe Malthustos, dropped his head and asked God's forgiveness.

"I'm holding Starbright in my hand!" Peter raised his hand, squeezing an unseen object.

"Ooooooooo!" he squealed. "It hurts! It hurts! I've cut my hand! Blood is dripping everywhere. *My* blood! Ahhhhhhhhhh!" His breathing was rapid and shallow. "I'm going to die! The deal is done! I will be reborn . . . REBORN . . . I will be Starbright's!" He went limp with no sign of life.

The psychiatrist immediately felt his wrist for a pulse.

A muffled groan of apprehension came from Cardinal Stamp. Moshe, seeing the intense worry on his face, said, "He's all right, isn't he, Doctor?"

"Sleeping," Kinninger confirmed. "He's exhausted. Worked very hard. Let's let him rest for a few minutes."

"This Starbright," Kinninger said, huddling with the two churchmen, "is someone Peter believes possesses magic. Someone powerful enough to fulfill his fantasies and make him perfect. Is this the devil figure?"

"We think so," Moshe allowed.

"But is he real, Archbishop? I doubt it!"

"He's real to Peter," Moshe said. "For the rest, I withhold judgment at this time."

Cardinal Stamp tapped Moshe on the arm. He had been scribbling on his pad and now handed him the note, "When I found Peter in the cave, I told you the name Starbright was mentioned. I remember that the demon also had another name. The Chinese called him Baz."

"Baz?" Moshe read off the pad. "It might be. In several eastern tongues, Baz would translate as 'light-carrier.' The name Starbright is close."

The exorcist turned to Rollo Kinninger. "I'm puzzled about one thing, Doctor," he said. "How is it possible for Peter to have made this pact, yet have gone about his business of praying, doing good, striving for Christ-like perfection? It doesn't make sense."

"Well," the psychiatrist said, "when Peter buried those wishes deep in his psyche, he at the same time kept alive a superhuman, compulsive drive for perfection. He thought it only normal. But in fact it was unrealistic. More than any Christian is capable of, or for that matter, any saint."

"It was the feeling of being inferior then that drove him? An overcompensation in the form of a superiority complex?"

"More than that again. You might call it a super-superiority complex. Picture his anguish. He could never afford to be normal, never allow himself to be anything but perfect. Is it any wonder he turned to a magical means to make him so?"

"But that still doesn't explain why it happened in the first place?"

"You're very perceptive, Archbishop," Kinninger said. "None of any of this could have happened without a character flaw. A flaw, which if I'm correct, Peter developed as a result of a traumatic event or events in the first part of his life."

Cardinal Stamp motioned him to pause. He wrote a short note, handed it to the psychiatrist.

"Yes," the doctor said, reading it. "Seeing his parents killed might have done it. Or simply being in a place like that cave, cut off from reality. Do you know how long Peter was in that cave, Cardinal Stamp?"

Livingston thought a moment, then shook his head.

"Well, I'll wager it was for quite some time," Kinninger said. "The loss of self occurs easily in places like that. It's even a common brainwashing technique. And on a young mind, it can be obliterating. That cave caused, in my opinion, a serious character flaw. When Peter emerged from there, he could not and would not accept who he was. He had to be someone special to be someone. Even his primary act of leaving the other children at the orphanage and going off by himself indicates that to me."

"But again, Doctor," Moshe observed. "We are coming back to his need for superiority."

"Not quite, Excellency," Kinninger said. "Peter's capability of doing everything he has done comes from a flaw best defined in Theology, your field. Someone once said that 'Pride precedeth the fall.' Peter's need for being someone special caused an inborn pride. It was that flaw that made him seize the opportunity and seek to be the son of a cardinal in the first place. And that same flaw made him later totally vulnerable to all that happened."

"But the meeting between Cardinal Stamp and Peter was only fortuitous."

"Yes," Kinninger said. "Perhaps if the Cardinal had never come along, Peter might conceivably still be in that cave. But then, of course, there is another way to look at it."

And that is?"

"Well, Archbishop, Cardinal Stamp, I am not a religious man by nature. But some might say the meeting was predestined. I mean, statistically, it was highly improbable. Psychologically, for both of you, it was a perfect match."

Cardinal Stamp quickly scribbled with his pencil, "This is what I have always felt, that it was predestined!"

He handed the note to Doctor Kinninger who read it and passed it to Moshe Malthustos.

"Perhaps, perhaps," the Archbishop said. "But why?"

"Peter spoke of a plan," Cardinal Stamp wrote. "Maybe his becoming pope was the design of this demon."

Malthustos nodded. "What you say may be true. But could a minor demon named Baz, one I have never heard of, put such a momentous plan into effect?"

For a moment, the three men sat in silence, listening to Peter breathe, pondering the proceedings. Then Cardinal Stamp wrote on his pad, "Because of my ambition, Peter made his pact. I created a vicious circle. To be my son, he thought he had to be perfect to please me. And to be perfect, he had to sin."

Moshe nodded to Livingston, agreeing with his analysis.

"It is my sin as well," the note finished. "I confess my guilt and I shall be punished for it. But what about Peter? Is he now free of his pact?"

"We shall see," the Archbishop whispered. "The time for exorcism nears." Pulling at his long, gray beard, Moshe turned to Doctor Kinninger. "Proceed, please."

The Doctor checked Peter's pulse, then bent close to the sleeping man. "Peter," he asked, "can you hear me?"

Bishop Peter Stamp stirred fitfully on the couch. He seemed annoyed by hearing his name spoken.

"Peter?"

"What? What do you want?"

"I'm going to count down from ten. And each time you hear my voice, you will come one step up, one step further out of the darkness. And when I say 'One' you will open your eyes and feel fine."

Moshe Malthustos now scrutinized Peter with special interest. Peter had been given a direct command. If a demon were present he would make some fuss before bowing to authority.

"Ten . . . nine . . . eight . . ." Rollo counted quietly.

Peter raised his right hand which was bandaged and laid it over his chest. Moshe caught the movement.

"Six . . . five . . . four . . ."

Peter's face furrowed, crinkling as though he were in pain.

"It's all right," Rollo Kinninger said. "You've kept everything in your unconscious. And that's where you've been right now. But when you awaken, you will remember all that you've done and you will accept responsibility for it."

"I've been bad!" Peter shouted suddenly. "I don't want to wake up!"

"You must!"

"I've done terrible things. I didn't behave like a good priest. I can never be forgiven!"

"You still want to be perfect," the Doctor said. "You forced yourself to be. But no man is perfect, Peter. When you awake, you will face that!"

Again, he went on counting. "Three . . . two . . . one!"

Peter cried out. He sat upright. Then, reluctantly, he opened his eyes. For a moment, he looked dazed. He took a deep, shuddering breath.

The exorcist, unseen, nodded his head. Peter had obeyed.

"Do you remember everything?" the Doctor asked.

"Everything."

"And how do you feel?"

"Ashamed. Very ashamed."

"And not angry?"

"No."

A small, even smile creased the lips of Archbishop Malthustos. Leaning toward Cardinal Stamp, he whispered, "You know possession means a lacking of things human. But it's very human to feel shame and guilt. And the fact Peter did not show anger means he is not acting from pride. It appears well!"

But Cardinal Stamp did not react to those words. He only continued to study Peter's face.

"So," the Doctor said, rising, "you're at least in touch again." He placed his notebook on his desk. Crossing to the window, he pulled open the drapes. A bright, autumnal light washed over the room.

"Why didn't I remember before?" Peter asked. "I'm so weak!"

The doctor smiled. "Ego and superego are strange bedfellows. The ego does; the superego passes judgment. Sometimes when they are in great conflict, new capacities are developed to reconcile them. You put the burden on Starbright, an imaginary playmate. It was he, not you, who wanted all that was not pure and holy."

"But, I made a pact. A pact with a devil!"

"Have you ever read any stories about devils, Peter?" the Doctor asked, after thinking a moment.

"In the Bible. And . . . I remember seeing the opera 'Faust' as a boy."

"Well, it seems that that story influenced you deeply. And no wonder. You were at an impressionable age. And having seen it, you wrote your own story in effect and then lived it. At the same time, you felt you were doing something bad. So you denied your script."

"You make it sound so simple, Doctor. But you can't just explain everything away. A devil gave me the power to find water! I saw three girls, his progeny, cause a huge jet plane to crash. What do you say about those things?"

"Well, first you don't know for a fact that you didn't find water. A person often punishes himself, denying his talents, if he believes he has done something wrong. The airport accident? Weird things happen all the time. Recently in a seaside resort in Spain, a truck loaded with propane went out of control and killed over two hundred vacationers. A tragedy caused by evil forces? I guess it would depend on your point of view. But," Kinninger concluded, "there are pieces to the puzzle which don't fit. I did some checking. No one in Bethany has seen the Calendar sisters since you left to find water."

"That has to prove something!"

"It proves there are questions to be answered. In this case, it's a deadend. I thought they may have perished in the crash so I contacted the airport authorities. They have recovered sixty-seven bodies from the fire. All have been identified as passengers. Not one is a child's."

Peter frowned at the news.

"Listen, whatever happened, happened. That's not the important part. You could come in here and tell me you just destroyed the entire population of New York. It wouldn't concern me. All that concerns me is that you're my patient. My only task is to assist you in sorting out these things, put them in some sort of healthy perspective and help you get well."

"And am I well, Doctor?"

"You've just skimmed the surface. In the days, months, years ahead, you'll continue to dream, continue to put your unconscious in touch with your conscious. It will be a revealing and healing process. But what I see today is that you've made the initial breakthrough and are willing to face up to and unearth what you buried."

Peter nodded, understanding. But he did not seem satisfied.

"Peter," Moshe Malthustos spoke now, "Doctor Kinninger and I believe in different things. He does not admit to the possibility of a devil here. I do. Do you fear you are possessed? That you are still under the influence of a demon?"

"Yes!" Peter said reacting fiercely. "That's it exactly!"

Moshe cleared his throat. "People possessed by a devil or under his will generally cannot conceal it. There would be some sign. Something God would not permit a devil to hide. Something we would openly see. From my previous exorcisms, I know there is a method which has never failed to detect a demon. Its purpose is to anger him."

"Anything," Peter said eagerly. "Tell me what to do!"

"Say the name . . . Jesus."

"Jesus!"

"Jesus Christ! Say it with feeling!

"Jesus . . . Christ!"

"Son of God, Saviour of the World!"

"Saviour of the World, Saviour of mankind," Peter said, his lips trembling.

"I love you, Jesus Christ!" Moshe started.

"I love you, Jesus Christ. Jesus . . . Jesus . . ."

"Say it again and again!" Moshe commanded. "Think about His name. Say it over and over and mean it! Tell Him you love Him!"

"Jesus God . . . Jesus . . ." Peter closed his eyes. "Jesus, I love you! Forgive me, forgive me! Jesus, Jesus, Jesus! JESUS CHRIST! My God, my all . . . I love youIloveyouIloveyouIloveyouIloveyou. . . ." He squeezed his eyes tight, tears oozed out. "Iloveyou-ILOVEYOUILOVEYOU. . . ." Bowing his head, he continued to mumble the prayers beneath his breath.

Moshe, observing Peter, leaned near Cardinal Stamp. "Nothing," he whispered.

"ILOVEYOUILOVEYOUILOVEYOU . . . JESUSJESUSJESUS-JESUS . . ." Peter mumbled, the words seeming to penetrate to his soul.

"The more convinced Peter is that he's possessed," Moshe whispered to Stamp, "the less likely the possession."

"But," the Cardinal scribbled, "is this method always effective? Shouldn't we proceed to exorcism to be sure?"

"It has never failed before," the exorcist affirmed, "but I will probe a final possibility."

The black-garbed Archbishop rose from his chair. He laid his hand on Peter's shoulder and the young Bishop stopped praying. But he kept his eyes closed, his head bowed, as though feeling for the impact of the words.

"Doctor," Moshe asked, "have you examined Peter?"

"Thoroughly," Kinninger said. "A complete physical."

Peter raised his tear-stained face and blinked inquisitively. For a moment, the exorcist studied Peter who was sitting dressed in his cassock and collar. Then the Archbishop's eyes dropped to the white bandage covering Peter's hand. He reached down and picked it up, cradling it gently. "Have you seen inside this, Doctor?"

"Why . . . no," Kinninger admitted, sheepishly. "I . . . saw no need to."

"May I?" the exorcist asked.

"Certainly," the Doctor said. He crossed to a white, glass-and-enamel cabinet and took out a number seven surgical scissors. Then, he returned quickly to the side of the Archbishop who was holding Peter's hand, observing his eyes, watching, it seemed, for any sort of reaction. But Peter showed none. Except annoyance that no one seemed to believe what he had so painfully and detailedly related.

While Cardinal Stamp watched with great interest, Moshe deftly slipped the flat-shoed bottom of the scissors beneath the adhesive tape and snipped. Down the middle of Peter's palm, he sliced, carefully peeling back the gauze and bandages as he worked. At Peter's wrist, he took one more snip at the adhesive and handed the scissors back to Doctor Kinninger. Then using his thumbs, he opened the bandage.

The Cardinal leaned forward.

There, scattered over the center of Peter's swollen hand were small gashes, closed by one hundred thirty-seven stitches.

"You cut yourself badly at the airport?" Moshe queried.

"Yes, on a window."

"Where is the scar you received that night of the wish?"

Peter glanced down at his hand. "It was there. I swear it!"

"Well, it's not there now," the exorcist said.

"You don't believe me!" Peter shouted. "None of

you do!" He stood up suddenly and agitatedly ran his hand through his blond hair. And he suddenly froze. "My face!" he said.

"What about your face, Peter?" Doctor Kinninger asked.

"I began to look like that demon in the cave. I'm ugly! Look at my eyes. My nose. Look at me."

Peter saw that everyone except his father was now grinning.

Rollo Kinninger reached over to his small table. He picked up and held out a mirror.

"Look at yourself," he said.

Slowly, Peter took the round, hand-mirror and raised it. To his surprise, his face, despite his ordeal, was again firm-skinned, his eyes soft, his expression boyish, resolved.

"You've been shriven," Moshe said.

"I've seen it happen too," Kinninger enforced. "Patients get in touch, change dramatically."

The Cardinal sat frowning. He scribbled to Moshe, "I am not convinced. If Peter thinks he made a pact, then the devil must also!"

"Perhaps," the Archbishop replied, huddling with the Cardinal. "But I sense no evil here."

"Is it hidden?" Livingston wrote.

"I tend to agree with the Doctor," Malthustos said softly. "It seems it was a prideful delusion. Peter has forgiven himself. God has too."

"But your suspicions...."

"The signals, the oddities, the small perversions I perceived were truly present. Your adopted son was in danger of losing his immortal soul. But recognize the new signs, Livingston. Look at him!"

Stamp raised and saw Peter studying his refreshened face in the mirror.

John Zodrow

The Archbishop whispered, "Livingston, you have my opinion. But you are a Prince of the Church. You have the right to order an exorcism. Tell me and I will do it."

There was a knock on the door and a secretary entered.

"I know you didn't want to be disturbed," she said, "but there's an urgent telegram for his Eminence, Cardinal Stamp."

Doctor Kinninger accepted the missive and handed it to the Cardinal. With puffy, still tender hands, he opened, scanned it, then handed it to Malthustos.

The eastern prelate read out loud:

> Lord Cardinal Karol Wojtyla, a Pole, elected Pope John Paul II. First non-Italian in four hundred fifty years. Step in right direction. Get well quickly.
>
> your brother,
> Mazande

Cardinal Stamp thoughtfully accepted back the telegram.

"It's finished," Moshe Malthustos said to Peter. "You are no longer a candidate!"

"Yes," Peter said, lowering the mirror. "It's over. Really over." He smiled faintly. "They failed. Everybody failed."

Cardinal Stamp sat brooding, preoccupied with his thoughts, taking no part in their celebratory mood.

"I would recommend more therapy," Doctor Kinninger was suggesting.

"I'll have the best," Peter said. "I'm going away to pray."

"Do you want that bandaged again?" the doctor asked, pointing to Peter's hand.

"No. Fresh air will do it," he said, flexing it.

He bent to his father. "Forgive me," he whispered. "I had convinced myself it was you who made the pact. I promise to make all this up to you." The Cardinal, in answer, squeezed Peter's hand. But his face yet held the worry.

Peter turned briefly to Archbishop Malthustos. "Good-bye, brother in Christ. God bless."

The old man nodded. Then he rose and leaned close to Livingston Stamp's ear and confided, "I shall continue to pray for your son."

The Doctor held the door open and Peter wheeled Cardinal Livingston Stamp out.

"Most progress I ever made in one session," Rollo said, opening a side door in his library. He pulled out a collapsible bar. "Not often that things are so clean."

"Yes, clean," the exorcist agreed, packing away a vial of holy water and crucifix he had not used. Then he swiveled on impulse and faced the closed door. "Very clean," he mumbled, sensing something he had felt before. The familiar emptiness of never serving the Lord to his fullest capacity. And with it a new feeling. The chance of a lifetime missed. A sense of having fumbled something important.

"Excellency?"

The Archbishop turned and saw the proffered bottle of cognac.

"What? Oh. Tea, perhaps," he said.

"Of course," the doctor apologized, ringing for his secretary. "Cream?"

"Lemon," Moshe said, the vague feeling nagging. "I'll have it bitter."

PART FOUR

. . . UPON THIS STONE . . .

TWENTY-SIX

On the easternmost of the three-pronged peninsula of Chalcidice was an independent republic composed solely of twenty monasteries. The monks, discalced and cloistered, prided themselves on the total silence that reigned continuously in their land. Only at prayer time were voices heard.

High in the sun-bleached, bouldered mountains, there stood the monastery of Daphni. Built in 1130 at the height of the Crusades, it was run by an order of similarly shoeless Cistercians. The blue Aegean surrounded it, refracting the brilliant light of the sun up to its ancient white walls.

From his cell window, Peter watched the sunlight play on the wind-ripples in the sea. His beard was full and untrimmed and his skin was tanned to the color of ripe bananas. His deep-set eyes were clear. And though he was not smiling now, his face looked always ready to laugh.

Over the years, he had found the ascetic discipline he had always craved for his soul. Long hours of uninterrupted meditation; nights spent in blissful, undisturbed sleep; hours of long labor in the orchards and gardens. While his body had grown hard and

muscular, his soul had softened and mellowed until
every bad memory, every unanswered piece of the
puzzle simply did not matter. What mattered only in
this life was the Master and trying to emulate him.

Catching himself daydreaming now, he forced his
eyes back to his breviary.

But soon he raised them again and stared out at the
sea. It had been this way for a long time now. A
growing listlessness, as though waiting expectantly for
something about to finish. What, he did not know
precisely. But he sensed it had something to do with
the deaths he had seen in the future. Every once in a
while, that psychic gift had returned and . . . .

He shuddered involuntarily and turned his thoughts
to pleasant things, things he had missed most. They
flowed in like the spreading Aegean sea below.
Bethany. His little town. Had the farmers done well
with their new water? How was big-boned Lerda and
little, fiery-tempered Francisco? Ramirez? Mrs. Riley?
What was the new pastor like?

Sometimes he thought of the Calendar Sisters, Doc
Heim, Father Brinkley and Cardinal Neil Wright. But
not often. Not very often at all.

In fact, the healing dreams that Dr. Rollo Kinninger had promised would keep coming, the continuing revelations of precisely what he had done, had
not continued at all. Though he suspected that he
dreamt frequently during the night, try as he might
he could not remember most of his dreams upon
awakening.

There was, however, one recurring and memorable
dream. Somtimes it came in fragments or merely in
snapshots, frozen in time. Ice crystals would form in a
sky and the very air would freeze. Then, a bearded
man on a dappled gray horse would appear and he

would ride toward Peter, his arm raised in greeting. As the man approached, just as Peter could almost reach out and touch him, he would feel a gun pressed into his hand. Then, the man's face would go up into the sky. Very big, enormous, covering horizon to horizon. Ice crystals for a halo. And the face in the sky would say softly, "'The Kingdom of God is taken by violence and the violent bear it away.'"

There was a knock on the crude door. Turning, Peter walked across the whitewashed cell, past the iron cot and straw mattress that served as his bed. He pulled the door open by its cast-iron ring and outside stood old Brother Theolonicus, the porter. The brother picked up the black slate writing tablet that hung from his waist and with a piece of chalk wrote, "VISITOR."

"For me?" Peter gestured by touching his chest.

The snaggle-toothed monk nodded and padded off barefoot down the cool cut-stone corridor.

Peter followed him through the ancient labyrinth of passageways, once used to garret Saracens. After descending three sets of forged metal stairways, they came to a room near the entrance. With a flourish, Brother Theolonicus opened a door for Peter.

Inside, there was a tapestried couch with threadbare padding, a rectangular table and two chairs. Seated at the table was a short, totally bald man. He was dressed in plum-colored robes and he grinned when he saw Peter.

Peter turned briefly to Theolonicus and made the monastic gesture to the mouth, seeking permission to speak.

The old monk nodded "yes," then pulled the door shut.

"I am Papal Nuncio Kapadapoulos," the Bishop

said, extending his hand and shaking Peter's. "It is a privilege to meet you."

Without speaking, Peter beckoned to the table and the two men sat across from one another.

"There are many who have talked about you," the Nuncio went on. "Many who have never forgotten."

Peter nodded, accepting the compliment.

Kapadapoulos said, "The Holy Father has died."

"He was assassinated," Peter added simply. "I was saddened at the short reign of Pope Pius XIII."

"I thought no news came to this island," the Nuncio said.

"No one told me. I just knew it happened. Let it go at that."

"You have a gift, then?"

"A . . . gift. Yes."

"Then you saw Pope John Paul II and Leo XIV die also?"

"I did."

"It is very odd the way these popes are going so quickly," Nuncio Kapadapoulos wondered.

"Who was the second and third pope?" Peter asked pointedly.

"You don't know?"

"I am cursed with only seeing them die."

"Pius XIII was Cardinal Mattingly from Australia," the Nuncio explained. "And Leo XIV was German."

"Three non-Italians, then, including Pope John Paul II?"

"Correct."

Peter Stamp nodded as if this was what he had guessed.

The Nuncio stood and reached around to a small, leather case. Swinging it up, he laid it flat on the table.

"You must come to Rome," he said. "I have brought your correct clothing."

He undid the snaps and raised the lid. Inside were the scarlet garments of a cardinal.

"You have made a mistake, my Brother," Peter said. "I'm only a Bishop."

"At the urging of many, His Holiness, Pope Pius XIII elevated you to Cardinal, consecrating you *in absencia* when you did not respond to his Vatican notification."

"Then *I* am a Cardinal?"

"Why do you keep the world from you?" the Nuncio asked. "What is it that you fear?"

Peter said nothing. Instead, he gazed at the crimson garments.

"I have more news," the Nuncio announced. "The current Camerlengo has asked you to serve as his assistant. Conclave begins tomorrow."

Duty fulfilled, the Greek snapped his case shut in punctuation, bowed and crossed the room to the door.

"I hope my news and instructions have not disturbed your life too deeply," he said.

Peter raised his eyes to his. "I know now that I've been expecting you," he said. "And there is no escaping what I must do."

The Nuncio bowed and exited.

Alone, Peter walked to the window. The hot sun met his face and warmed his chest. He watched as the bald prelate took his time working his way down the difficult and steep stone steps. The blue-green sea was beneath him as he descended.

Then as though some invisible force tugged him around, Peter turned slowly back toward the center of the room. The sun flared in over his shoulder, touching the robes. The ruby red garments bathed the simple, whitewashed room in ruddy splendor.

Mesmerized, Peter gazed at the kinglike clothing, pondering, weighing, his face growing flushed.

"Forgive me, Lord Jesus," he said softly. "I can hide here no longer."

TWENTY-SEVEN

ROME

During the two different plane flights and even as he was making his way through the Leonardo Da Vinci airport, Peter's mind was whirling with the kind of thoughts that had lain dormant these past years. Clean-shaven, dressed in Roman collar and a simple black suit, he boarded a bus for the forty-five-minute ride into Rome. As he rode, he continued clicking off possibilities and entertaining strategies. The closer he got to the Eternal City, the more his mind seemed an independent creature reeling with newborn imagery.

He knew his father would be waiting. Yet he could not bring himself to go to his apartment first. There was another place. A place from boyhood, like a private shrine to him.

At the downtown terminal, he slung his single bag onto a number 64 bus and rode to the Vatican. He hopped off at the Via di Angelica and strode under the Colonnade of Saints and out onto the magnificent expanse of St. Peter's Square.

Up the steps of St. Peter's he ran, entering the Basilica, and turned to the left. To his surprise, he saw that there was a ticket-taker behind a desk. Beneath his desk a sign stated: "CUPOLA CON ASCENSORE."

"Five hundred lira," the suited man said automatically in English.

"*Sino da quando denaro?*" Peter asked. When did you start charging?

The man, in the act of tearing the red ticket, looked up. His eyes widened. "*Pietro, Eminencia!*" he exclaimed. He hurried around from behind the desk and kissed Peter's hand. Then he straightened. "*No prezzo!*" he exclaimed proudly. He ushered Peter onto the elevator and said. "*Benvenuto a casa!*" as the doors closed.

Carrying his bag, Peter alighted from the lift and turned up the ramp that led to the circular catwalk high inside the dome of the Basilica. Entering, he felt the familiar blast of air ruffle his clothing. He paused momentarily, peering far below to Bernini's baldacchino which covered the papal altar.

Then turning, he exited, dancing out the door and up into a winding, narrow shaft. Running now, he began to ascend the ultimate nine hundred and ten steps of the cupola itself. The thick walls narrowed, making it difficult for even a child to squeeze up. He moved faster, more determined, obsessed to reach the top. The width of the steps shrank to a foot. He pounded up the worn steps, certain in his heart that somehow the final imprimatur to his ideas awaited him above. Breathlessly, he climbed, wedging the suitcase through the narrow twists and turns.

The steps narrowed again. The walls of the cupola were taking the shape of its curved exterior, pressing closer on him. Claustrophobic now. The only light from slits in the wall's thickness. Upwards, sideways. Round and round the dome itself. As though slipping through the tunnel of a narrow-walled cave.

Then up a twisting iron staircase, pulling himself by an aiding rope, knowing that now, he was near the pinnacle. Shoe leather on cast-iron steps. The rush of wind and he was outside. Below him lay Rome!

On the wind-swept cupola, Peter stood and breathed deeply. As he gazed at the brownish Tiber, the distant Palatine with its ancient Roman Forums, the new Piazza Venezia, seat of the present Italian government, the Colosseum where Christians had died to amuse Romans, the far-away hill of the Pincio near the Villa Medici, he saw them gathering. Every color marching toward him. Some with arms, in uniforms. Crucifixes held high like challenging banners.

One billion Catholics. The most powerful, untapped force in the world. A sea of faithful marching to a single, enlightened theme. Christian soldiers! And all of them under order of a pope who had only to issue the command of "Ex-Cathedra." At that, every Catholic was duty-bound to obey under pain of eternal damnation!

And the Vatican would become overnight a most effective country. A nation to do real good. To right every wrong.

Peter took a deep breath.

The armies of Catholics faded. Rome was as it was. He smiled, his dream of the bearded priest in the sky confirmed. Turning, he clung to the rope, descending leisurely down the iron staircase and the tight, narrow steps of the cupola's dome.

*   *   *

Monsignor Charles Kalki, transferred from San Francisco, served espresso in tiny demitasse cups as he kept up a light, flowing conversation. Peter sat across from his father and waited for Kalki to finish and leave them alone.

"Most generous," the darting-eyed Monsignor said in praise of his benefactor. "Cardinal Stamp brought me here shortly after his accident. To tell you the truth, when I wrote him, asking to serve in Rome, I never imagined. . . ."

Cardinal Stamp raised a withered hand, signaling it was enough. The Monsignor broke off in mid-sentence.

"Of course," he said, "I've been prattling like an old woman." He set the coffee on its warmer on the silver tray and extended his hand toward Peter. "Let me welcome you," he said unctuously. "Welcome back where you belong." Bowing, he left the room.

Peter turned his eyes toward his father. The old man had written no messages since Peter had arrived. His face covered with the too shiny skin of burn victims was expressionless. But there seemed to be a worried look in his eyes as he sipped his espresso, palsied hand shaking.

"You know, father," Peter said, "I expected a warmer welcome from you."

Livingston Stamp balanced the coffee cup and saucer on the arm of his wheelchair and pulled the white note pad from a side-pocket.

"I *have* missed you!" he wrote.

"But you thought it was better I stay in the monastery?"

"I've broken off relations with Mazande. This is his doing."

"Father, I've faced myself. I know now that I'm ambitious. But so were you. And you managed a lot of good in your time. I want that same chance."

The aged Cardinal wrote hastily, "The devil may be gathering you in again."

Peter read it and nodded. "I've gone over that a thousand times in my mind. But I believe I've shaken him. I've faced who I am. I'm free!"

The Cardinal scrawled again, "The ultimate sin of pride is to think you can outwit evil by yourself!"

Peter rose and walked to the open doors of the apartment. It was sweltering outside, the beginning of a long, Roman summer. Yet, here, inside the marble-lined apartment, it was cool and comfortable.

"I remember many days spent here," he said, looking out on the Travertine saints atop the Bernini colonnades. A flock of pigeons rose above the balcony wall, circled above St. Peter's Square, then lighted among the statues.

"You know," Peter continued, still staring out the tall window-doors, "when I arrived, there were many people who recognized me. The Swiss Guards, though they're not the same ones I knew; *uscieri, sampetrini*; clerks; passing clergy. All knew me."

For a moment longer, Peter held. Then, he turned and walked toward his father.

"Livy," he said enthusiastically, his china cup and saucer rattling as he sat, "the good I could do would outweigh any risk. I want to work exclusively as a cardinal for the Third World. To erase their poverty, put them on their feet. Practical things. Things you always wanted to do."

"What things?" the Cardinal wrote.

"You remember the man I killed in the Atacama desert? The one you thought was a bandit?"

The Cardinal nodded, rheumy eyes glistening.

"Well, he was a priest. And before dying, he whispered that the only way the Third World could ever right its social evils was by revolt and war."

In agitation, Peter began pacing. He did not notice the Cardinal's hands tighten in alarm as they clasped the armrests of his chair.

"What I will do," Peter said, "is siphon off some of the immense wealth of the Vatican to finance Christian revolutions in the Third World. To implement fully the Theology of Liberation! What governments like Brazil, Chile, Argentina, Nicaragua, Rhodesia, Uganda, South Africa, understand is force! Another thing! It's time for the Church to realize that Marxism, as an economic concept, is valuable in the Third World!"

He spun back toward his father and noted the shock on his face.

"Oh, I know you think that Marxism is the Church's greatest enemy. But times change, father! In my eyes, both Marxism and capitalism are godless. And face the facts: there are certain countries in the world where Marxism is destined to work better! We can't force systems on nations."

Excitedly, Peter marched back and forth across the room, driven by his visions. "Something else," he practically shouted. "The Vatican should have its own army. We could be more effective in keeping peace. Why, if we had any force at all, we'd have settled the Middle East crisis by now!"

He began to slap his fist down in his open hand.

"We need to de-Romanize Catholicism. Take the Italian out of the Church. Make it more universal. Maybe move the Vatican out of Rome entirely. Jerusalem would be a good place to set it up."

He spun and knelt quickly before Livingston.

"Think of it, father! To re-establish the Church where Jesus walked and taught. To go back to our true seeds of Catholicism!"

Peter, noting the old Cardinal's lack of enthusiasm, grinned. "I know it sounds too radical," he said. "But new things always do. It's a lot to accomplish and it will take time. But those things are what I intend to work for as a cardinal."

Peter strutted across the marble floor, his shoes tapping to the time of his words.

"I thought it all out," he said. "The Church needs revitalizing. You said that yourself once upon a time. I plan a coalition of cardinals who think like myself. Then, gaining the power, we intend to fight for equalness in the Church. One vote apiece. The Pope as a sort of President."

In shock, Cardinal Livingston Stamp grabbed up his pad and wrote, "The Church a democracy?"

"Right!" Peter agreed. "Just like the American concept you always wanted. A real democracy!"

"You're not talking like a cardinal now," Stamp scribbled. "You sound insane!"

"Oh, don't be silly, father," Peter said glancing at the message. "I hear the Italians will win back their power this time."

"But what if it were offered to you? What if you were actually elected pope?"

"Then," Peter said, his eyes narrowing with his vision, "I would take it gladly!"

The Cardinal reached up and snatched hold of his wrist. He turned his son's right hand up and studied the palm. Two major scars had remained. They resembled joined, wobbly circles.

"See anything?" Peter asked, amused.

The Cardinal shook his head, picked up his pencil. "Does Mazande know of your changed ideas?"

"There's plenty of time to tell him later."

"He will not support you if he knows!"

"Father," Peter said, extending his right hand and laying it gently on the old Cardinal's shoulder, "I know your fears. But I'm my own man now. And while I may never be pope, as cardinal, I can make myself heard. None of this could have happened without you."

Quickly, the Cardinal began to write another imploring message but the sound of the door clicking shut roused him. He looked up and saw that Peter had exited.

For a moment, he sat motionless, pondering Peter's state of mind. The old obsessiveness had returned. Or else, he thought, it had never diminished. Why? Who was putting these insane ideas into his head? It was almost like hearing someone else talk through Peter's mouth.

The Cardinal lay the white note pad on his left knee and drew two round circles that touched one another. They were like the ones in Peter's palm. A sort of standing up infinity sign: "8."

Tracing them over and over, Stamp sat deep in thought. Suddenly, he paused and stared at the two circles. With his pencil, he drew a line through their middles, then lifted his pencil. He moved it an inch down page and wrote half of the figure: "S."

Starbright? he wondered. Did the "S" stand for that demon's name?

He brought up his pencil, drew two fresh circles: "8." Then he drew a line down one side and a "B" appeared. Was the "B" for "Baz"? And what did the

name Baz mean anyway? Distantly, he recalled Archbishop Malthustos had translated it as Light-Carrier.

LIGHT-CARRIER . . . STARBRIGHT. . . .

Funny, he had never noticed before but those
names were similar to that of Lucifer, the King of
Devils. His name meant Morning Star and Light-
Bringer.

LIGHT-CARRIER . . . STARBRIGHT . . . LIGHT-BRINGER
. . . MORNING STAR.

The pencil broke as he finished the last word.

Lurching toward his nearby desk, he pressed a
buzzer. Monsignor Kalki entered.

"Yes, Eminence?" he asked solicitously.

The Cardinal attempted hurriedly to write on his
pad. But the pencil was leadless.

"You've broken it," Kalki said. He handed him a
fresh one from the desk.

"Get me my scrapbook," the Cardinal wrote, "and
the Bible."

The Cardinal sat there, heart pounding, trying to
put the pieces together.

Could it be that Baz, alias Starbright, was the Evil
One himself, masquerading as a minor demon? Was
that the reason Moshe Malthustos had not detected
the possession? Had Lucifer himself, the fallen angel
who once was second only to God, outsmarted him?
If so, why all the effort to conceal himself?

Kalki reentered and laid the scrapbook on the desk,
cradling the thick Bible open in his hands.

"Now, Eminence," he said, thinking that the Cardinal desired his short period of meditation for the day,
"is there a special passage you wish?"

The Cardinal wrote quickly, "Daniel and Revelations. The prophecies."

"I presume you mean the prophecies concerning

the Anti-Pope?" Kalki concluded. He snapped shut the big book and said, "There is no need for me to look them up. After all, I taught Divine Scripture for years."

The Cardinal motioned for him to proceed.

"Six signs to look for," Kalki noted. "Restoration of Israel; Creation of Common Market; Six-Day War between Israel and Egypt; Russia allied against Israel; unusual number of earthquakes; and, after a final war in the Middle East, the temple in Jerusalem is to be gloriously rebuilt. Then, of course, the Anti-Pope takes the temple over and the Jewish nation rises up against him."

The Cardinal's eyes were focused on something outside the veranda windows, far beyond the towering face of St. Peter's Basilica.

"Somebody," Monsignor Kalki went on a little nervously, "somebody asked a colleague of mine once if a conservative might misjudge a liberal as the Anti-Pope and vice versa." He tried to chuckle but the sound died. He did not notice the old Cardinal frown and a questioning doubt settle in his eyes.

"In Revelations," Kalki said, "in Chapter Thirteen, there is a favorite prophecy of mine. Often overlooked. It says, 'He doeth great wonders, so that he maketh fire come down from heaven on the earth in the sight of men and deceiveth them that dwell on the earth by means of those miracles.'"

The Cardinal scribbled on his pad, "Enough of that. What's the gossip about my son?"

"There is still no one as popular with the Third World, Oceania and Eastern Europe," Kalki said succinctly, understanding the political question. Indeed he suspected it was his expertise—since Cardinal Stamp was unable to get around as he once did—that had brought him to Rome years ago. "Talk is, he still has a good chance to be the first American Pope elected."

Livingston pointed a finger at his leather scrapbook. Kalki handed it to him and asked, "Anything else?"

Stamp wrote, "Call Mazande!"

"But, Eminence," Kalki objected, "I thought you weren't talking. . . ."

"NOW!" Stamp wrote vigorously.

Kalki hurried out the door.

The Cardinal held the portfolio-sized scrapbook on his lap. The book bulged with newsclippings of the events most important to him of each year. But Stamp did not seem fully aware of this history. He was again staring, seeing something far off.

If I am right, Stamp thought to himself, then I have been the dupe of the devil. I have participated in the most evil thing ever to befall mankind. I have paved the way for the end times.

Kalki stuck his torso into the doorway. "Cardinal Mazande has gone to Conclave already," he announced.

Livingston sagged disappointedly.

Slowly, he began to leaf through the fat scrapbook, hoping he would not find the dreaded prophecies.

The day of his ordination, March 9, 1933. Quickly, he scanned other clippings. Not until May 14, 1948, did he stop turning pages. Carefully, he read the item to make sure. Then he brought up his pencil and circled the newsquote:

> May 14, 1978. The free state of Israel proclaimed in Tel Aviv as the British evacuated Palestine.

Clippings: *Osservatore Romano; The New York Times.*

To the left of it, in his own hand, he wrote, Note: SIGN NUMBER 1, recalling that nineteen hundred and forty-eight was when he had found Peter in the cave. Then, quickly he paged forward through the scrapbook, to his consternation, finding again and again other signs, marking them as he progressed.

TWENTY-EIGHT

In the newly constructed, hotel-like Domus Mariae that housed most of the arriving cardinals, his Eminence, Cardinal Mazande, temporary Pope and Camerlengo to the coming conclave, sat in a makeshift office and thought about why he had lied to Livingston Stamp's secretary. Because Livingston had grown senile, he told himself. In fact, he had not been the same since the airport accident.

Lately, when Mazande had devised a plan to get his son Peter back into action, Livingston had avoided him. At first he had wondered why. Did he have some reason for giving up on Peter? Why was he never spoken of? And why was his son hiding himself in that monastery? Questions never answered. Well, let Livingston Stamp rot in his senility! He, Mugabwe Mazande, still had the fire.

Turning his attention back to the "Upper Room" seating chart spread out on his desk, he checked one last time for any slipups. Cardinals had to be seated according to seniority. Glancing across the boxes, he saw that like all of his grand preparations, it appeared perfect.

Normally, the Secretary of State served as Camerlengo in these functions. But Cardinal Ugo Masticci had suffered a paralyzing stroke shortly after Pope Pius XIII's murder. So the Curia, casting a bone to the Third World, had appointed his Eminence, Cardinal Mazande, and summoned him from pastoral rounds. He was on Lake Victoria, visiting his boyhood Swahili village when he received the message.

Arriving in Rome, he had shakily approached the cadaver in the Apostolic bedroom and tapped its forehead three times with a silver hammer, each time asking in the prescribed manner, "Richard Mattingly, are you dead?" Then, taking the Fisherman's Ring from the Holy Father's fourth finger, he had broken it with a hammer.

Having sung the Requiem Mass with Cardinals Stromboli, Kaszus and Baggio, Mazande had seen to Vatican protocol and singlehandedly planned the next conclave. While Pope Pius XIII lay in state and thousands of faithful filed past his bier, Cardinal Mazande of the Third World calmly went about his business.

On the ninth day of mourning, Mazande had watched as the *sampetrini*, attendants at St. Peter's, had hammered gilt nails into the cedar-wood coffin, then lowered the body into a sarcophagus near the tomb of Simon Peter.

Then under Mazande's astute direction, the Vatican workers had prepared for Conclave.

Electronic surveillance crews had continually swept

the "Upper Room" where the Conclave would be held, searching for any listening or recording devices. Food, medicines and enough purified water for a small city had been gathered into the kitchens. Doctors, nurses, translators, electricians, carpenters, plumbers, barbers, a dentist had been hired. Five ordinary priests to act as confessors; nuns to cook the meals. A total of two hundred and fifty cardinals, assistants and personnel would be locked in Conclave starting late this afternoon.

Three different sets of vestments had been made also. A large, medium and small white cassock, white slippers, skull cap, rochet, cloak and stole. One of the Vatican tailors had added gold embroidery to the smallest set. A private wager that Stromboli, the finely featured Italian Cardinal, would be the next pope.

Mazande leaned back and felt very satisfied with his preparations. Many churchmen would think twice before calling Africans "backward" now. He lit up a yellow-paper Gauloise.

He had only minutes before he had to dress. But he propped his big shoes up on the desk enjoying this quiet moment.

Exposure was the key right now. Get Peter back in the limelight. He smiled, allowing the thick, aromatic smoke to curl up around his ebony face. With Pope Pius' body lying barely cold upstairs, he remembered the questioning, nearly panicked look on Stromboli's face.

"You have our support completely," Mazande had reassured him.

"The Latins? The East Europeans and Asians?"

"They will follow."

"But the new Cardinal? Do you really need him as

an assistant? He will stay in the background. No up-staging?"

"He seeks only to help, Eminence. Despite his popularity, he is very humble."

"This is dangerous," Stromboli had said. "Very dangerous!"

"But it will make *us* most happy," Mazande had assured him.

There was a knock. Mazande pulled his feet off the desk and stepped over several boxes containing maps of the Vatican.

Bdimiji, one of his Bishops, stood without. "The Exhortation sermon begins shortly," he said in Swahili.

"Did you deliver the position papers to the late arrivals?"

The rotund Bishop from Rwanda nodded.

"And have you seen our brother Stamp?"

"Here in the Domus Mariae. I showed him his room. He is dressing now."

"Do many know he has come?"

"Many. The word is spreading fast."

"Good," Mazande grinned. "Bring him in last. Then right up to my bench on the stage."

Bdimiji bowed and padded away.

As Mazande closed the door and unhooked his Roman collar, he paused a moment, remembering something.

Who was it who said the best way to beat these bastards was to agree with everything, then get into Conclave and fight like hell?

And as the Tanzanian hurried into his bedroom, he realized it was the old rebel himself, Cardinal Livingston Stamp, who had once espoused that tactic.

Back at number 52, Via della Conciliazione, Kalki

nearly had the Cardinal dressed. He threaded Stamp's arms through the surpluslike, white rochet, slipped it over his head and smoothed it down in back of him. The Cardinal was not cooperating.

"We're ready," Kalki said, unperturbed.

The Cardinal did not look at him. He was scribbling with his pencil beside a 1978 newspaper clipping.

"I'll just change into my good vestments and then we're off. All right, Eminence?"

When the Cardinal did not reply, Kalki's eyes danced nervously. He started to say something else but stopped himself instead and exited.

The Cardinal at last closed the book and bowed his head. It was his fault. His great sin had led the one he loved to this unforeseeable end.

But what if I am wrong? he asked himself. What proof do I have? Could my son really be the Anti-Pope? Peter, the last man in the world this should happen to! Moshe Malthustos did not sense it! Am I a monster to doubt him?

He sat there now, faltering. Torn.

Absently, he turned, shifting his gaze to the papal balcony that overlooked the Piazza. The same balcony that would be used to announce the new Pope: the spot where he would stand and bless the entire world.

"*You are Peter....*"

Suddenly, he knew he had been mistaken all these years. Communism was not the greatest enemy of the Church. Pope John II as a Cardinal in Poland had proven that. It was only a worthy adversary. Indeed, a mild form of Communism existed within the communities of the Church itself!

The only thing that could destroy the Catholic Church was democracy!

"*. . . and upon this* STONE. . . ."

He saw it all now. Clear as a moving picture. The Church disintegrating; factions bred by equal, clamoring voices; a spiritual world subverted into a temporal, military power; the emergence of the Four Horsemen of the Apocalypse: pestilence, war, famine and death. All unleashed by a blinded man who wanted only to do good.

And the proof, the final proof for it all, was that all the prophecies about the Anti-Pope had come true in this one young man's brief lifetime.

There was no doubt. There could not be. Peter was him.

Painfully, he gripped the rubber tires on his chair and rolled himself behind his desk.

Unlocking a drawer, he fumbled inside and withdrew a black-handled revolver he had purchased long ago for protection in Washington, D.C. He slipped it into his voluminous ruby-red cloak.

Closing his eyes, he begged God to make his aim steady and his will strong.

TWENTY-NINE

There were not many Romans in the city this time of year. Being a Sybaritic and health-conscious people, striving for the elusive *bella figura*, most had gone to the beaches of Ostia or Civitavecchia. But the Via Condotti, with its Gucci and Pucci shops, and the Veneto, with its glass cafes and high-priced whores, teemed. Rome had filled up with tourists who had come to witness the outcome of this Conclave.

As a consequence of their influx, a throng of one hundred thousand filled St. Peter's Square and pressed forward from the Via della Conciliazione, hoping to catch a glimpse of the Cardinal-voters and *Papabili* as they arrived in the buses from the Domus Mariae.

At precisely four o'clock, the five buses left the walls of the "House of Mary," and rolled slowly through the crowd. Entering the Square, the vehicles, guided by police on motorcycles, picked their way down the narrow path held open for them by the *Carabinieri*.

A man broke through their cordon and ran to a moving bus. He slapped his open palms against a window. The *Carabinieri* attempted to pull him down. He fought them until the Cardinal inside blessed him, then, peacefully, sagged and allowed himself to be dragged away.

The buses stopped at the Egyptian obelisk and the cardinals, according to seniority, now began to alight. Slowly, in a serpentine double file, they flowed past the thousands of faithful who were clapping and shouting as they welcomed the famous men.

In the distance, the Roman sun was setting already. It was unusually early. But dark, purple clouds had bunched up in the west and it looked as if it might rain tonight.

The two oldest Cardinals, Comenici and Zapruder, led the way up the steps to the Nervi Hall, now renamed after Pope Paul VI, and entered the open doors on which was etched the religious history of man. Here in the "Upper Room," after the Exhortation sermon, each Cardinal Elector would be sworn in.

Then all of them would listen with their minds, hearts and souls for the movement of the spirit, that inexplicable force that would guide them in making the heavy choice.

Many now, as they boarded the elevators, were examining their Cardinal colleagues. Many, too, were stealing glances at the slightly bowed dark-haired Italian named Stromboli. Not a few silently noted that he was "of a piece." An almost tangible aura surrounded him.

Near the papal stage, close to Fazzini's bronze sculpture of the Resurrection, Peter stood with Bdimiji, watching the other cardinals cross the theatre to the elevators.

As the last Princes of the Church boarded, Bdimiji turned and said, "Now, we go, Eminence. We go in last, then straight to the front. We sit at Mazande's table to help."

Peter nodded and followed him.

In the "Upper Room," cardinals in their red robes were filling the small senatorial desks in the half-moon gallery. Below them sat the long, oblong desk of the Camerlengo and his two assistants.

The confessor priests, assistants, doctors, some workers and the nun-cooks, allowed momentarily in the "Upper Room," watched respectfully from a rear door as the churchmen entered.

Monsignor Kalki wheeled in Cardinal Livingston Stamp and pushed him toward his rightful place in the gallery. But the old prelate lifted his hand and gestured to the large, double-entry doors. Kalki bent and objected about the protocol.

"I want to see everyone!" Stamp wrote on his pad, then impatiently motioned again to the twenty-foot doors.

Monsignor Kalki parked him near the great bronze portals and took up his stance nearby. Cardinals of legendary note slowly filed past them. Most bowed in greeting to Cardinal Stamp.

Mazande entered, his eyes searching the room to spot anything amiss. Strolling past Stamp, he nodded yet managed to ignore him completely.

Stamp tugged at Kalki's sleeve and handed him a quick note. Kalki looked at the name on the outside and saw it was intended for Mazande. Snatching it, he rapidly strode forward, catching up with the African.

The black Cardinal seemed annoyed at the intrusion.

"Sorry, Eminence," Kalki said and he motioned regretfully toward his boss.

Imperiously, Mazande opened the note. Then he folded it and creased it once.

"No reply," he said.

Kalki, sheepfaced, returned. "No reply, Eminence."

Fool! Stamp thought. You could have stopped it even now! Reaching inside his left sleeve, he curled his index finger against the trigger. And as he did, there was a murmur from the assembled and he looked up to see Cardinal Peter Stamp fill the doorway.

The young American paused, as if taking in the august gathering, then straightened proudly. His dark brown eyes glowed as with some mysterious inner light and his blond hair, combed straight back off his forehead, made him appear even younger than his years.

Turning his head, Livingston Stamp saw that Mazande, behind his desk, was smiling.

You double fool, he thought, you engineered this!

Peter finished his sweep of the room and spotted his father hidden in the niche. Smiling, he strode toward him.

"Livy," he said in greeting. "What are you doing over here?"

"He wanted to see everyone enter," Kalki explained.

"Well, it's time to join the others," Peter said kindly. "Come on, father!" And he stepped toward the wheelchair.

A low-key scattered applause started from behind him.

"They're welcoming you," the assistant offered. He motioned with his head to what was happening.

Puzzled, Cardinal Peter Stamp swung from the wheelchair. He saw that the African Cardinals had their arms extended in an "embrace" sign and were politely clapping. Several Latin America prelates joined in the proper, respectful applause.

"They love your son," Kalki said, bending to Livingston and thinking the large tears rolling down his cheeks were tears of happiness. "Listen to them!" He straightened and began to clap. The workers at the rear door joined also. They knew about this saintly young man.

The Asians, Eastern Europeans and Australians, as though rehearsed, rose to their feet. They began to applaud louder. The Americans stood also.

Cardinal Stromboli swung about and searched out his Italian cohorts, seeking the answer to why this was happening.

Then realizing he had been betrayed, he swiveled slowly toward the desk. There, the black Camerlengo was applauding also.

Peter, his back to his father, stood and received the accolade.

Cardinal Stamp eased out the revolver. Everyone's eyes were on his adopted son. With a trembling hand, he aimed the muzzle at the flatness of Peter's redrobed back. And as the applause built to a veritable roar, he prayed, "Lord Jesus, forgive me!" and pulled the trigger.

But the only sound was an empty click.

Monsignor Kalki discreetly pried the gun away from the shaking old man. Surreptitiously, he dropped it into his cassock pocket. Then he bent, opened his other hand and showed Livingston six bullets.

"If it's any consolation," Kalki whispered beneath the thundering applause, "you guessed right."

The Cardinal, overwhelmed, looked up. He reached to grab Kalki. But as he did, the Monsignor stepped behind him and gripped his neck. Unbelievably strong fingers pressed into Livingston's carotid arteries. His mind blurred.

"Look," Kalki breathed in his ear. "See truth at the moment of death."

Stamp, squirming helplessly, lifted his eyes. Peter, drawn by his reception, had moved several feet from the wheelchair. His face had changed! Eyes small and piglike, lips thick, forehead folds of flesh, the nose a snout. The figure from the stone talisman!

Could no one see? Fools! Stamp screamed inside himself. Look! Look!

Before darkness took the Cardinal, ending for his ears the frenzied applause his son was receiving, his thought was, for a great man, a seeming foolish one. Mockingly, the memory came of a voiceless chihuahua he had seen in the Mexico City airport. The dog's vocal cords had been cut to keep it quiet. Quivering from head to toe, it was trying desperately to bark and warn its owner of some imagined danger.

Mazande was beckoning to Peter. As the young Cardinal made his way down, row after row bade him welcome. Only the French and Italians remained quiet as he passed.

He ascended the Camerlengo's platform and Mazande gestured to his place at the long table.

Peter raised his hands to silence the applause. As he did so, Comenici, the oldest Cardinal present, came to his feet and stretched out a quivering finger toward the stage.

"*Signo!*" he cried loudly. The sign!

A gasp went up from the assemblage.

A tongue of fire had exploded over Peter's blond

hair. Its heat was so intense, everyone in the "Upper Room" could feel it. Yet, Peter did not seem affected.

"Fiero caeli!" Kalinov, a Russian Cardinal, shouted. Heavenly fire!

Some Cardinals fell to their knees. Stromboli, the prime candidate, rose slowly and stared at the bobbing strip of flame. The blood left his face.

Mystified, Peter turned toward Mazande. But the expression on the face of the black Cardinal was of primitive terror mixed with intelligent awe.

"Spiritu Sancto!" Lavalier, a French Cardinal, exclaimed.

"The Spirit! The Spirit!" the magic word spread like a grass fire.

"Ita!" some began to cry. *"Ita!* ITA!"

Smiling, Monsignor Kalki removed the hand that had rested inconspicuously on the neck of Cardinal Livingston Stamp. He allowed his charge's chin to settle peacefully on his bony chest. Then turning he ran his nervous eyes up the gallery to the workers.

There, in the rear, standing by themselves were the nun-cooks. Black, brown and white-skinned, they wore modern habits, and so the front of their hair was revealed. The three of them, faces mature and handsome, looked in their early twenties. Even beneath their habits, the outlines of their bodies were voluptuously pretty.

We will always have him, Kalki mused with satisfaction, gazing at them.

The black and brown-skinned nuns, as though feeling his thought, turned and smiled down at Kalki. Only the strawberry-blonde, hand lifted slightly and held out before her, continued to concentrate on the bobbing fire above Cardinal Peter Stamp.

*   *   *

Out on the darkened Square of St. Peter's, it had begun to rain lightly. Many of the people were drifting off.

The crews of TV cameramen on their scaffolding towers were winding up electrical cords and stowing their cameras for the night when somebody from the BBC spotted it. He shouted down to the Piazza. Several English-speaking faithful spun and verified it.

Lit by a nearby spotlight that always shone on the Basilica, a white stream of smoke was spouting from the roof pipe on the Sistine Chapel.

EPILOGUE

ISMIR, TURKEY

Since that long-ago day in San Francisco, he had not been well. If it was not his stomach, then it was a lingering cold or the flu. Some virus. The doctors did not seem to know. All his life he had been robust, seldom sick. But since that day, his life had changed. Still, Moshe Malthustos visited his dioceses, keeping his appointed rounds, preaching to and exhorting the faithful. Only a few moments ago he had finished delivering a homily of hope to the lepers of Smyrna. They were housed in a clean, black-walled enclosure near the edge of town.

Now, as he picked his way through the narrow, crowded streets, fish vendors in sweat-stained fezzes and bloodied aprons, "ooo-loo-ooohed" the day's catch.

A local Bishop, Musadah Kiafey, accompanying him, quietly described his next appointment in Manisa, on the Gediz River.

A low-life bar lay ahead. As they passed the dark and smelly hole, someone inside yelled to them.

"He says it's something about the Pope," Musadah Kiafey explained. Striding quickly back to the open door, he yelled into the bar: "Turn up the radio so his Excellency can hear from outside!"

Moshe Malthustos forced his weary feet back to the sour-smelling door.

Amidst the cheering crowd on the radio, an announcer said: "This evening, in an unexpected move, the College of Cardinals has elected another foreign Pontiff."

Distantly heard, a tiny voice in St. Peter's Square shouted through a microphone *"Habemus Papam!"*

The crowd roared: *"Viva! Viva!"*

"He is," the voice strained, "Lord Cardinal Peter Stamp who has taken the name of Peter the Second."

Archbishop Malthustos, as though struck an unseen blow, reeled into the street. He brought up his hands and tore his black gauzy robes.

"Peter . . . Peter, the *stone!*" he cried.

"What is it?" Bishop Kiafey asked, whipping around.

The Archbishop, howling, tore tufts of hair from his gray beard. A crowd from the street gathered around him; drinkers from the bar poked out their heads.

Bishop Kiafey, seeing the attention he was getting, stepped into the street. He took hold of the old man's arm. For a moment, Moshe Malthustos sagged as though he carried a monstrous burden. Then he looked up, his eyes clear and fierce. He shook off the younger man's hand.

"Go home," he shouted to the crowd. "Go home and pray for yourselves! And while you're at it, pray for me!"

With that, he pushed through them.

Kiafey, hurrying after him, noted that he did not walk like an infirm old man now. And as he disappeared around a corner, it was as though the Archbishop was marching, to some distant battle.

Dell Bestsellers

- [ ] **COMES THE BLIND FURY** by John Saul $2.75 (11428-4)
- [ ] **CLASS REUNION** by Rona Jaffe $2.75 (11408-X)
- [ ] **THE EXILES** by William Stuart Long $2.75 (12369-0)
- [ ] **THE BRONX ZOO** by Sparky Lyle and
  Peter Golenbock $2.50 (10764-4)
- [ ] **THE PASSING BELLS** by Phillip Rock $2.75 (16837-6)
- [ ] **TO LOVE AGAIN** by Danielle Steel $2.50 (18631-5)
- [ ] **SECOND GENERATION** by Howard Fast $2.75 (17892-4)
- [ ] **EVERGREEN** by Belva Plain $2.75 (13294-0)
- [ ] **CALIFORNIA WOMAN** by Daniel Knapp $2.50 (11035-1)
- [ ] **DAWN WIND** by Christina Savage $2.50 (11792-5)
- [ ] **REGINA'S SONG**
  by Sharleen Cooper Cohen $2.50 (17414-7)
- [ ] **SABRINA** by Madeleine A. Polland $2.50 (17633-6)
- [ ] **THE ADMIRAL'S DAUGHTER**
  by Victoria Fyodorova and Haskel Frankel $2.50 (10366-5)
- [ ] **THE LAST DECATHLON** by John Redgate $2.50 (14643-7)
- [ ] **THE PETROGRAD CONSIGNMENT**
  by Owen Sela $2.50 (16885-6)
- [ ] **EXCALIBUR!** by Gil Kane and John Jakes $2.50 (12291-0)
- [ ] **SHOGUN** by James Clavell $2.95 (17800-2)
- [ ] **MY MOTHER, MY SELF** by Nancy Friday $2.50 (15663-7)
- [ ] **THE IMMIGRANTS** by Howard Fast $2.75 (14175-3)

At your local bookstore or use this handy coupon for ordering:

DELL BOOKS
P.O. BOX 1000, PINEBROOK, N.J. 07058

Please send me the books I have checked above. I am enclosing $_____
(please add 75¢ per copy to cover postage and handling). Send check or money
order—no cash or C.O.D.'s. Please allow up to 8 weeks for shipment.

Mr/Mrs/Miss_____

Address_____

City_____State/Zip_____

Comes the Blind Fury

John Saul

Bestselling author of
Cry for the Strangers
and *Suffer the Children*

More than a century ago, a gentle, blind child walked the paths of Paradise Point. Then other children came, teasing and taunting her until she lost her footing on the cliff and plunged into the drowning sea.

Now, 12-year-old Michelle and her family have come to live in that same house—to escape the city pressures, to have a better life.

But the sins of the past do not die. They reach out to embrace the living. Dreams will become nightmares.

Serenity will become terror. There will be no escape.

A Dell Book $2.75   (11428-4)

At your local bookstore or use this handy coupon for ordering:

Dell	**DELL BOOKS** COMES THE BLIND FURY $2.75 (11428-4) **P.O. BOX 1000, PINEBROOK, N.J. 07058**

Please send me the above title. I am enclosing $ _____
(please add 75¢ per copy to cover postage and handling). Send check or money order—no cash or C.O.D.'s. Please allow up to 8 weeks for shipment.

Mr/Mrs/Miss _____

Address _____

City _____ State/Zip _____

California Woman

Daniel Knapp

The first novel in a new series

A sweeping saga of the American West

Esther left New England a radiant bride, her future as bright as the majestic frontiers. But before she could reach California, she had lost everything but her indomitable courage and will to survive. Against the rich tapestry of California history, she lived for love—and vengeance!

A Dell Book $2.50 (11035-1)

At your local bookstore or use this handy coupon for ordering:

Dell	DELL BOOKS CALIFORNIA WOMAN $2.50 (11035-1) P.O. BOX 1000, PINEBROOK, N.J. 07058

Please send me the above title. I am enclosing $ _____
(please add 75¢ per copy to cover postage and handling). Send check or money order—no cash or C.O.D.'s. Please allow up to 8 weeks for shipment.

Mr/Mrs/Miss _____

Address _____

City _____ State/Zip _____